undying HEARTS

UNDYING LOVE SERIES BOOK 1

CAITLIN CHERISE

For Mark, my Aussie, my shot of caramel, my 42, my best friend, thank you for everything you have given me, for everything you have done for me, for everything that you are, and for loving me the way you do #athousandways

CHAPTER 1

*L*ily's finger inched back the yellowing lace curtain, her fingertips skimming along the cool glass. She peeked out the window, between the thin plywood boards shielding them from view. Darkness settled in the sleepy neighborhood. The world around her was quiet except for the never-ending moans of the infected roaming just outside the house.

An infected shuffled past the window, its pale blue smock streaked with dirt, blood, and diseased flesh that dripped down its clothes like muddy jelly. Behind the walking corpse, moonlight glinted off a car window. Stars sprinkled the blue frosted sky above. With no streetlights, no lamplights, and no candlelight, the rest of the neighborhood was black and invisible.

"Mommy?" Sammy asked. "Can you read me a story?"

"In a minute, sweetie. There are a few monsters outside. I have to take care of them first. Remember what we practiced?" Lily shot her daughter a pointed look, one she'd perfected over the years—a listen-to-your-mother stare.

Four-year-old Sammy sighed with exaggerated disappointment. Her mess of red curls fell forward as she slouched her shoulders. "Yes." Her little voice sounded like a deflated balloon as she stood and dragged herself the steps.

Lily heard the bedroom door shut, then the waist-high bolt lock slid into place.

Her daughter was safe for now. Safe if she didn't come back.

But Lily always came back.

She peeked through the old curtains one last time. Three infected roamed around the street and their moans were soft and distant. No hordes waiting for her in the darkness. No surprises.

"You've got this," she murmured to herself as she dropped the curtain back into place. She reached down for the machete at her feet and she slid it from its homemade aluminum foil holster.

Careful not to make much noise, she walked toward the front door and peeked outside the peephole. The world stretched out before her in a tiny bubble. The porch swing swayed even in the humid summer air.

Lily checked beyond the swing in the corner, past her mother's rose bushes which were beginning to grow a bit wild. She stared harder. A thin strip of scarlet streaked across her view. "Damn," she murmured, yanking the stray piece of hair behind her ear.

She checked again. No infected at the front door.

The door chain jangled as she unlocked the door. She paused, twisted the doorknob, and stepped out into the night.

A wall of humid air slammed into her, moist heat sticking to her skin like sweat. Her hands gripped the machete tighter as she surveyed the street, at least what she could see of it. She missed streetlamps.

Her stomach rolled as adrenaline pulsed through her

system, ramping up her senses and flooding her body with a weird high—she liked it.

To the right, a soft moan grew louder like a choking animal. An infected wandered up the front gate toward her. The walking corpse wore a mailman's uniform, caked with congealed blood and bits of decaying skin. Its glossy, dead eyes stared at her as it hobbled toward her.

Lily stepped off the porch steps, raising her machete in the air.

Whack!

Lily's bicep stiffened as blade met bone.

The infected chocked on its last moan before crumbling to the ground at Lily's feet. Clotted blood dripped off the blade, still half-raised where the skull had been a moment ago.

"Gross," Lily winced as a chunk of decayed yellow bone fell from the tip. The smell of death churned her stomach like that liquid pink stuff her mother used to give her when she had indigestion.

She stepped over the corpse in search of the other two infected she knew were wandering near her mother's house. "Come out, come out wherever you are," she taunted to the empty night sky.

Another moan echoed further down the block, steadily coming toward her. Lily whistled as she walked along the white picket fence, getting closer to the infected moving toward her. Its tattered plaid t-shirt whipped in the summer air around its rotting torso. Dried blood and chunks of flesh stuck in its long beard.

"The lumberjack look doesn't suit you." Lily raised her blade and sliced downward, the machete cracking its skull with a loud thunk. "Like splitting a coconut," she said to the corpse as it fell in front of her. Clotted blood and bits of decayed brain oozed from the gap. "Like splitting a nasty, diseased-ridden, dead coconut."

Lily hummed "Put the Lime in the Coconut" as she continued to roam around the front of the house, careful not to stray. A shimmy of movement caught her eye and she stopped walking. A fresh wave of adrenaline rushed through her veins.

The third corpse hobbled out behind an SUV parked right in front of the house. Its left ankle twisted at an odd angle. It limped toward Lily with outstretched arms. The guttural moans gargled from its throat as dead eyes stared at her. The nametag on the pale blue smock read "Heidi."

Lily's gasp echoed in the thick air as surprise punched her in the gut.

Heidi had been her mother's favorite neighbor. The young woman visited Lily's mother often when Lily and Sammy moved away from Ohio and out to sunny California. Heidi and Lily had been childhood friends. They'd played hopscotch and gone to school together.

Heidi had been the person Lily called when her mother didn't answer the phone. Heidi had been the one who found her mother dead on the sofa, watching the news about the infection and the world going mad.

This infected Heidi bore no resemblance to the bright, youthful woman Lily remembered. Instead, a walking corpse with decaying skin and a broken ankle stumbled around, moaning and wearing Heidi's nametag.

All infected used to be people.

"I'm so sorry." Lily raised her machete again and froze.

Two headlights flashed into view on her street.

A car.

Another person.

The infected turned its attention to the lights and away

from Lily. She stepped forward and plummeted the machete deep into Heidi's skull.

"Fuck," Lily said again as the machete stuck in Heidi's head, the corpse dropping to the ground and pulling the blade down with it.

"Damn it, Heidi," Lily murmured, ducking below the SUV and trying to jiggle the blade from Heidi's skull.

The lights faded away. The engine died. The door slammed.

Whoever was out there had seen her, and her only weapon was four inches deep in her childhood best friend's skull.

Lily let go of the handle, careful to keep herself ducked down below the SUV's windows.

The front door to her house was unlocked. If whoever was out there didn't notice her, she could—

"Hello?" A deep voice rang out in the dark like a church bell in the otherwise quiet neighborhood. A man's voice.

"Oh hell no," Lily mouthed to herself. No one was going near her or Sammy, especially not a strange man.

Somewhere in the back of her mind, she heard her mother's cheery voice. *Don't talk to any strange men, Lily. And remember, all men are strange.*

"You can come out now." The voice sounded closer, the bass tone rippling over her skin. Fear pricked the back of her neck like a mosquito. She heard the crunch of his boots as he stepped over the dead lumberjack in the street. He was moving closer to the SUV and further away from her front door.

Lily knew it was now or never. She'd have to run.

With a start that would have impressed her old track coach, she launched herself from behind the SUV and darted toward her front door.

"Hey, wait!" His heavy steps sounded on the concrete

behind her, but she wouldn't look back. She burst through the front gate, leaped up the porch steps, and grabbed the handle, twisting the knob. She hurried through the front door.

"I just want to talk to you!" The man's voice was right on top of her.

Lily slammed the door shut behind her, fumbling at the chain to lock the door before he could—

The door flung open with such strong force Lily had to step back before she lost her balance.

A tall figure filled the doorway. A sword shone in his hand as he stared down at her with gleaming sapphire-blue eyes.

Eyes that were very much alive.

"Mommy?" Sammy's voice floated from the top of the steps.

Lily's heart pounded faster. Sammy had left the bedroom. The stranger knew Sammy existed.

"Get away!" She growled at the figure, but the man froze, glancing between Lily and Sammy.

"You have a daughter."

"Sammy, get in your room and lock the door," Lily said as she rushed toward the steps.

A strong arm wrapped around her waist, yanking her down to the floor as the man's weight crushed her.

Pain shot through her knees as she fell to the floor. Her hands scratched against the old rug.

"Mommy!" Sammy shrieked.

Lily flung her head back into the stranger's chin with a hard thump.

"Ow! I don't want to hurt you." He released Lily and took several heavy steps backward that seemed to rattle the entire living room floor.

Lily panted as she turned on all fours.

Her heart lodged itself in her throat. The steady thumping reached into her brain as she watched Sammy jump off the bottom step toward the stranger.

"Leave her alone!" Sammy said, stomping her foot only two feet away from the man.

He paused, staring down at the little girl in front of him. Lily's heart hammered out of her chest as the man smiled down at her daughter. His teeth gleamed in the dull moonlight. "Well, hello there. What's your name, princess?"

"I'm Sammy McLaughlin," she said, placing her hands on her hips as she frowned at the stranger.

"Hi, Sammy. My name is Flynn."

Sammy gasped. "Like in *Rapunzel?*"

"Yes, just like in *Rapunzel*. Sammy, is this your mom?"

Flynn's sword gleamed in his hand as he pointed the tip toward Lily. Even in the darkness from several feet away, the weapon seemed razor sharp. Moonlight glinted from the tip. Red drops of thick, clotted bloodstained the cutlass.

His hand reached out toward Sammy, moving closer.

"Get away from her!" Lily screamed and launched herself toward him. Flynn's head shot up, his gaze locking with Lily's. He froze in place, his hand inches from Sammy's mess of red curls.

Sammy spread her arms out, protecting the stranger from her mother. "No, Mommy," she cried, "don't hurt the prince." Sammy flung her arms around the man's waist, wrapping him in a tight hug to keep him safe.

Lily froze, fear choking her as her throat tightened.

He had Sammy. Her daughter was hugging a man holding a bloody sword.

An invisible fist squeezed Lily's throat and panic rose in her belly, making it almost impossible to breathe. "Let her go," she pleaded, her heart pounding so loud she could hardly hear herself speak.

The stranger stood frozen, sword in one hand, the other still suspended in midair. Through the darkness, Lily could still see his blue eyes blazing, locks of dirty, black hair shielding half of his face from view.

Panic pulsed through her veins as she wracked her brain for an idea.

The sword.

If she had his sword, she would have a bargaining chip.

"I'm not going to hurt her." His deep growl of a voice pierced through Lily like a lance. The roughness in his voice made her shiver.

"Let her go," Lily said again.

On the floor, less than five feet from her was a long, silver candlestick that held a half-melted taper. The metal might not be heavy, but a blow to Flynn's head would hurt him enough to distract him. Lily inched closer.

Following her gaze, the stranger moved with her. Sammy still clung to his waist. "I wouldn't do that, Sweetheart," he taunted.

Lily lunged for the candlestick.

Flynn shoved Sammy from his waist and rushed toward Lily to stop her.

She was faster.

Lily grabbed the candlestick. The taper clattered to the floor and rolled under a couch. She glanced at the candlestick in her hand, to the stranger who stood still, only a few feet in front of her. He stood between the girls, sword still in hand.

"I'm not going to hurt her," he said, his voice echoing around the living room. He slid his cutlass into a sheath that belted around his waist, like a modern knight. He held up both hands in surrender. "See, now I'm unarmed," he paused. "You wouldn't hurt an unarmed man, would you?"

"You touched my daughter," she growled. Red blurred

Lily's vision as she lunged, her arm swinging downward with a tight grip on the candlestick.

The stranger's hand flung out and caught her wrist, dragging her closer to him.

Lily's grip loosened in shock and the candlestick dropped to the floor with a loud bang.

His arms twisted, turning her around and pressing her spine to his chest, her arms pinned in front of her. "Now, I said I wouldn't hurt her. I don't want to hurt you either, but you're making this extremely difficult." His breath tickled her ear, shivers of awareness slithering down her back. His hard chest was like granite as he pressed her body closer to him. Even caked in blood and dirt, he smelled like sandalwood and something tropical.

Her blood boiled under her skin, frustration mounting as she struggled to break free. She writhed in his grasp.

His grip on her tightened with each movement.

She swung her legs, trying to kick him, but she couldn't seem to reach her target. "Get off of me, you son of a bitch!" She could feel his cock stiffen and grow against her bottom. Was this getting him off?

Lily fumed.

"Let go of her," a small voice shouted behind them.

With a loud "Ouch," the stranger released her and crumpled to the floor. "She kicked me," he murmured in surprise as he fell to one knee.

"Sammy!" Lily called to her. Sammy ran behind her mother and clung to her leg.

Lily reached down and pulled the sword out of its sheath, pointing it between the stranger's eyes. She should do it. It was the only way she knew they would be safe. He knew where they were hiding…

"Mommy," Sammy's weak voice crackled behind her. "Don't hurt the prince. He didn't hurt us."

Suddenly the sword seemed a hundred pounds heavier in her hand. Sammy was right. Her four-year-old daughter was better at keeping a level head than her.

Lily sighed and stepped away, allowing the stranger enough room to rise off the floor. He wobbled and stood, leaning against the wall. He kicked his leg out once, twice, before finally putting some weight on his injured knee.

"Smart girl you've got there," he said.

"What do you want?" Lily snapped, keeping the sword held in front of her.

"I saw those zombies moving toward the house. Then I saw you. I haven't seen another person for weeks now."

"Why did you follow me?" Lily asked.

"Like I said, you're the first person I've seen in a long time." He paused. His powder blue eyes gleamed through the darkness as his gaze bounced between Lily and Sammy. "Did you really think I was going to hurt your daughter?"

"I don't know," Lily said. "I don't know you. You don't know us. You're the first face we've seen in almost two months. I wasn't sure anyone else was… out there."

Lily glanced down. Sammy still clung to her thigh, tiny fingers gripping her tight.

Lily shook her head. "I'm not talking about this in front of my daughter."

He nodded like he understood her concern. "What's your name?" he asked.

Lily thought for a second. Should she tell him? Why not? It's not like she had to worry about some stranger identifying her on the street or stealing her identity online. There was no online. Strangers didn't roam the streets anymore. Only infected could walk outside freely.

"Lily McLaughlin," she said.

He smiled, his white teeth catching in the moonlight.

"Lily," he repeated, testing her name as if he was deciding something. Lily couldn't figure out what though.

"Who are you?" she asked.

"Flynn Irving," he said. He started to hold his hand out for a handshake, but Lily pointed the tip of the sword toward his arm. "Okay, so we're not friendly yet. Point taken," he pulled his hand away. "No pun intended."

Lily fought back a small smile.

Flynn sighed. "Lily, I'm alone. I'm not looking for trouble. You have me unarmed and at a serious disadvantage. I was scavenging supplies on my way to a refugee camp and—"

"Wait," Lily stopped him. "There are others? Alive?"

Could it be true? Were there other people who survived the disease?

"I've seen signs along the highway," Flynn replied. "I can't guarantee their legitimacy. They could be Trojan horses for all I know, but I figured it's worth the risk. My plan was, if they're a real camp, perhaps I could persuade them to take in an outsider. I have some knowledge about cars. I built hot rods as a hobby before the infection spread. I guess I'm a mechanic by the loosest of terms."

He glanced at the tip of the sword again before glancing back at Lily. Those startling blue eyes caught her off guard. "I was a history professor before the disease. Medieval history. Clearly, that's not very useful to anyone right now."

"Was it really useful to anyone before all of this?" she asked, raising an eyebrow.

Flynn tossed his head back as he let out a bark of a laugh that boomed like a gunshot through the house. "Touché, Lily." He glanced at the sword again. He pointed. "That is a prized cutlass from my personal collection. It was the only weapon in my collection worth taking. The only thing worth bringing. Most of the other swords were too large and bulky. Maces and battle axes are poor weapons against the infected.

Too much blood flying about. Too easy to get it in your eye or your mouth and turn you."

"You can get turned without them biting you?" Lily asked. "I thought it was like in the movies where they had to bite you to become infected?"

Flynn shook his head, locks of dark hair swooshing along the edge of his jacket. "No, I saw someone get a bit of infected blood in his eye and within twenty-four hours, he had turned. His wife—" Flynn shuddered. "His wife shot him in the back of the head. Instant kill. The poor woman turned the gun on herself afterward before they could stop her."

Sammy whimpered.

"I'm sorry," he apologized. "We shouldn't be discussing this in front of your daughter."

Lily froze, her mind whirling. Why did he care about what Sammy heard? That seemed so…human.

"As I was saying," he continued, "I was on my way to a refugee camp when I passed through here. Driving on the back roads is better than trying to use a highway. Too many jammed-up cars. Too many infected."

"Where's this camp?" she asked.

"Out near Lancaster, Pennsylvania. I far, but right now, it's my only option. It's that camp or wandering around until I find something else, assuming there is something else."

Flynn paused before a grin broke out over his face. "Come with me."

Lily tried to hold back a laugh, but she couldn't help herself. The harsh sound burst from her chest like a gunshot. "What?" She lowered the sword to her side, careful to keep a safe distance between the bloody blade and her curious daughter.

Flynn smiled. "There's safety in numbers. You're not safe here."

"You broke into my house," Lily began. "You pointed a

sword at me. You scared my daughter. I don't know you from Adam."

"Well, my name's Flynn, so you know that." His smile shifted into an easy grin that was almost…charming?

Lily's stomach fluttered in a strange way. "How do I know I can trust you?" she asked.

"You don't. Not yet, anyway. Let me stay the night," he suggested.

"Let you stay? In my house? With my daughter? You're insane."

"No, I'm not," he said. "Besides, I know where you live. I know what you have. I know you don't know how to use that sword. You can barely hold it in front of you. Your grip is all wrong. Oh, I was a fencer in college by the way. Notre Dame. Add it to the list of marketable apocalyptic skills." He chuckled, but when Lily didn't laugh, he kept talking.

"You can make me leave, but who's to say I won't come back in the night? If I wanted to hurt either of you, I could have done it a hundred times by now. Obviously, I don't want to hurt you."

Lily stayed silent, observing him. It was like studying a lion in a cage. She had him trapped, but he was eying her with a restrained hunger she couldn't quite understand.

Flynn's hand rose, running his fingers through his dirt-slicked hair. "Look, as I've said, you're the first person I've seen in a long time. Probably about a month since my old camp broke up. There was a horde that came and we scattered. I haven't seen any of them since. I have no interest in hurting either of you. Honest. I was looking for a safe spot to sleep and maybe find some food when I saw you. A woman, wandering the streets alone, killing infected. I was curious. And relieved to see another living person. Come with me."

Lily paused, weighing her options. On the one hand, he was right. She couldn't just kill him. How could that protect

Sammy, watching her mother become a cold-blooded murderer? On the other hand, she couldn't let him leave. He knew too much. She needed time to think, to mull over her options. What better way than to keep him here right under her nose for a few hours while she thought? Keep your friends close and your enemies closer.

But was he really an enemy?

"You'll have to stay in the bathroom," she said. "I'm going to lock you inside. There's nothing but a straight fifteen-foot drop onto the ground if you try to get out. And I'm a light sleeper."

"Thank you," he breathed out in relief. "My cutlass?" He reached out a hand for it.

Lily pointed the tip toward him again, the blade inches from his outstretched fingers. "No. This is mine for now. Until I say so."

Flynn shielded himself with his hands and laughed. "And though she be but little, she is fierce. Alright, your house, your rules. Now, where's the bathroom?"

CHAPTER 2

For nine hours, Lily tossed and turned, drifting between sleep and uneasy consciousness. Sammy slept beside her, her little limbs sticking out everywhere as soft mewling sounds slipped from under the covers. Her daughter loved to sleep with the blankets tucked up to her nose.

The sword leaned against the bedside table, along with a long steak knife she had taken from the drawer downstairs.

Just two rooms away, Flynn slept in the bathroom. He was locked in with no weapons, besides a few pill bottles and a shower curtain. His snores proved he was sound asleep, probably curled up in the bathtub or sprawled out of the floor.

Something about him pushed Lily's nerves on edge, more than the infected, more than the knowledge that there were other people still alive. Something about *him* rocked her to her core.

At seven o'clock the next morning, Lily couldn't take the curiosity anymore. Sammy began to stir beside her, yawning and stretching out her arms.

"Morning sweetie," Lily murmured beside her little girl.

"Morning mama." Sammy yawned.

"Did you have any good dreams?" Lily asked, trying to stick to Sammy's morning ritual, although her mind was focused on the stranger two rooms away.

Sammy nodded. "Yes."

Sammy's sleepy eyes blinked open and she rubbed the tiredness away with her small fists.

Lily's heart melted as she watched her daughter wake. "And what did you dream about?"

"Fairies," Sammy said. "They were dancing and I danced too and they made me their Queen."

Lily kissed her daughter's unruly curls. "My little fairy Queen."

"They had wings," Sammy beamed at her mother with her beautiful, innocent eyes and curious stare.

Lily's curiosity pricked at the back of her neck. "Let's go see if Flynn is awake," she said to Sammy.

"Is Prince Charming still here?" Sammy asked.

Lily laughed, the happy sound feeling foreign but welcome. "I don't know if he's so charming," Lily said.

"I think he's charming. He's Prince Charming." Sammy stuck her chin out with childlike stubbornness.

"Come on, fairy Queen." Lily slid the covers away and grabbed the sword in one hand. Its weight pulled on her arm, but she kept her shoulders straight as she left their bedroom. Like a little duckling, Sammy followed behind her.

Lily flicked open the bathroom lock, and the door swung open on its loose hinges.

Stretched out inside her tub was a man in his early thirties. A trace of a beard covered his cheeks and chin while his dark hair fell in thick locks around his face. He curled into himself, biceps straining the fabric of his stained, white t-shirt. His jeans had a small tear in the left knee. Gray grime and blood caked his boots. His denim jacket hung over the showerhead.

Lily's heart revved in her chest like an engine, her body humming on edge like she was watching a horror movie and waiting for the jump scare. He was almost attractive.

"Morning, sunshine," Lily barked.

Flynn jolted upward, his arm slamming into the porcelain soap holder against the wall. "Ow, mother fucker!"

"He said a bad word," Sammy whispered from behind Lily's leg.

"Yes, he did," Lily smirked. Something about him, about this situation, seemed amusing, almost funny. Maybe it was because sunlight ripped through the open window and she could finally see him. Maybe it was because she knew he was defenseless. Or maybe it was just because she hadn't seen a man in so long.

Must be the light.

"Sammy needs to use the bathroom," she said.

She thought about offering him some of their water to shower. The dirt on his body almost hid the color of his tanned skin. His hair was matted like a lion's mane, and he could use a shave. But until she knew him better, she wasn't about to waste hard-earned water. She had spent weeks collecting bottles and jugs from neighboring houses with infected roaming around.

He'd have to earn her water.

Flynn rubbed his injured arm and smiled at Sammy as she stepped from behind her mother's leg.

"Of course." He rose from the tub, ducking below the curtain rod, and retrieved his jacket. He slipped past them, his eyes darting between the blade and Lily's face. Lily watched him from the corner of her eye, her body shielding Sammy. She closed the door and left her daughter alone.

"Let's go downstairs," she suggested.

He nodded, walking down the stairs with his head turned sideways. Perhaps he was just as wary of her as she was of him. Smart man.

Lily gripped the sword's handle a little tighter. The cold metal felt comforting, even though the decorative designs dug into her palm. Perhaps she would keep the sword after all.

"Are you hungry?" he asked as he reached the bottom step.

"Excuse me?" Lily froze halfway down the steps.

He faced her. A soft smile lit his face. Even under the dirt, he was an attractive man. And the only one she'd seen in over a month. That must be why her stomach was twisting into knots, right?

"Are you hungry?" he asked again. "I have some food in my car. I'm not sure how stocked up you are, but I have some canned peaches and cherries. They're not so bad once you get used to the sweetness and the metallic aftertaste."

"Um," Lily said, completely thrown off-kilter by his kind gesture. "Alright, thank you. But no funny business. If I hear that car engine, I'll use my gun," she warned.

"You're lying." He smirked at her. Damn, that smirk… That smirk was dangerous alright.

"No, I'm not." Lily stuck her chin out, her chest puffing up as her shoulders lifted.

His eyes dipped down to her breasts. His brows furrowed for a second, the tip of his tongue darting out to lick a corner of his lip.

Something pulled in Lily's lower belly, teasing her…That tongue…

His eyes returned to her and she wondered if he was blushing underneath the dirt.

"I know you're lying because you would have used it on me last night. If you had it upstairs, you would have gotten to it once you had my sword and Sammy was safe. If it was down here, you would have reached for that instead of the candlestick last night. There are only two floors in these newer houses, maybe an attic. So, I know you don't have a gun."

Lily's jaw unhinged, hanging open like a fish. "How did you…?"

He shrugged. "I'm going to get those peaches." He peeked through the peephole before stepping outside the house.

Lily moved to the window, watching him. He pulled a few cans from the trunk of a Toyota Rav4. No infected lurked nearby. Good. She didn't feel like saving his ass first thing in the morning.

Would she have saved him though?

Lily stepped away from the window. Of course, she would. She was still human after all.

He returned a moment later with two cans of peaches in hand and a small backpack. "Breakfast is served." He strolled into the kitchen like he owned the house.

Lily followed behind him. "Why are you sharing your food with us?"

He rested his bag and the cans on the counter before answering. "Because you gave me a safe place to sleep last night."

"Did I have a choice?" she asked.

He shrugged and said nothing else. He busied himself by rummaging through drawers, searching for a can opener. When he found one, he pulled some bowls and mugs from the cupboard.

Lily rested her hip against the kitchen doorway as Flynn continued to invade her pantry. The muscles in his shoulder strained through the thin fabric of his shirt as he pushed aside cans and boxes. He pulled down a few packets of sweetener and an open container of powdered milk.

"How do you take your coffee?"

"The stove is electric. It doesn't—" she began.

Flynn unzipped his bag and pulled out a French press and a camping stove, setting them on the kitchen counter. Grabbing a water bottle, he emptied the water into a small pot and placed it over the open flame. He scooped a can of Maxwell House Breakfast Blend from a shelf in the pantry.

Lily smelled the coffee from across the room the moment he opened the lid. The memories of lazy weekend mornings and peace wafted around her for a moment. "I haven't had coffee in so long," she admitted. She saw him smirk for a second. That smirk…coffee wasn't the only thing she hadn't had in so long…

Lily's mouth went dry as she found him staring at her, waiting for her answer. "Black, three Sugars."

"I should have guessed you like it sweet."

"Like what sweet?" she asked.

A hint of a smile flickered at the corner of his lip before he busied himself with breakfast and pretended to ignore her question.

Lily felt a blush creep up her cheeks as she realized what it must have sounded like. "I didn't mean—"

Flynn chuckled. "I know what you meant, Sweetheart." He turned toward her, those blue eyes smoldering as his gaze locked onto her. Lily's feet froze to the kitchen floor, like prey stuck in an animal's claws. "But tell me, Lily…do you like *that* sweet? Or do you need it darker?" he growled, his voice layered with a husky need.

"I… We're not talking about coffee, are we?" she asked.

"No." Flynn's eyes slid over the curves of her body. His eyes locked on her chest and her nipples responded by puckering into tight points, stretching toward him.

Her thighs squeezed together as a tingling spread between her legs. How long had it been since a man had looked at her like that? How long had it been since her body reacted so immediately to a man's gaze? "Flynn," she said, the name sliding from her tongue and almost filling her mouth before leaving. "I need—"

"Mommy!" Sammy shouted as she jumped off the bottom step onto the floor. "I'm hungry."

Lily's stomach dropped, her spine stiffening as her daughter flounced into the room with a cheery grin. The little girl dissolved the tension crackling in the air moments ago. Lily missed that tension.

Sammy dashed over to her mother, her eyes wide as she eyed Flynn up and down. "He's dirty." Her nose wrinkled in disgust like she could smell something nasty radiating off Flynn that Lily could not.

Flynn let out a bark of a laugh, the booming sound echoing around the kitchen. The tension slipped from the air, but Lily could feel her nipples rubbing against the cotton of her tank top.

"Sammy, that's not a nice thing to say." Lily scolded, resting her hand on top of her daughter's head while keeping an eye on Flynn.

"No, she's right. I'm a mess. I stink. My clothes are so dirty they're almost brown." A knowing smile flitted across his dirt-smudged face as he set their breakfast on a table like it was a typical Sunday morning. "Coffee will be ready in a minute."

Sammy ran toward the table and jumped into a chair with surprising enthusiasm. Sammy was not a morning child. Most nights Lily struggled to get Sammy to bed at a reasonable hour and wake her up at a normal time.

Flynn slid a bowl of fruit across the table toward Sammy along with a spoon and a bottle of water. Sammy dug into the sweet fruit cocktail as Lily waited for the coffee to finish brewing. "You can wash up if you'd like," Lily said.

"Are you sure you want to waste the water?" he asked, his eyebrow quirking up in surprise. "There's a stream only a few miles down the road."

She nodded. "Yes, I'm sure. I wouldn't have offered otherwise. I can spare a little water in exchange for your peaches."

"Well, I already said the peaches were for your hospitality," he said.

"Well, then maybe you owe me something for the water," she teased.

"Whatever you want from me, Sweetheart," he growled. He winked as he poured coffee into mugs for each of them and spooned some Sugar into her cup. "Enjoy," he said, placing her mug in front of her with a smile.

Lily held the warming mug between her palms, letting the smell of fresh coffee waft around her like smoke. She sipped from her cup and let out a soft moan as the strong brew swept across her lips and lingered on her tongue before sliding down her throat. Her body relaxed, sinking deeper into her chair as her eyes closed. Heaven in a cup.

"Remind me to make you coffee all the damned time." Flynn smirked from across the table before taking a drink from his mug.

She shrugged. "Sorry. I just haven't had coffee in so long. None of the houses nearby have had any way to make it. I found coffee filters, but with no electricity or way to heat the water, they're useless."

"Mommy," Sammy interrupted. "Can I go?"

Lily ruffled the top of her daughter's wild hair. "Sure, just stay downstairs where I can see you."

Sammy scurried off to play with a box of LEGO while Lily and Flynn watched from the kitchen. "It's inspiring to see a kid playing again," Flynn said. "It's been too long." His eyes glistened with sadness.

A silence stretched before them, Flynn's eyes darkening as

though his mind was reaching back for some distant memory. "I had a daughter."

Lily's heart pinched. *Had?*

"What happened?" she asked.

"She had cancer, and when the disease spread…She had no immunity from the chemo. She caught the virus, or whatever the hell this thing is." His shoulders slumped as his smile faded. His cheery attitude disappeared and for a moment, Lily glimpsed a man whose heart had been ripped from his chest. A tortured soul, but one that kept smiling.

"I'm so sorry." Lily reached across the table, placing her hand on his arm, just below a small gash that was scabbed over. Warmth flooded through her palm, the hair on his arm tickling her fingers.

"What was her name?" she asked.

A smile returned to his lips, but not a happy smile. A bitter one. "Hope," he replied. "I've made my peace with her death. I don't know if she was meant for this new world. She was too sweet. Too innocent for what the world's become. I don't think she could have survived."

He rose from his seat, dislodging her hand from his arm. "I think I'll go wash up now." Grabbing a water jug from near the useless refrigerator, he marched up the steps with slow, heavy footsteps.

An anchor pulled Lily's heart down to the bottom of her stomach.

Poor Flynn.

She couldn't imagine the pain and heartbreak of losing a daughter to the disease. She shuddered, imagining a little girl with those deadened, pale eyes and gray skin, limping around like those monsters who used to be people. Her heart ached for him, from one parent to another.

The coffee in Lily's stomach churned as she watched Sammy. Her four-year-old scrunched her eyebrows together, examining her LEGO building with some gaps and dips between the pieces. It wasn't a perfect building, not even close, but Sammy continued to build, happy with her little creation.

Sammy was sweet and innocent too. Would she survive?

A pinch of fear hit the base of Lily's spine. Shivers wracked her body.

Sammy would survive.

Lily would fight, steal, cheat, kill, whatever she had to do to keep Sammy safe.

She moved into the living room, sitting in an overstuffed armchair. The book she had been reading was lying on the coffee table. She picked it up and continued where she left off, letting her mind disappear from the world around her.

Half an hour later, Lily heard a loud creak at the top of the stairs. Flynn stood on the landing. Droplets of water dripped from his dark brown hair and his blue eyes gleamed under thick, dark eyelashes. He had changed into a fresh pair of jeans and a navy t-shirt. His jacket and back-pack were slung over his shoulder and bounced against his back with each step he took as he descended. He's picked up his sword and scabbard and buckled them around his waist.

"I'm leaving today. It's not safe here," he announced as he reached the bottom step.

Panic slithered up Lily's spine. Leaving?

"Come with me. It's not safe in this house," he said again.

"You think I don't know that?" Lily snapped. She shoved a bookmark between the pages and glared at him. "I've been looking for a map or something for weeks. Trying to find some sort of escape out of here. I have a car too, you know. It's packed and ready to go at a moment's notice. But I won't leave until I know there's somewhere safer for us."

"And you haven't found anything?" he asked. He rested his

hip against the banister at the bottom of the steps. His eyebrow quirked up at her.

Anger boiled beneath her skin. Lily wanted to slap the expression right off his face. She couldn't tell if he was mocking her or thought she was a moron for staying. "Obviously not or we wouldn't be here."

"I know a place." The sing-song notes in his voice left bubbles of annoyance rolling in her belly.

"Oh, and where might that be? You do know Narnia doesn't exist, right?"

He chuckled. "I was thinking Hogwarts."

The bubbles popped. A small pain spread over the tip of Lily's tongue as she bit down on it to stop herself from laughing.

"So where is this place?" she asked, resting her book on the coffee table, and tucking her feet under her. "You had my interest. Now you have my attention."

"It never takes me that long to get a woman's attention," he smirked. A small metallic clinking noise filled the air as his nails drummed along the handle of his sword.

"Well, I'm not like most women."

His deep laugh bounced off the walls. Locks of hair slid around the collar of his shirt as he tossed his head back, revealing his Adam's apple.

For a second, Lily wondered what it would be like to kiss it, to trace her lips over his neck and up the rough stubble of his jaw.

"Penny for your thoughts?" he smirked.

Lily rolled her eyes. "Money's useless nowadays. Unless you want to use it as kindling to start a fire."

"Or paper to wipe your ass," he added.

"Oooh." Sammy's attention snapped up from her LEGO. "He said a bad word." She pointed her small finger and glared at Flynn. Her brows scrunched in irritation, probably because he could say words that she couldn't in front of her mom.

"Sorry," he apologized.

Lily's heart fluttered for a moment. He was blushing!

"So, what do you think we should do?" she asked.

Flynn coughed. "A few more weeks and this place will be overrun with infected. I'm going to try to find that refugee camp in Pennsylvania."

"Do you think it'll be safe there?" She leaned against the arm of the chair and gazed at him. She hadn't noticed the dimple on his left cheek when he smiled. And he smiled often. How could someone who'd lost so much smile like that?

"It's supposed to be safer than anywhere else I've been. I heard a few people talking about it when everything started to fall apart. I heard about the place on a radio broadcast before all the towers died. I figured it would be my best chance. If that doesn't work, I'm going to a small island off the Jersey Shore. I'll clean out the island of infected if I have to and try to make a camp there. There should be enough supplies on an island to last me until they find a cure for this thing or until I die of boredom. Whichever comes first."

"Well, we'll keep you company. Boredom won't be an option with Sammy around. But we're taking your car. Mine is, well, it's a piece of junk," she admitted.

Flynn's laughed. "Fine. I'm driving."

Lily opened her mouth to speak, but before she could say anything, Flynn strolled across the room and held a hand up to stop her. He sat across from her on the couch, leaning into the seat with one leg propped up on his knee.

"He's what we do. You and Sammy pack up some necessities. I'll carry some of the food to the car. And we get the hell out of here. We'll drive until we find a place I can get more gas. I'll keep you both safe. I promise."

Lily pursed her lips together. "I've been keeping me and Sammy safe just fine, thank you very much."

The corners of Flynn's lips creased, revealing that dimple of his cheek. "Sweetheart, I have no doubt you can keep yourself safe. But, maybe I need someone to watch my back, too. Did you ever think of that?"

His eyes twinkled as he reached across the coffee table, the rough pad of his thumb tracing small designs over her knuckles.

Tiny electric sizzles shot into Lily's hand and up her wrist. Another person's touch. How long had it been? Two months since she had touched any living person besides her daughter? And to be touched by this man—someone who seemed so strong. Someone who wore his heart on his sleeve and a smile on his face, even in this horrible hell.

"Alright," she nodded. "You better get the stuff out of my car."

His grin lit up the room brighter than the morning sunshine. "Great, I'll get packing." He stood, and in three long strides, he closed the distance between them. He leaned low, his face inches from her. "You won't regret this, Sweetheart." His rough lips brushed against her cheek. His stubble tickled the delicate skin. His warm breath teased the tip of her ear. "Trust me," he whispered before walking into the kitchen.

Lily's heart thudded like an African drum, her mind whirling so fast she thought she would fall out of her chair. A man hadn't been this close to her in years. The strange feel of his lips invited her for more. A dull ache steadily grew throughout her body. She remembered that ache. She hadn't felt it in so long, but he sparked something deep inside her. She missed that feeling. Of being wanted. Of wanting.

"Mommy," Sammy said, derailing Lily's devious train of thought.

She smiled at her daughter, her heart still fluttering like a hummingbird. "Yes, sweetie?"

"Where are we going?" she asked.

So, her daughter had heard their conversation. She sat on the floor, playing with toys, and gave no hint that she was still listening to the adults. Clever girl.

Lily beamed with a little bit of maternal pride. "We're going to go find some more people. Maybe some more kids for you to play with," she said.

"Yay!" Sammy squealed, bouncing up and down.

"Shh!" Lily said, pressing a finger to her lips. "Remember, they're still outside."

Sammy cupped her tiny hands over her mouth. "Sawwy," she mumbled from beneath her fists.

Lily laughed. "Come on now, fairy Queen. We have to pack."

She watched her daughter rush up the steps to their bedroom, her tiny curls bouncing on her shoulders as she hurried along in excitement. Lily followed Sammy up the stairs to the second-floor landing. She glanced down at the bottom of the steps.

Flynn leaned against the wall, watching her walk. His lower lip was caught between his teeth, raw hunger flashing in his eyes. When he noticed she had stopped, he winked, before returning to the kitchen.

Lily blushed. This was going to be an interesting trip.

CHAPTER 3

Flynn roamed around the block one last time to wipe out any lingering infected that might be blocking their path. He held his gleaming sword in one hand, while Lily gripped the steak knife she had slipped between the laces of her boot. She also kept a second knife tucked away in a makeshift holster against her hip. Some thick cloth, the covers of a few leather-bound books, and a belt made for a sturdy, homemade holster.

Sammy hopped into the backseat of the car before Lily handed her a bottle of water.

"I'm tired of water," Sammy pouted, crossing her arms over her tiny chest.

"I know, sweetie, but you need to drink some," Lily said, placing the bottle beside her daughter. She shut the door before twisting open the cap on her own bottle. She took a sip, the lukewarm liquid flooding her mouth.

God, she missed ice.

The sun gleamed high above them, heat pounding down on their shoulders and the tops of their heads. Sweat trickled down Flynn's broad chest and dampening his new shirt.

Lily wanted to peel that shirt off him inch by damp inch, like unwrapping a very naughty Christmas present.

"Ready to go?" he asked.

She blinked and realized that she had been staring at his chest for God knows how long. Heat crept up her neck where the sun didn't touch her. "Yes," she squeaked.

"Was I interrupting something?" Flynn stepped closer, his breath tickling the damp skin on her cheek. His body hovered an inch from hers.

Lily's pulse raced as the intoxicating smell of him filled the air around her. Earth, sweat, musk, man—it was enough to drive her wild with need.

She needed air.

Lily stepped away from him, but her back pressed against the side of the warm car. Heat surrounded her from behind as Flynn smiled down at her, his eyes sparking with hunger. She was trapped. And she liked it. Her blood raced, heated by more than the hot summer sun. "N...no," she stammered.

His hands flew up to the sides of her head, pinning her between them. The weight of his body pressed against her and she gasped. Her nipples grazed against her shirt, squished against the hard muscles of his abs. Sizzles of awareness bolted from her chest down into her lower belly, stirring a need deep inside her core.

"What were you thinking about, Sweetheart?" he whispered in her ear, the tip of his tongue flicking out to taste the sensitive area against her jaw.

Lily whimpered. Her panties dampened between her aching thighs, her mind whirling. Touch. She wanted his touch. Needed it like she needed air.

A soft moan came from her right. But it wasn't Flynn. An infected had stumbled out from a back street and was hobbling toward them, teeth bared like a shark.

Flynn moved as quickly as a lightning strike. He pulled

himself from her body and gripped his sword. Yanking it from his scabbard in one fell swoop, the infected's head severed from its body and rolled against the ground like a gory bowling ball.

The growling sound continued until Flynn stabbed the tip of his sword through its eyeball. "Stab them in the head," he said. "It kills their brains. Otherwise, they're technically still alive. It's fucked up," he murmured quietly enough that Sammy couldn't hear that last part.

"We should go," Lily said. A chill slithering under her skin, cooling her in a way that made her stomach heave. For a moment, she thought she might be sick all over the sidewalk. She choked the feeling down and inhaled long, slow breaths to calm her nerves.

Flynn opened the passenger door for her. "Are you sure you have absolutely everything you need?"

"Yeah, I have medicine, clothes, soap. Did you clean out the pantry?" she asked.

He nodded as he closed her door and walked around to the driver's seat.

Lily watched the house disappear in the passenger side mirror as Flynn pulled away. Already, Lily missed that house. It had become a haven when all hell broke loose.

"Are you ok?" Flynn asked.

Lily sighed. "I'm fine, just feeling sentimental is all." She ran her hand through her hair, catching her fingers on some of the knots. She gripped her hair and tugged it up into a ponytail, keeping it out of her face and off her neck.

"Was that your house?" he asked.

"No, it was my mom's house," she said. "My mom died there. Just as the disease started to spread."

"I'm sorry." Flynn reached across the car, taking her hand in his. His rough fingertips rubbed the back of her hand, sending goosebumps rising on her arm.

"She died watching TV. The news of the disease literally scared her to death." Lily glanced in the rearview mirror. Sammy was busy staring out of the window, but she didn't know how much more she could say with her daughter within earshot.

"Did she T-U-R-N?" Flynn spelled out, giving Lily a nod toward the back seat—after all, little children have big ears.

"No," Lily said. "A neighbor found her. I was only there to make the funeral arrangements and sort through her final affairs. Then they closed the airports and the train stations, and Sammy and I were stuck just outside of Columbus."

"I'm so sorry, Sweetheart." Flynn's voice filled with genuine sadness. He squeezed her hand one last time before letting go.

Cool air washed over the skin where his skin had touched her. Lily missed the warmth of his touch, but she said nothing.

They flew down the road behind the house, littered with debris and abandoned cars. The road stretched beyond them for miles, with a few twists and turns along the way. The SUV's windows were rolled down, letting the warm summer air blow through the car.

After about an hour of quiet driving, Sammy's head drooped, and she napped in the back seat. Lily turned, checking on her daughter occasionally like this was somehow a normal family drive. They could be going on vacation, or going to visit family, or just out for a drive.

For a few hours, she felt normal again.

The car was running on fumes as they passed a gas station near Pittsburgh. "I'm going to try and fill up here," Flynn said as he steered the SUV into the parking lot. "Maybe you could go in and raid the convenience store. I'd kill for a Snickers bar right about now."

Lily rolled up the windows and opened the door. She

gazed at Sammy for a moment, watching her daughter, who was still sound asleep. Her little head lolled to the side, her eyelids fluttering.

"Can you keep an eye on her?" Lily asked Flynn.

"Of course," he said. He stepped out of the car and carefully shut the door behind him. "Don't worry. The child safety lock is on. She can't get out unless she climbs in the front seat." He strolled off toward one of the abandoned cars and grabbed an empty gas tank from a stack next to a broken ice machine.

Lily yanked a duffle bag from the trunk, careful not to wake Sammy. She locked the car doors and strolled into the store. Like every convenience store, the inside looked dirty and dim. A thin layer of dust had settled over the packaged food. Lily scanned the aisles, but there was no moaning, no infected to be found.

She pulled out her knife just to be safe.

Some of the shelves had been picked clean, but there was still enough food to keep them well-fed for weeks. Yanking open her bag, she emptied boxes of protein bars, candy cars, pop tarts, chips, beef jerky, and bottles of water. She even grabbed a few Cokes for a special occasion. She crouched down to check the dates on a few bottles of Gatorade on the bottom shelf.

"What do you think you're doing?"

Lily's stomach dropped as a water bottle fell from her hands. Her blood iced as she turned her head to face the scratchy voice behind her.

The stranger grabbed onto her ponytail pain exploded over her scalp as he yanked her up from the floor by her hair. Her body froze as pain rocketed from her scalp down her spine. She lost her grip on the knife and it clattered to the floor.

The man spun her around to face him. Yellowish teeth

and beady black eyes towered over her. He reminded Lily of the orcs from *Lord of the Rings*, only much smellier. Clearly, he hadn't showered since the breakout began.

"Hey guys, look what I found," he said, calling over his shoulder.

Two more men stepped out of the employee break room. One man was scrawnier, with a long, thin scar on his cheek. The other looked like the Orc's bald twin.

"Nice catch," Scarface said, his eyes roaming over Lily's body. She lashed out, trying to free herself, but the orc tightened his grip.

"Are you alone, precious?" Orc asked.

Precious? She would have pointed out the irony of the Orc calling her Precious, but now didn't seem like the time for jokes. "Yes," she lied.

Let these creeps know Sammy and Flynn were just outside? Over her dead body.

"Liar," Baldy said. "We heard car doors close outside. Too many for just a little bitch like you."

"Lock it," said the Orc. Scarface went over to the store's door and slid the bolt quietly into place.

Lily screamed like a banshee, fighting and kicking, but the Orc wrapped one strong arm around her arms, trapping her to him. "Come on. In the backroom you go," he teased, dragging her into the break room.

She kicked out, her feet slamming into the ground, into shelves, but missing her mark. Their laughter drilled into her ears as gunshots fired outside the store.

Flynn! Sammy!

Lily fought harder.

"Hold still, precious. We'll let you go when we're done," Orc breathed in her ear.

Lily's stomach twisted into knots. She wanted to vomit,

but fear gripped her stomach like a vise, keeping everything in.

Baldy grabbed at one leg while Scarface unzipped his pants. His aroused cock poked out from his dirty underwear.

Lily screamed again, but they kept laughing.

Another gunshot echoed, but louder this time. Scarface shrieked, falling to the floor as blood squirted from where his ear had been.

Lily swung her foot upward, the toe of her boot colliding with Scarface's jaw, jerking his head upward.

"Let her go," a fourth voice said from the back doorway.

"Fucking hell," Baldy said, pulling a pistol from his back pocket. But before the barrel of the gun was fully out of his pocket, the fourth man shot Baldy, his brain scattering across the wall and falling to the ground.

"Let her go," the man said again, pointing his gun at the Orc. Sunlight streamed in behind the man, clouding their vision. The Orc let go of one of Lily's arms to shield his eyes. His fatal mistake.

Lily reached down and yanked her knife from her boot-laces. With a sweaty grip, she tugged, twisted and pulled her arm upward into the Orc's side. The blade sunk into his skull with a satisfying, sucking motion.

Orc's hand fell away from Lily's body as he collapsed in a heap at her feet. He was dead before he hit the floor.

"Bastard," Scarface shouted from the floor. He stood on shaky legs and lunged for the stranger in the doorway.

With another bang, Scarface collapsed to the ground, a bullet entering his chest, piercing his heart and exiting out between his ribs. The bullet landed on the floor before he did.

"We have to go. The roamers are coming," the stranger said, holding out his hand.

Lily bent down, tugging her knife from Orc's head and slipping it into her holster. "No, my daughter's outside."

Turning her back on him, she raced back to the refrigerators. She grabbed her duffle bag and the knife that had fallen to the ground before she bolted to the front door.

The man followed behind her, but she ignored him. He didn't lunge at her. He made no attempt to stop her. Instead, he just watched her and grabbed a pack of Starbursts on his way out.

As they stepped outside, Lily froze. A dozen infected surrounded the car. Sammy screamed from inside the car.

Tears burned Lily's eyes. She dropped the duffle bag, gripped her knife tighter, pulled her second knife from her boots, and ran into the horde.

Flynn slashed at them with his sword, one after the other falling at his feet, but more infected poured out from the forest beside them.

"Lily!" Flynn shouted. An infected fell in his path and his sword came down, severing its head in half.

The stranger pulled out a long knife from his side, joining Lily in the fight. They slashed and stabbed, with the infected falling to the floor like dominoes, one by one.

Sammy screamed from inside the car as blood smeared the windows. "Mommy!" she shrieked.

"Sammy! Stay inside the car!" Lily yelled, tears streaming down her cheeks.

The tip of her knife sunk into an infected's eyeball and slid deeper before she yanked it back out. Blood stained her arms, but Lily ignored the icky feeling. She needed to get rid of these infected. She had to get to Sammy. Her daughter needed her.

More infected. More screams. More deathblows. More blood.

Finally, after what seemed like an hour-long battle with

the infected, the last one fell from Flynn's sword. Lily dropped her knives and fumbled in her pocket for the keys, her hands trembling like she was in an earthquake as she tried to unlock the door.

The stranger took them from her hand and unlocked the door for her, pulling open the driver's seat. He hit the unlock button for all the doors and watched.

Lily flew into the backseat, clutching her crying daughter like she might disappear from the earth at any second. "Oh, Sammy," she cried into the child's bushy hair. "Sammy, my baby girl. Sammy." Lily wept, holding onto her daughter for dear life.

Relief flooded her system, overwhelming her. Her daughter was safe and in her arms. Throat-clenching panic gave way to bone-deep relief.

The two men stared at her. "Thanks for that," Flynn said, nodding toward the stranger.

The stranger nodded back without a word, his fingertips tapping against the end of his knife before sliding it back into its holster.

There was a long pause without another word from the men. The stranger walked off and turned on a tap on the side of the building. He rubbed the blood and grime from his hands and arms. Flynn followed him and did the same. "What happened in there?" Flynn leaned over and asked. "I heard her scream, but I couldn't see her. I tried shooting out the glass, but…"

"The glass is bulletproof. Think about how easy was for people to rob convenience stores before all this shit happened," the stranger mumbled. "Bet your shots are what brought the infected right over to us."

Flynn shrugged. "Perhaps you're right. I hadn't considered the noise. I just knew I had to get in there."

The stranger stood closer to Flynn, standing a few inches

taller than him, his crew-cut, blond hair and streaked with dirt. "You hadn't considered it? You know loud noises attract those fuckers, right? Brings them right to where you're standing. You almost got us killed with that stunt."

"What went on in there?" Flynn asked again, ignoring his barb.

"She was almost raped, that's what," the stranger said.

Flynn's face flushed red, his lips upturned in a snarl before jumping on top of the stranger, his fists crashing into whatever skin and bone he could reach. "You touched her! You son of a bitch. I'm going to kill you. I swear to God I'm—"

"Stop it!" Lily shouted.

Fists flew as both men tried to get the upper hand. More blood splattered the ground.

"Stop," she yelled again, before darting between them. She stretched out her hands like a teacher holding back two of her students from starting a fight.

"Ooh," Sammy's small voice echoed from inside the car before shutting the door, closing herself off from the adults and their fighting.

They stopped and glared at Lily, their gazes darting to Sammy in the car, then back at her. "What the fuck?" Flynn spat.

"He saved me," she huffed. Her chest constricted as she stood between the two men, power and testosterone pouring from every inch of their bodies. And she was caught in the middle. She shivered, but not with fear.

"There were three guys in there," she said. "They were trying to…well…and he came in and killed them. Just shot them right in front of me."

"She stabbed one of them," the stranger said with a hint of a proud smile teasing the corner of his lips. A glint of amusement flickered in his eyes.

Her gaze mirrored his own. She finally saw this stranger in full light. His warm, brown eyes glistened like a shiny bowl of melted milk chocolate, and his tan skin was almost as dark as his dirty blond hair.

Muscles strained under his clothes, rolling under the fabric as his body moved. His sharp gaze watched her like a predator. Was she his prey? The tip of his tongue darted between his full lips, calling to something deep inside Lily.

"You killed one of them?" Flynn asked, the harsh edge in his voice jolting Lily back to the present moment.

She stared into Flynn's piercing blue eyes. Instead of tamping down her fire, he stoked it. His stare seemed to rip through her, adding fuel to the flames building inside her. She mentally pulled herself together, piece by piece, trying to remember what was happening. The air heated as she felt both men gazing at her, her body warming in response.

"Yeah, she stabbed one of them in the head," the stranger said, staring between Flynn and Lily like he was trying to solve a puzzle.

Flynn blew out a long breath, ruffling his hand through his hair. "Flynn Irving," he said after a long minute, dropping his hand to shake the stranger's hand.

"Grant Duff," the stranger answered. They shook hands, glaring at one another like angry bulls, waiting for the other one to shoot first and start a war.

"We need to get back on the road," Lily said before either of them would say something that ended in another tornado of fighting men. "The sun will be going down soon. We still have a long drive ahead of us," Lily said. She walked to the tap and scrubbed the blood and grime from her hands before shutting off the water.

"Look, why don't you come with us," she heard Flynn offer, taking them all by surprise.

Grant shrugged, "I'm better off by myself I think." His

gaze roamed over Lily again, soaking in her curves.

"Mommy!" Sammy whined inside the car, lifting the water bottle beside her. "It won't open!"

"Hold on, sweetie," Lily said. She went to open the back door of the car and twisted off the flimsy plastic cap before handing the bottle off to Sammy. She sat on the seat beside Sammy, keeping her attention focused on the men. She heard snippets of the conversation between Sammy's gulps and annoyed mumbles.

Flynn coughed. "Look, I think we're better off in larger groups."

"I think you and your family are just fine on your own," Grant shrugged.

Flynn shook his head. "I just met them yesterday. But, things have already gotten off to a rocky start, and there are two of them to protect. Lily's a fighter, but it's not easy protecting a four-year-old. The more people in our company, the safer for all of us."

Grant's gaze flickered from between them. "Where are you guys going?"

Flynn rubbed the back of his neck. "There are rumors of a refugee camp in Pennsylvania, out near Lancaster."

Grant rolled his eyes. "That's still really far from here, especially if you're staying off the highway. That's hours of driving ahead of you."

"I know," Flynn said. "But it's the only piece of information I have at the moment unless you know a better place."

Grant paused before shaking his head. "No, I haven't heard of any sort of camp at all. Not til now anyway."

"Come with us," Flynn said.

Grant paused, then nodded. "Okay. But what's with Lily? Where's the little girl's dad?"

Flynn shrugged. "Honestly, I have no idea. But there was no man around when I found her yesterday. I don't know if I care enough to find out. Frankly, I'm happy she's not attached to anyone, or we'd have a problem."

"Same here," Grant said, his eyes sharpening as he stared Flynn down.

But, Flynn stared back. "What makes you think I'm not already involved with her?"

"Are you?" Grant asked, his brows crinkling together.

"Look, I'll be straight with you. I'm not. That's not going to stop me from trying."

Grant shrugged again. "Why not see what she wants? Cause I like her. She's fierce. A fighter. I like that about her."

"You barely know her."

"You've only known her for one day," Grant pointed out.

"In this world, that might as well be a year." Flynn paused, rubbing the stubble on his chin. "We've both just met her. I'm not going to stand in your way, but don't stand in mine. Let her choose. This whole place is screwed up enough. I don't want some jealous punk tagging along if it's going to cause problems."

"I don't think there's anything to be jealous of. But fine. And I'm not stupid enough to cause any trouble. The world's a rough enough place without starting a fight over a girl. Grow up, kid."

"Kid?" Flynn leaned back with an amused smirk. "How old are you?"

"Thirty-five." Grant crossed his arms over his chest. "I lost track of time a couple of weeks after the infection spread. Just got back from Iraq when the world went to hell, a few months ago. Maybe longer. What about you? What's your story?"

"I used to be a professor at Notre Dame. Medieval history. I started heading east from Illinois when I heard about the refugee camp. And I turned thirty as of last week," Flynn frowned a bit.

"Well, happy birthday, kid," Grant smirked.

Flynn laughed, the small bark shaking a couple of nearby birds from a tree. "Thanks, old man."

Grant glanced back at car toward Lily and Sammy. His face softened and a small light illuminated behind his eyes when he saw Sammy. The men talked a bit quieter, but Lily could have sworn that she heard her name. She knew for sure she had when both men watched her, a primal hunger burning in both sets of eyes.

The fluttery, anxious feeling returned while she was stuck in their gazes, like a fly caught in a dangerous web. But she liked this feeling. She wondered if she would be feeling it more often if Grant joined them.

Grant nodded and both men came to the car. Grant climbed into the passenger's seat while Flynn grabbed her fallen duffle bag and packed it in the trunk. He rummaged through it and pulled out two Snickers bars. He handed one to Sammy and kissed Lily full on the mouth. Her lips tingled as his crashed down onto her, consuming and overpowering her. Her hand snaked up his hard chest as he entwined his fingers into the hair at the nape of her neck.

"Mommy, where'd the cap go?" Sammy holding out her water bottle.

Flynn smirked as he broke their kiss. "I think someone needs else needs your attention right now, Sweetheart," he said before closing her door and taking the wheel.

They said nothing as they drove away on a full tank of gas. Lily's lips tingled, a little bruised but no worse for the wear.

Grant's gaze slid back to her, a faint frown tugging on the corners of his mouth. He turned his attention back to the road in front of them, giving Lily just enough privacy to reach up and touch her swollen lips.

How long had it been since she'd been kissed like that?

CHAPTER 4

The car creaked along a wooden bridge before winding its way back up to the main road somewhere outside of Pittsburgh. Lily and Sammy snuggled close to one another and Sammy rested her head on her mother's arm as she listened to Lily read her a tale about Hobbits and Elves and a magic ring. Sammy wanted a magic ring, "just like the one in the book." The adults laughed, and Sammy couldn't figure out why that was funny.

"How far until we reach the refugee camp?" Grant asked as he kicked his feet up on the dashboard.

"If we keep taking back roads, I'd estimate two more days," Flynn said.

"I'd estimate," Grant mumbled, imitating Flynn's rumbling voice. "Who talks like that?"

"College professors," Flynn growled.

"Do you think it would be worth it to try the highway?" Lily suggested, trying to ease the building tension as she closed the book.

Grant shook his head. "No, I tried that before. Too many cars just stopped in the middle of the lanes, too many infected roaming around the cars, and broken-down cars are the perfect place for scavengers."

Grant swiveled in his seat and gave Lily a pointed look. "You know what they can be like. Best to stay off the main road."

"Like Frodo," Sammy said.

Lily and Grant blinked, their heads turning toward the little girl in shock as Flynn laughed. "Clever girl," he chuckled.

"Guess she takes after her mom," Grant winked at Lily before swiveling back in his seat.

Warmth spread over Lily's cheeks as her heart melted in her chest.

"Wonder how many people will be there," Grant said.

"I'm hoping dozens if we're lucky," Flynn said. "More than that could be dangerous. Fewer than that and they might be struggling too much to be of any use to us. Frankly, I miss large groups of people. I never thought I'd miss being stuck in a crowd, but I'd give anything to be in the middle of a baseball game right now."

"Or a rock concert." Grant shifted in his seat, performing an air guitar solo that had Sammy in tears. Pearls of little girl laughter bounced around the car.

Happiness expanded in Lily's chest as fat little tears rolled down Sammy's cheeks. Grant's hair swished back and forth in time with his scratchy vocals, cranking out a gritty solo of "Wild Thing." He added a drum solo, which made Sammy shriek with laughter. The easy smile brought a light to his eyes. His smile was infectious and Lily found herself wanting to launch across her seat and kiss him.

"Watch out!" Flynn shouted. He slammed his foot on the breaks, but it was too late.

Lily flung her arm out to keep Sammy pressed against the

seat. Their bodies slammed against the seat belts, knocking the wind from Lily's chest.

The tires shredded against the asphalt and the car wobbled as the Rav came to a sudden stop in the middle of an empty road. The air filled with the sound of deafening silence. No birds. No crickets. Only nothing.

The four of them climbed out of the car, surveying the damage to the tires. Grant pointed to the ground behind them. Police grade tire shredders lined across the road, spray-painted black to match the tar.

"Fuck," Flynn shouted. He kicked a shredded tire, looking around to see who had placed them.

Right on cue, a loud shriek came from between the trees. A battle cry. Then the popping sounds of gunfire filled the air. Bullets sprayed in their direction, bouncing off the SUV and hitting the ground by their feet.

"Behind the car," Grant shouted, shielding Sammy as he ushered them behind the SUV. He yanked opened the door and grabbed his shotgun from the passenger seat. A bullet shattered the window just inches above his head.

Flynn yanked his gun from his jacket pocket and reached over the car's hood, shooting in the direction of the bullets.

Lily looked around. She only had her knives. She never thought she'd be the person to bring a knife to a gunfight, but here she was. Useless.

Another bullet shattered a window, glass raining down into Sammy's curls like heavy raindrops. The little girl sobbed, cupping her hands over her ears. "Make them stop, mommy."

"Get her out of here!" Flynn barked. His wild eyes shone with fear as the rest of his body tenses, priming him for fight mode. With a lingering stare, he pulled his attention back to the fight and aimed his weapon.

Lily's chest tightened. Fear gripped her throat, unable to

speak. What if they didn't come back? What if they were separated?

Sammy sobbed, pressing her head against her mom's arm. They needed to leave. Now.

She lifted Sammy in her arms and, crouching low, she bolted into the woods. She heard shouts and more gunfire before she disappeared into the cluster of trees. Lily's feet flew like she was running on air. Twigs and leaves crunched under her boots as she lifted Sammy higher, clutching her close to her chest. "It's ok, sweetie" she panted. "We're ok."

Sammy whimpered against her mother's breast. Her small body bounced as Lily jogged farther and farther away from the banging gunshots. Soon the only sounds were crackling leaves under her feet and the heavy gasps escaping her chest.

Setting Sammy down on the ground, Lily whipped around, taking in her surroundings. The road disappeared somewhere behind them. Or in front of them. Maybe to the left?

Lily's gaze wandered from tree to tree. Her heartbeat thudded in her chest, air drawing into her lungs like small ice shards.

They were lost. She didn't know if either of the men had survived. Was the fight still going on? How long had she been running? It felt like hours. Her calves throbbed in pain, and her shoulders stiffened from carrying Sammy through the woods.

She huffed again, staring at the sun as it set a little lower beyond the trees. The sunlight seemed to dim with every passing minute.

Sammy's short arms hugged her mother's thigh tightly.

Lily rested her hand in Sammy's bushy curls and shards of glass rubbed between her fingers.

Fear crept up her spine. Someone had shot at Sammy, and this terrified her even more than the infected.

Sunlight glinted off the flecks of glass in her daughter's fiery hair. "Close your eyes," she heard herself tell Sammy, though her voice sounded foreign. Like listening to herself talk in a dream.

Lily brushed the thick curls between her fingertips, glass falling around Sammy's feet like snowflakes.

"It's okay, Sammy," Lily said, trying her best to sound confident and relaxed. Her heart beat like a wild animal in her chest as fear slid through her skin and pierced her heart.

Sammy screamed, her hands balling into fists in front of her face. The shriek echoed around them, filling the air.

"Shh," Lily said, pointing a finger to her lips.

"Mommy!" Sammy cried, pointing behind her mother.

Lily turned to see two infected wobbling toward them, their jaws stretched, oozing blood and bone. Slivers of flesh stuck in their gnawed teeth like pieces of human spinach. Their dead eyes gleamed like monsters from a nightmare as they made their way between overgrown bushes and gnarled branches.

Lily yanked her knife from its holster and stood, blocking Sammy from them.

Sammy ran behind a tree.

One of the infected lunged at Lily, its mouth hung open like a decaying piranha. Its rotting stench tested her gag reflex. Decaying skin and infection filled the air around her, and Lily had to take a step away from the creature to catch her breath. She jumped toward it, but it moved. Her knife sunk to the hilt into the infected's shoulder. It kept walking toward her, unaffected by the blade in its side.

Sammy screamed and ran as the second infected came up to Lily's side and knocked her to the ground. Lily's blade slid out of the infected's shoulder as she fell, her hand tightening so hard on the hilt her knuckles turned ghostly white.

The first infected fell to the ground on top of her, its teeth chomping like a rabid dog. Adrenaline pumped through Lily's veins, filling her with a need to fight. Flight wasn't an option. She thrust the knife into its temple. The infected stopping moving and died on top of her.

Lily squirmed under the corpse, its weight pinning her to the ground.

The second infected fell to its knees beside Lily, grabbing onto her arm, her knife slipping from her fingers. Its mouth opened, its grip too tight on her arm to move. She struggled and squirmed as the infected's mouth lowered toward her fleshy underarm.

A loud pop ripped through the air.

The infected crumpled in a heap next to her, half of its head blown to bits on the dried grass nearby. Then the forest was quiet, except for the sound of crunching leaves and Lily's heavy breathing.

"Lily!" Flynn kneeled on the ground beside her, pulling the corpse off her. "Lily! My God, are you hurt? Did they bite you?"

Warmth drained her body, leaving her numb. The sound of the gunshot rang in her ears. The image of those hollow eyes, those gruesome mouths, the smell…

She heaved up the contents of her stomach onto the second infected's body. Her muscles contracted as she heaved over and over again, her brow glistening with sweat. When her stomach was empty and her mind cleared, she spat to clear the taste in her mouth.

"I think she's alright." Grant's gaze roamed over her he helped her stand on shaky legs. "I don't see any bites or scratches. She's just scared."

"Sammy," Lily croaked out. "Where's Sammy?"

"She was with you," Flynn said. "Sammy!" he shouted out. No answer. Not even a leaf moved.

"Sammy!" Lily tried. Nothing.

"Sammy!" she shouted louder. Silence filled the air. Lily walked around on trembling legs. Fear clenched her throat as her stomach squeezed in a vise. "Sammy!" she cried out, doubling over. "No, no…Sammy!" she screamed. Tears stung her eyes as she stared out at the vast crop of trees around them.

"Sweetheart, stop." Flynn wrapped her tightly in his arms. She rested her head against his hard chest as she sobbed. "We'll find her, I promise," he said. "She can't have gone far."

"She went this way," Grant said. He crouched down and lifted a broken twig fifteen feet away from them. "Let's go before it gets too dark out."

"She's afraid of the dark," Lily whimpered.

"Shh, it's okay. We'll find her. She won't be alone when it's dark outside." Lily nodded against his chest before moving away from him and in the direction Grant pointed.

Lily stayed quiet as they trudged through the trees, her eyes scanning every corner, every tree, every bush.

"So how'd you know she went this way?" Flynn asked.

Grant shrugged. "I was in the Marines. They train you for a lot of stuff in the Marines. Before that, my uncle used to take me and my sister hunting, sometimes fishing. Not much to do in Hazelton when you're a kid."

"Hazelton?" Flynn asked. "Never heard of it."

Grant ground out a bitter laugh. "Most people haven't unless you know the area. Small little town. Everyone knows everyone."

"That must have been nice," Flynn said.

"It was hell," Grant added.

"I think this is hell," Lily huffed as they walked up a steep hill, her calves burning, her heart racing so loud it sounded like background noise to their conversation.

Thump, thump. Thump, thump.

Find her. Find her.

"Nah, Sugar, this ain't hell. Hell is the desert." Grant paused and nudged a tree branch with the toe of his boots. "She made a left here." They altered their path and followed Grant's directions.

"This is hell for me," Lily murmured. "Hunting, Scavenging. Staying quiet for so long that you think you're going to go insane. Worried you might snap and scream until your lungs burst. Watching people around you die and morph into monsters that try to eat you. This new world is its own kind of war zone."

They stayed silent for a moment.

"At least the forest is a hell of a lot nicer than the desert," Grant said. "Tracking down a bunch of terrorists in a sandstorm wasn't quite what I was expecting when I signed up to be a Marine."

"What did you expect?" Flynn asked.

Grant rolled his eyes. "Paperwork."

Flynn laughed. "If you wanted paperwork, you should have been a teacher. You would have been drowning in it."

Grant shrugged. "Couldn't afford college. It was the military or the Hazleton warehouses. I chose the military. My sister joined the National Guard. My dad gave her so much shit, joining the weekend warriors."

"Weekend warriors?" Flynn asked. "Sounds a bit disrespectful."

Grant barked a harsh laugh that left a squirrel running from behind a bush. "Yeah, well my dad wasn't the most stand-up, politically correct guy out there. He said what he thought and didn't give a damn about hurting anyone."

"Is he still out there?" Lily asked.

Grant shrugged. "Don't know. Don't care. I haven't seen him in five years, just before my third tour."

"What about your sister?" Flynn asked.

"You ask a lot of questions kid," Grant grumbled, walking past Lily to the top of the hill.

"She changed direction again." Grant stopped and walked east.

At least Lily thought it was east. Maybe it was south?

She followed Grant through the thick trees, the light getting dimmer by the minute. "It's getting dark," she said. "What if Sammy…"

If anything happened to Sammy… Lily couldn't go down that road of 'if.' She'd lose her mind.

"She'll be okay. She's a bright girl," Flynn said. He rested a hand on Lily's shoulder, the soft weight pressing down on her like it was supposed to be comforting. Nothing would calm her until she had Sammy back safe and sound.

Grant led them onto a back road with homes lined up in a neat little row. "She might have gone into one of the houses," Grant said.

"Sammy!" Lily shouted, running to the street, looking into the windows of the empty houses. "Sammy!"

Grant ran up behind her and covered her mouth with a rough hand. The taste of sweat and heat lingered on her lips. "Shh, you'll bring every infected to our position if you keep shouting like that."

"Mommy!" The soft cry echoed down the road.

Lily struggled against Grant's grip, trying to run in the direction of the sound.

"We know she's near, but drawing the infected out might get one of us killed, or maybe even get her killed. You need to stay calm," he barked into her ear.

Lily stopped fighting, her body tensing up against him. She knew he was right, but she wouldn't relax until she had her daughter safe in her arms again.

Flynn gripped the handle of his sword and walked toward

the sound. Lily and Grant followed, with Grant keeping a tight grip around Lily's shoulders to stop her from running.

Flynn crept into the backyard of a nearby house, his sword held tight. He raised his hand, halting Grant and Lily in their tracks. Peeking around the corner of the house, he checked out the backyard before waving them forward to him.

"There's a group of infected in the backyard," he began. "Maybe about a dozen of them. Sammy is hiding in a tree-house out of reach."

A whimpering sound echoed around them. The men stared at her for several seconds before Lily realized she was making that noise. "Sammy," she croaked.

"Shh, we'll get her. She's safe," Grant said, placing a hand on her shoulder. To keep her from running or to comfort her, she didn't know.

"We'll clear them out," Flynn said. "On my mark."

Flynn peeked around the corner again. He raised his hand. It hovered in the air, each second dragging.

Each second was another second Sammy was surrounded by infected.

Lily wrenched herself from Grant's grip and rushed around Flynn, bursting into the backyard.

She froze.

A swarm of infected moaned and walked beneath a tree-house in the back of the yard. Sammy was huddled by the entrance, her tiny body tucked into a ball. Infected wandered around, hunting for Sammy, smelling her, hearing her, but seeing no one.

"Mommy!" Sammy's scared shriek pierced Lily's heart like an icy needle.

"Stay there, sweetie! Mommy's coming!"

The infected turned toward her as Flynn and Grant burst

into the yard. The trio moved in cautious steps toward the treehouse.

The infected's attention shifted to the fresh meat in front of them. They wobbled and wound their way around the yard, stumbling over lawn chairs and rocks to get to them. A pink flamingo was crushed as an infected fell over and began crawling toward them.

"Get ready," Grant said, pulling out his handgun.

Lily grabbed both of her knives, one in each hand. She watched her daughter, moving around in the little treehouse, out of the clutches of the corpses below. She had to get to her. She had to keep Sammy safe.

Lily lunged into the fray, one knife sinking into an infected's skull before either of the men had moved out of formation. The corpse hadn't hit the ground before another one stumbled toward her. Her second blade shot upward through the bottom of its jaw, slicing through its mouth and stopping somewhere in its brain.

The men flanked out behind her. Grant, to her left, bashed in an infected's skull with the barrel of his gun. Flynn, to her right, slashed through an infected's skull, severing its head in half. Close together, the three of them fought like maniacs, inching toward Sammy. Corpses fell like paving stones in front of them, covered in slashes, gashes, crushed bone, and rivers of blood.

The group grunted as they fought through the horde, but Lily's focus fell on Sammy's cries and whimpers as the little girl watched the bloody battle below. Fear lingered in the air.

Her daughter might never want to leave the treehouse after watching them fight this mass of monsters—monsters that must have looked like people from that treehouse. From the air, Sammy wouldn't be able to see their pale eyes and bloodstained mouths.

As her blade sunk into an infected's eyeball and exited the

back of its skull, Lily wondered what had happened to her in the few hours they had left the house. This morning, she had a civil conversation with Flynn while sipping coffee and eating peaches, while watching her daughter play on a threadbare rug.

Now, she fought like a Spartan warrior to protect her daughter. Before the end of the world, Lily had only held a knife to cook. Now she sliced through flesh, muscle, and bone, trying to destroy these monsters that ruined Sammy's life. Ruined her life. Even if there was a cure tomorrow, Lily knew that the world would never feel normal again. And she hated these monsters for destroying her daughter's future.

As the last infected fell to its knees, Flynn's sword gleamed in the dying sunlight before crashing through its skull with a sickening thunk.

Lily's boots pounded on the dry grass as she rushed toward the treehouse steps nailed into the side of the trunk. Splinters dug into the tips of her fingers as she climbed, but she ignored the stabbing pain.

She needed to get to Sammy.

Lily hoisted herself through the small hole and into the tiny, musky treehouse. Aging wood creaked under her weight as she sat down.

Sammy flung herself into her mother's arms before Lily fully climbed inside, her little arms wrapping around Lily's waist.

"It's okay, baby. Mommy's here," Lily crooned, rocking her daughter from side to side. Relief punched through her chest as she felt Sammy's little arms cling tightly to her. Her daughter's messy curls tickled her chest as Sammy's little face buried against her bosom. "I love you, Sammy. It's alright. Everything's okay."

Sammy blubbered into her mother's side, drenching a small spot in Lily's t-shirt.

She lifted her daughter onto her lap and rocked her like she had when Sammy was a baby. She shushed and cooed, letting Sammy vent her fear and worry for a bit until finally, her little body went limp with exhaustion and relief.

"Sweetie, we need to get out of the treehouse," Lily said.

Sammy shook her head against Lily's chest, her curls whipping around her face.

"Yes, it's safe to come down now. There are no more monsters in the backyard. But it's going to be night time soon, and we need to find a place to sleep."

"We can sleep here." Sammy's muffled voice pinched Lily's chest.

"No, sweetie, we can't sleep here. We can't all fit in the treehouse. Flynn and Grant need to sleep, too."

"I don't want to," Sammy said.

"Come on, my brave fairy Queen. Sometimes we all should do things we don't want to. I promise, we'll keep you safe," Lily said.

"But who will keep you safe?" Sammy asked, pulling her head from her mother's chest. Her round eyes gleamed with fresh tears.

Lily smiled and ran a hand over her daughter's hair. "I have Flynn and Grant to keep me safe, sweetie. And I'll help keep them safe. We all need to watch out for each other. Now, come on down so we can find a good spot to sleep tonight."

Sammy paused before sliding out of her mother's embrace toward the opening in the treehouse. "Mommy, will Flynn and Grant keep me safe too?"

Lily brushed away a stray tear on her daughter's cheek. "Of course they will, Sammy. We'll all keep you safe."

"Okay," Sammy said before turning toward the steps.

Lily helped Sammy climb down, careful to avoid the splinters on the corners of the wood. Grant reached up and caught Sammy around the waist. "You're okay, baby girl. I gotcha," he said. He kneeled to set her down on the ground, but the four-year-old wrapped her small limbs around him.

Surprise pinched Lily's chest as she watched how comfortable Sammy was with Grant. Sammy feared men, and Lily used to blame herself for not dating or having no male friends for Sammy to be comfortable with. Other than the neighbors and the dads at daycare, Sammy's life was testosterone-free. Watching her daughter rest her head against a man's chest was…comforting.

Flynn held out his hand and helped Lily off the rickety steps. She winced, splinters digging deeper into her fingers. "Are you alright?" His brows furrowed with concern as his gaze slid over her, eying her for anything wrong.

"Yeah, just a few splinters in my hands," she shrugged.

"Come on," Grant said, "we need to get back on the main road. It's almost sunset. It'll be dark in a few more hours."

"What happened out there?" Lily asked.

Grant shrugged. "We shot. They shot. Eventually, they stopped shooting. Either they died or they ran out of ammo. Either way, when it stopped, we came to find you."

"We should have checked to see if there were still any of them out there," Flynn grumbled.

"If we did, Lily would have been bitten," Grant snapped. "Don't argue with me, kid. I've been through this shit before…And don't make me curse in front of Sammy." Grant shot Flynn a piercing stare before walking off, Sammy still held in his arms.

Flynn sheathed his cutlass and mumbled something about crotchety old men as he followed Grant out of the backyard.

Lily tucked her knives back into their spots for safe-keeping and walked behind him. Ahead of Flynn, Sammy's head nodded, dipping lower and lower until she finally fell asleep in Grant's arms, the movement of his body rocking her to sleep.

She strode past Flynn toward Grant. "Do you want me to take her?" she asked, holding her arms out to take Sammy.

She waited, but Grant shook his head. She tried to look him in the eye, but his gaze was focused on Sammy. A faint smile painted his lips as he watched the child sleep in his arms. A sweet affection twinkled in his eyes as he brushed aside a stray curl from Sammy's cheek. "I've got her." The tenderness in his voice left Lily's knees weak.

Exhaustion overcame her as her eyes shut and the world went black.

CHAPTER 5

"There she is." A deep voice floated over her, tracing her skin like velvet. "Come on Sweetheart. You fainted. Time to wake up, Sleeping Beauty."

Lily blinked as she stared up at the wide expanse of sky freckled with stars. Flynn's face slipped into her view.

"What happened?" The dryness in her mouth left her voice cracking.

"You fainted back there." Grant's cautious voice echoed beside her.

Lily lifted her head and saw Sammy sound asleep in Grant's arms. Her head pounded as she tried to take in her surroundings. Flynn's strong arms held her bridal style as they walked along the smooth tar road.

"We're on the road now," Flynn said. "The car is just up ahead."

"I can walk," she murmured.

"When we get to the car, I'll set you down. You need something to drink. You're dehydrated and you've gone through more than one shock for today."

Lily nodded and rested her head on his chest. Sandalwood. Sweat. Mint. Earth. A scent that was distinctly Flynn cocooned her like a safety blanket.

"Fuck," Grant whispered, loud enough for Lily to hear but low enough that Sammy continued sleeping soundly in his arms. Lily craned her neck over Flynn's shoulder to peek at the Rav.

Ribbons of tire rubber scattered along the road along with three corpses and dozens of bullet casings. "So, we're back to where we started. What now? Do we find another car?" Lily asked. "How much farther to the camp?"

"It's a couple more days if we find a car." Flynn grimaced, clutching his arm. "We need to find somewhere to hold up for the night, get some sleep and try to find another car tomorrow." He popped open the trunk of the Rav and yanked a water bottle from one of the bags, twisting off the cap before handing it to Lily.

"Drink," Grant said as Flynn zipped the bag shut.

"There were houses scattered along the road just a couple of miles back," Flynn said. "We could hole up in one of those for the night and reconvene tomorrow."

"It's getting too dark out." Grant frowned. "Forest on either side along the road. Too easy for scavengers and infected to spot us. I don't want to mess around with this area in the dark."

"Right," Lily agreed. "Maybe there's someplace nearby with a fence or something around it. A car dealership or someplace like that."

"Some schools have fences around them too," Grant said.

"We'll see what we can find before it gets too dark," Flynn said. He winced.

"What's wrong?" Lily asked, reaching for his shoulder. A small tear in the jacket caught her attention. "Were you shot?" She moved his arm and examined it more carefully.

She tugged the jacket's sleeve off his shoulder. A small

smear of bright red blood streaked over his shirt, rivulets of the sticky stuff trickling down his arm.

"You were fucking shot! And you didn't say anything!" Lily jabbed her finger into Flynn's chest. She winced as one of the splinters in her finger rubbed against his chest. "You idiot! You fought with a fucking gunshot wound, and you didn't say a damned word. Not even on this whole walk back. What is the matter with—"

"It's just a flesh wound," he smiled.

Lily glared at him.

"Monty Python? No? Really, Lily, it's just a scratch. The bullet grazed me. Though I'm glad to see you care, Sweetheart." He winked.

Lily stomped her foot like Sammy throwing a tantrum. "This is serious! You should have said something."

"Why? All of our medical supplies are right here," he nodded toward the car. "And we don't know how many infected were back in those woods."

"Infected. That's all the more reason to get out of here now," Grant said. "We can treat you when we find a place to stop for the night."

"We have to treat your splinters, too. Something like that can easily get infected if we're not—" Flynn began

Lily shivered. "Please don't say the word infected. It makes me think of them."

Flynn winced. "Sorry, Sweetheart. We should leave before it gets any darker." He opened the trunk of the car. "Everyone grab water, food, any medical supplies you can carry. We're leaving the rest behind."

Lily moved to grab a bag and a backpack from the trunk, shoveling any bottled water and food she could carry into the duffle bag. She loaded the pack with first aid supplies, bottles of pills, tablets, gauze, bandages, alcohol wipes, peroxide, whatever prescriptions they had from her mother's house.

"Ready?" Flynn asked, hoisting a shotgun out of the back and lifting a heavy bag. Some of their clothes were stuffed in there, along with all the weapons in the trunk.

Grant bent down and grabbed two handguns from the corpses on the ground and pointed east, careful not to jostle Sammy. "Let's go," he said.

The group walked up the road in silence, the sun slowly setting behind their backs. Streaks of pink flashed across the sky. Rays of orange and red light moved above them like flames, teasing them. Darkness was moving in.

Grant stopped, staring around him "We need shelter soon."

Flynn grumbled. "Let's find a house for the night and tomorrow we can search for someplace more secure."

"I know they weren't the best places to hide," Lily began, "but I'm sure we can stay in one of the houses on the back-road for one night."

Grant paused, his eyebrows crinkling in concentration. Lily could almost hear the gears in his mind grinding as he considered their limited options. "Let's go." He hoisted Sammy higher up onto his chest, walking back toward the woods. Flynn and Lily followed.

They said nothing as the group stayed in tight forma-tion. Their footsteps echoed in the silent forest. Grant led them back to the clump of houses near the treehouse. The first house had a shattered window, so they moved to the next.

Flynn hustled inside, sword in hand. Slinking from room to room, he checked every floor, every room, every closet, cabinet, and pantry before he declared it safe.

Lily went in next, followed by Grant and still sleeping

Sammy. "Are there any rooms with no windows?" Grant asked as he laid Sammy on a couch.

Lily tugged a blanket down, shook off some of the dust, and tucked her daughter in for the night.

Flynn nodded. "The small bathroom on this floor, right down the hallway."

"Good," Grant said. "I need candles or a flashlight and a first aid kit. I need to take a look at your arm before it gets infected. It might need stitches."

Lily shivered as though an icy hand had traced its fingers down her spine. "Don't say that word," she hissed.

Flynn rummaged through one of their bags and tossed a first aid kit to Grant, who caught it with one hand.

Grant picked up a jarred Yankee candle and a pack of matches in the other hand. "Let's go," he said, marching down the hallway. Flynn followed.

Silence flooded the house, the eeriness settling into Lily's bones and rocking her nerves on edge. Needed to move, to do something—anything—Lily left Sammy sleeping in the living room and decided to explore the first floor of the house. The kitchen used to be state of the art, but without electricity, it seemed like it was all for show now. A waste.

She rummaged through the cabinets, pulling out cans and boxes of food. The pantry was stocked well with natural, all organic food. Boxes of organic crackers, protein bars, cereals, peanut butter, pasta, jarred spaghetti sauce, and cans of low sodium vegetables and fruits.

She continued to rummage until she found a bottle of Jameson behind a box of linguine pasta. "Jackpot," she murmured to herself, grabbing the neck of the bottle and carefully leaping off the counter.

With the spoils of her search sitting on the kitchen counter, Lily moved to the dining room. A fancy bowl filled with plastic fruit sat on a dusty dining room table. A portrait of a smiling family with identical blond hair stared down at her. They looked happy. Happy to have a stranger in their home. Happy that their house was covered in dust. Happy that their lives would never be the same.

Maybe this family became infected when the breakout started.

Their smiles tugged at Lily's heart. She wanted to reach through the picture, hug these strangers and explain why she was there, in their house, without their knowledge, without their permission. A few months ago, Lily's group would have been breaking and entering. Now they were just trying to survive.

"Your turn, Sweetheart." Flynn's voice yanked her back to reality. He walked into the dining room and draped his uninjured arm over her shoulders. The stubble on his chin scratched her cheek as he gave her a soft kiss.

Lily's stomach fluttered like a giant butterfly. She slid from his arms and wandered off to find Grant.

The small, peach bathroom smelled like fresh pine Christmas trees and spicy apple pie. Printed pictures of daisies lined the walls in matching frames. Her stomach grumbled as she sat down on the closed toilet lid, covered in a rough rug cover with a daisy design. Grant sat on the edge of the tub, rummaging through the first aid pack. He pulled out a pair of tweezers, some alcohol wipes, and got to work.

"This might sting a little bit." He pulled out a wipe and cleaned her fingers. Small white-hot needles dug into her skin where the splinters remained. She winced when the tip of her pinky began to throb.

"I'm sorry. It'll be over soon, Sugar," he said as he cleaned the tweezers with a fresh wipe.

"Do you call all the girls you know, 'Sugar?'" She teased, hoping she could encourage him to talk to her. He'd said maybe five words to her all day, and she wanted to get to know this stranger who Sammy had already taken a liking to.

A small smile flickered across his face, but it might have been a trick of the candlelight as it disappeared in an instant. "No, just you."

His honesty took her by surprise. Lily opened her mouth to say something. "Ouch," she winced as he tugged the first splinter free.

"Sorry," he mumbled again.

"It's alright…ouch." She bit her cheek. "I know they need to come out. I just have a low pain tolerance I guess and —ouch!"

"It'll be over soon. Only one more on this hand, I think," Grant said.

"You think?" she asked, raising an eyebrow.

"I'll know for sure once it's daylight. I can barely see in this light." He pulled out the splinter on her thumb. "Now, give me your other hand." He grabbed it before Lily had the chance to move.

His rough hands worked methodically over hers, poking and rubbing to see if there were any more splinters as he moved from one finger to the next. Small tingling shivers raced up her arm under his warm grip. Lily tried to focus on something else, but the more she tried not to focus on his hands, the worse her reactions became. The air in the room seemed to burn ten degrees hotter, sweat beading on the nape of her neck. Soon she was squirming on the seat, trying to ignore the heat in her thighs and the dizziness in her head.

"So, tell me about Sammy," he said, his fingers still tracing her hand.

"She's my world," Lily said. "I'd do anything for her."

"Every good mother says that," Grant nodded. "But what about you and her? What happened with the two of you?

Flynn said he found you holed up in a house somewhere just outside Columbus. You don't sound like you're from Ohio."

"No," Lily said. "We're from Boston, but Sammy and I moved out to San Francisco two years ago. My mother passed away and I was home to get her affairs in order when they closed the airports and the train stations."

"I'm sorry," Grant said. "Was she bitten?"

A bitter laugh escaped Lily's lips before she could stop herself. "No, her neighbor found her on the sofa with the news playing on the TV. She died just before the infection spread to Columbus. She had a heart attack. News of the infection literally scared her to death."

Grant paused, his eyes gleaming down at her, flickering like amber in the candlelight. "I'm sorry." He dropped his gaze and continued to treat her fingers.

"Thank you," she murmured. Her mouth felt dry as she tried to remember where she'd left off in her story. Those eyes…

"At least she didn't have to see what the world's become. She was lucky in that sense," he said. His tone was soft and easy, almost comforting as his touch warmed her to her marrow.

"Yeah, I guess so…Oh, mother effer!" she huffed as the last splinter was yanked from the tip of her pinky finger.

"This is going to sting a little," Grant said, as he pulled out another alcohol wipe.

She groaned. "I'm starting to think that you get off on torturing me."

Now he smiled, lighting up the room brighter than the Christmas candles. "Not this kind of torture, Sugar."

Lily winced as he pressed the wipes to her fingers. The hot stinging took several seconds to ebb away after he moved the wipe away, the cool air making her fingers blaze hotter. She flexed her hand and wiggled her fingers. Despite the lingering tingles and awful alcohol smell, they moved and flexed as good as new. "Thanks," she mumbled.

"Don't mention it." He packed up the first aid kit and tossed the wipes and wrappers into a small wastebasket. Even the wastebasket had cheerful daisies on the outside.

Lily leaned over and pressed her soft lips against his scruffy cheek.

As she pulled back, Grant's hand rose, his fingers slipping around the back of her neck, capturing her. He leaned forward, the spicy smell of sweat and man mixing with the pine-scented candles and summer air. He leaned closer, his lips hovering over her for a moment before closing the gap between them. Warm breath teased her before his lips finally found hers.

Lily's heart hammered in her chest, her mind swimming like she'd drunk too much wine. The dark, heady taste of him filled her mouth, lingering on her tongue as the tip of his tongue traced over the seam of her lip.

With a sigh of disappointment, he broke their short kiss. A faint smile lit his face, the candlelight tracing soft shadows over him. His eyes twinkled with something she couldn't make out in the dark.

A small thump sounded outside in the hallway, like something heavy had fallen over. They heard Flynn swearing from the living room.

They said nothing as she stood and left the room, a pulsing heat radiating in the air around them.

"We should eat," Flynn said, his body shifting on a chair as he saw her leave the room. He bent lower, retrieving a large can of chili that had fallen on the floor. "And we should take shifts, keep watch for anything outside."

"I'll take the first shift," Lily volunteered. "I want to be here if Sammy wakes up."

"Alright," Flynn said. "Grant, can you check upstairs, see if there's anything we can bring with us tomorrow before we leave? Medicine. Supplies. Anything you think we'll need, grab it."

Grant stepped out from the small bathroom and nodded before moving upstairs. They covered the windows with the curtains and bolted the front and back doors shut. Silence hung in the air like heavy drapes, weighing them down. Every cricket, every gust of wind, sent shivers down Lily's body like snakes sliding through her muscles.

Tomorrow the madness will be over.

She told herself that every night, chanted it in her mind like a mantra, but she stopped believing it long ago.

Flynn thrust a bowl of organic chili under her nose. The tinny, meaty smell made her stomach growl and grumble. A few months ago, she might have turned her nose up, but world-ending disasters can really change a person's palate.

She spooned chili into her mouth and watched her daughter sleep. Sammy's hair was a matted mess that she would have to brush out when they found a safer spot. Sammy screamed whenever Lily brushed through her hair, even when it's been soaked through with detangling spray. Her daughter's carrot top reminded Lily of her own when she was younger before it began to straighten out. But Sammy's eyes matched her father's. Sammy was the only good thing he'd left behind. Lily could still remember his green cat eyes, shining in the dark on the other side of her bed.

The last thing she remembered before he disappeared that night. Snuck out like a burglar while she was still sound asleep.

Sammy's eyelids fluttered, and Lily wondered what her daughter was dreaming of. Playgrounds filled with kids and laughter. A candy store. Going off to preschool with a Barbie backpack and her princess Belle lunchbox.

"What're you thinking about, Sugar?" Grant asked, sitting next to her and offering her a tissue. She hadn't realized she'd been crying. Both men stared at her with the same heavy look of sympathy that made her feel pitied and guilty. Everyone lost their old lives when the breakout started. She was no different. They shouldn't pity her.

"Just thinking about Sammy," she shrugged, taking the tissue and shifting her attention back to her daughter. Lily dabbed her eyes and blew her nose into the Kleenex, the loud trumpet sound echoing around the quiet living room. *Well, that's attractive...*

"She'll be alright. She has you to protect her." Grant wrapped his strong arm around her. She leaned against him, her head resting in the crux of his neck, wondering how her world turned upside down in such a short time. "We're all here to protect her," his voice whispered in her ear, a soft kiss touching the top of her head.

Lily nodded, crumpling the damp tissue in her hand and breathing in Grant's spicy smell. "Thank you," she said. "But you both should get some sleep. I'm taking the first shift."

The men nodded, looking at one another before walking up the stairs. "If you need us, just holler. I'm a light sleeper," Flynn said.

"I doubt I'll get any sleep at all tonight," Grant smiled and winked down at her.

Some of the knots in Lily's chest unraveled. She smiled back and watched them retreat to the second floor. Their bodies tensed as the men moved up the steps. Two doors opened, then clocked shut.

Lily rose from the couch and wandered back into the kitchen, listening to the shuffling of feet upstairs. She grabbed the bottle of Jameson by the neck, twisted off the cap, and took a long swig. Crisp amber liquor burned down her throat, sending warm tingles into places she thought had gone numb.

Grabbing a chair from the kitchen table, she eased it beside the front door so she could peek through the glass side panel. She slid her knife from its holster and placed it on her lap, watching, waiting.

The darkness swallowed up the trees and houses around them. If anything was out there, it was invisible until daylight. Lily shivered, staring outside at the front porch, overgrown hedges, and stared into the blackness.

CHAPTER 6

Sunlight crept through the thin lavender curtains, warming Lily's cheeks. She sighed, sinking deeper into the musky, overstuffed couch. A small body wiggled against her chest, snuggling closer. Lily knew Sammy was there without even opening her eyes. She'd know that little person anywhere. Mother's intuition.

"Good morning, Sweetheart," Flynn whispered, planting a gentle kiss on her heated cheeks. "Time for you two to wake up."

Lily's eyes blinked open, sunlight clouding her vision until she lifted herself into a sitting position with Sammy laying across her lap.

Sammy yawned, shaking her head into the couch cushion.

"Come on sleepyhead," Lily crooned, gently nudging her daughter awake.

Sammy yawned bigger and louder than before, stretching out on the couch and slowly waking up. She rubbed her sleepy eyes and sat up on her mother's lap, looking around at the house. "Where are we?" Sammy asked.

"We're safe in a house," Lily answered.

Flynn crouched down until he was eye level with Sammy. His cheery smile shone in the morning light. "We're going to go back out and find an even nicer place to stay. We're going to find a place with toys and maybe some kids for you to play with. Would you like that, Sammy?"

"Yes!" With a sudden burst of energy, she jumped off her mother's lap and bounced up and down on her feet.

"We should eat before we move out." Grant strolled toward the dining room, but paused and turned around, leaning against the doorway with a soft smile on his face. "Sammy, I found a special treat if you eat your breakfast." He laughed at Sammy, watching her jaw drop, and her eyes light up like she'd woken up in Disney World.

"Up," Sammy said, pointing to Flynn's head and putting her tiny fist on her hip with a sassy attitude. He laughed, the deep chuckle rumbling the air as he lifted the child onto his shoulders.

Lily followed them and helped set the table in the dining room. Her heart thudded hard against her ribcage as she watched the two strong men interact with her daughter, like Sammy mattered to them.

Sammy could sneak her way into anyone's heart, but who would have thought a four-year-old would have these two tough guys wrapped around her little finger in less than a day?

Lily wondered how long this would last before something happened to one of them, or one of them decided to leave. A heavy sadness weighed down on her drumming heart, slowing it to a dull beat.

"You okay, Sugar?" Grant's voice dragged her back to reality. He grabbed a few jars of canned fruit cocktail from the counter and nudged a chocolate pudding pack hidden behind a box of pasta before holding a finger to his lips. "For Sammy. You know, after breakfast."

She offered him a smile, but tears stung in the corners of her eyes.

Grant's lips tilted downward as he placed the cans back down and walked up to her. The rough pad of his thumb tilted her head upward to look him in the eye. "What's wrong, Lily?"

Warm, honey eyes glistened with concern. For her. When was the last time a man was concerned about her? Sammy's father hadn't cared enough to even tell Lily his last name before disappearing in the morning. Four years as a single mother to the most wonderful little girl. Now that the world was ending, someone cared. Truly cared.

For a moment, she caught the musky scent of him and she wanted nothing more than to fall into his arms and sob. Something about Grant felt safe and warm, like walking into a heated house after walking a mile in the snow.

Lily lifted herself on tiptoe and kissed him. The soft touch of his lips on hers made her knees liquefy. She broke the kiss, all too soon, before she ended up collapsing into a pile of mush at his feet. Her head swam like she'd drunk too much Jameson on guard duty, but she knew that wasn't why.

The man was one hell of a good kisser.

Grant bent down, capturing her lips to his again, his hand reaching up to cup her cheek. His rough thumb traced along the curve of her jawline as the tip of his tongue pressed against the seam of her lips, asking for entry.

Her lips parted, inviting him inside her body. He tasted like heaven-- warm whiskey and mint. She could kiss him like this until the end of the time. She didn't want it to end.

But end, it did. "We should go," Grant murmured, breaking the kiss though his hand still lingered on her cheek. Without thinking, she closed her eyes and leaned into the warmth of his large palm, the hard callouses rubbing against her skin. He kissed the top of her head before releasing her.

With a sigh, she opened her eyes and found herself standing alone in the kitchen.

"Breakfast." Grant's voice rang like a dinner bell in the dining room.

Lily followed him, smiling her usual fake smile— the smile Sammy wasn't old enough to see through yet—and pretended that this was all she needed for now.

Both men were giving Sammy their undivided attention as the little girl struggled to open the tab on the can lid. "Phew, this is hard," she said before tugging on the top and trying again.

"Want me to help?" Grant offered.

Sammy heaved a dramatic sigh and handed it off to him. "I guess, but it's really, really hard."

"I'll try my hardest," Grant smiled, taking the can from her. After a couple of seconds of exaggerating huffing and puffing, pretending to lose the fight to the flimsy metal tab, Grant yanked the top open. "Phew. Got it!"

"Looks like it was touch and go there for a moment," Flynn teased before spooning a slice of pineapple between his plush lips.

"Good job." Sammy nodded in approval, rewarding Grant with a big grin as he drained the fruit into her bowl.

The men laughed.

Lily tried to smile again, but her lips stayed flat. What if Sammy became attached to these men? And what if they left? Or worse…

"Are you alright, Sweetheart?" Flynn asked.

"Yeah, I'm alright. Just still a bit tired," she lied.

"Well, this will wake you up," Grant said, nudging a bowl of fruit with his finger. "You need your strength. We're leaving today. We have to make it to a gas station for a map."

"Why?" Lily asked. "We know we have to go east to find the refugee camp. Why not just keep moving east?"

Flynn shook his head. "It's not straight east. It's a bit northeast from here and I'd rather not get lost on the way. It could take days to get back on the right track if we take too many wrong turns."

"Besides, we might find another car on the way. Can't hurt if we leave early enough," Grant added.

"Gross," Sammy said, picking a cherry out of her bowl and throwing it across the room. The men laughed. Lily's heart pinched as she smiled, tears brimming in her eyes. Could this last?

CHAPTER 7

*A*n hour later they had washed up with some distilled water they found bottled in the basement. Probably for emergencies, like a snowstorm or an extended power outage. Lily wondered if that picture-perfect family in the portrait thought they would need gallons of water for a zombie outbreak. She doubted it, but some apocalypse-crazed people prepared for the end of the world with shelters and supplies and self-sustaining houses.

Now that the old world was over, those fanatics didn't seem so crazy.

The group hustled out of the house, carrying their bags and some supplies. With Sammy walking around, awake and alert as any four-year-old, Grant had a free arm for this trip to carry more equipment.

They hiked their way back to the main road, trudging through the grass, trying to keep in the shade of the trees. The high sun beat down on the backs of their necks and shoulders. By the time they reached the main road, the blacktop was hot, sticking to the undersides of their shoes.

Heatwaves rippled up from the never-ending stretch of tar ahead of them.

Above them, eagles circled overhead, watching from the safety of the skies. The group slinked between abandoned cars with flat tires and piles of bones that might have once been human. Their eyes traced over the trees, scanning for any more ambushes or infected roaming the area.

Flynn passed a bottle of water down to Sammy. Her small hands twisted the top before chugging the lukewarm water with a wince. "I'm hot," she whined.

"I know, sweetie. Mommy is too. We'll be at the station in a few minutes, ok? Just a few more steps," she said. As she spoke, the top of the gas station came into view. For a few seconds, Lily wondered if it was just a mirage, but can someone hallucinate when they are hydrated in the middle of a forest?

"See, Sammy, we're almost there. It's just up ahead." Flynn ruffled the top of Sammy's head. "It will be cool and shady in there. We can rest for a few minutes, ok?"

Sammy frowned. The little girl was getting grumpy in the aggravating summer heat.

"Look over here, Sammy," Grant said, wandering to the end of the road. "Wildflowers." He pointed to a patch of weeds with a few wild daisies and roses poking through the tangle of crabgrass and dandelions. He bent and snapped a few flowers from their stems, giving the tiny bouquet to Sammy. Her little smile sparkled, the excitement beaming in her eyes as she rushed back to her mother.

"Look, Mommy. Flowers!" she cheered.

Lily laughed as her daughter held the tiny bundle half full of weeds under her nose. "Very pretty," she said.

"Thank you." Her little voice pinched Lily's chest, her heart fluttering at the sight of her daughter's happiness shining her in innocent green eyes.

"We're almost there," Grant said as he quickened his pace. The rest of them followed along in silence until they reached the gas station.

Grant and Flynn tugged at the automatic doors, which refused to open without the aid of a crowbar and two sets of large, bulging muscles. Beads of sweat dampened their shirts as they muscled their way through.

Flynn stepped inside first, sword in hand. He roamed through the convenience store, checking to be sure this one was empty. He signaled to Grant that the coast was clear and the rest of the group slipped inside, slipping the door shut behind them.

Sammy ran toward the candy section at the front of the store. "Mommy, can I have one please?"

"Yes, you can eat one for now. I'll pack some in my bag for later." She crouched down next to her daughter, who had pulled a bag of gummy worms from the bottom shelf. Lily slit open a corner of the bag and handed them to Sammy.

"Thank you." Sammy began munching on insect-shaped sweets while Lily packed some of whatever she could find into her bag, including several packs of gummy worms. Candy was energy, and they would need plenty of it if they wanted to make it to the refugee camp in good time.

"The maps are over here," Grant said, as he stood beside a rack with local maps and brochures advertising a water park, a haunted cave, a winery, and some quaint bed and breakfast for adults only.

"How far is the winery from the refugee camp?" Lily asked. "Maybe they'll let us in if we bring a few bottles."

Grant chuckled, a flicker of amusement lighting his eyes. "Very funny, Sugar."

"Nothing wrong with a good Malbec. Hell, I'd even take a bad one right about now. God, one thing I miss is a sweet, red wine. With a bar of dark chocolate." Her eyes closed, trying to remember the silky feel of dark chocolate melting on her tongue, chased by the sweet taste of grapes with a hint of orange.

Without warning, Grant's lips pressed against hers.

Shock flooded her system, her body freezing at the surprise invasion before the surprise melted into need. A sudden wave of desire crashed over her. His hands slid up to cradle her neck, his rough fingertips running through her hair. With a belly-deep groan, her body surrendered over to him, her breasts crushing against his hard chest as she sunk deeper into his kiss.

Her tongue tasted like something distinctly him, a spiciness like cinnamon and heat like whiskey. Delicious. Her fingers trembled as they slid to his waist, keeping a firm grip so he wouldn't disappear.

A low grown in the back of his throat sent shivers rushing down her spine. Her mind whirled at the feeling of kissing a man... A man who wasn't Flynn.

My God, she'd kissed both of them!

"Ahem," Sammy coughed behind them.

The adults stopped, a blush creeping up Lily's already warm neck and tinting her cheeks.

"Someone just got caught," Flynn teased as he strolled down their aisle. Lily's heart pounded as her eyes met Flynn's, searching for some clue as to what he was feeling, thinking. He'd caught her kissing Grant. But his eyes sparked with a fire Lily hadn't known existed inside him.

"Sammy, why don't you see if there are any good sodas left in the fridge?" he suggested, giving the adults a few minutes alone.

Sammy hustled toward the refrigerators in the corner while Lily's gaze shot back and forth between the men. What had she done? Kissed both of them. This was unlike her.

Would they make her chose one of them? Would the other leave? Would they…?

"Relax, Sweetheart," Flynn said. "You look frightened. Are you alright?"

"You. Him. What am I doing?" she blurted out.

"I don't know." Grant took one step forward. "What do you want to do?" he asked, slinking behind her, one arm wrapping around her waist.

"I don't know." She gazed into Flynn's icy blue eyes while Grant's rough touch inched lower, tracing along the bare skin at the bottom of her shirt.

"What do you want?" Flynn closed the gap between them.

"I…I," she stammered.

Grant fisted her ponytail in his hand, the gentle tug on her scalp sending an erotic thrill through her. With a gentle jerk, he tilted her head upward to face Flynn.

Flynn's lips pressed against hers, the taste of cherries and smoke lingering as his tongue thrust between her lips, taking her mouth in every way he could before Grant pulled her head back. Before Lily's mind could clear, Grant's lips descended on hers, tasting, devouring every bit of her. An aching need pulsed between Lily's legs as Grant's tongue plunged and danced with hers. Tasting. Teasing.

"I can't reach," Sammy shouted from across the store.

The three of them broke apart, their chests heaving, lips bruised and burning. Lily felt caught between their hard, hot gazes, their tall bodies between her, overpowering her. But her daughter was there. They couldn't…not here.

"I'll be right there," she shouted to Sammy before walking away. She raised a finger to her tingling lips with a smile she couldn't suppress.

Sammy reached up for something on the top shelf. Lily pulled down a bottle of cola and handed it to her daughter, who twisted off the cap and began to gulp down the soda. "Not too fast or you'll get a stomach ache," Lily said.

Her daughter paused, finally coming up for air. "But I'm so, so thirsty," she said.

"You had plenty of water on the walk here. Soda dehydrates you."

"What's dehydrates?" Sammy asked.

"It means your body doesn't have enough water, so it starts to get sick." Lily grabbed a bottle of lukewarm sparkling water from the fridge and took a few sips. The bubbles popping on her tongue did little to help clear her mind.

Her nerves jolted around like they were dancing on live wires. Being pinned between two powerful men left Lily with an aching need low in her belly that didn't seem to ebb away. She needed their touch, their kisses. She needed more, but it had been so long since...years since she'd been with a man.

And now two were vying for her attention.

Flynn strolled down the aisle toward them, the map unable to hide his smirk. His gaze devoured her as his stare traced every curve of her body. Like he was undressing her in his mind. "There's a school a few miles up the road, and a hotel a little bit further. If we can locate a working car, we can get there in less than an hour."

"Well, let's find a car. There are some behind the station. Maybe one of them works," Grant suggested, moving toward the back door.

"Good idea," Flynn agreed, and followed Grant out to the parking lot.

"Cheers!" She clinked the top of her water bottle with Sammy's soda.

"Cheers!" Sammy giggled before chugging more of the molasses-colored soda.

While Sammy finished eating her dry protein bar, Lily watched the men work through the open back door. Flynn's torso was half-hidden under the hood of a burnt red Pontiac Sunbird, but it gave Lily a perfect excuse to stare at his ass. Damn, he had a nice ass. His strong legs flexed under the denim as he moved, manipulating the machinery beneath his nimble fingers. His shirt clung to his sweaty body like a second skin, revealing every hardened muscle beneath. They rippled as he wiped his brow and closed the hood with a soft slam.

Lily's mouth watered. Her fingertips tingled as she imagined what it would feel like to touch those hand muscles. Feel them tense under her palms as he held his hard body above her. Then Grant moved into view and she thought she might combust from too much testosterone in one place.

His smile caught the light like a diamond glittering in the sun. His grin reached his eyes, revealing a once easygoing man who'd fought through hell and back.

He strolled to the driver's door and leaned down, trying to jumpstart the engine. As he bent over, Lily could see how well he filled out his pair of jeans. Damn, since when did she have a thing for asses?

She didn't know, but her mouth watered and her nipples puckered, scratching against the rough fabric of her bra. If only she could have some time alone, just the three of them. She missed the feel of a man in her bed. Two would only be making up for lost time, right? Nothing wrong with playing catch -up...

"We're ready," Flynn shouted as the engine roared to life.

This time, Grant slid into the driver's seat of the beaten-down Hyundai, and Flynn took the passenger's seat.

Lily and Sammy joined the men, slipping into the back seat. Then they were off.

The group drove in silence as the Sunbird pulled out of

the gas station and onto the main road toward the school. "We should gather as many supplies as we can comfortably carry," Flynn suggested. "The school will hopefully be safe enough for us to camp for the night. We can continue the drive to the refugee camp tomorrow."

"Agreed," Grant said.

Lily nodded, and Sammy continued to stare at the passing trees.

"One," Sammy said.

"What's that?" Lily asked.

"Two," Sammy said.

"Sweetie, what are you counting?" Lily asked.

"Counting the monsters outside. Three. Four." She pointed out the window as the car drove past two infected who trudged by, trying in vain to chase the car.

Even at fifty miles per hour, Grant picked up speed. "They can't catch us. Don't worry," he said.

"Okay…Five," Sammy said.

Lily cringed. Sammy used to count cars passing by, naming colors, seeing how many red cards drove past them. Now, she counted the dead as they tried to catch their car. The world had gone mad, and they were living in a hellish Wonderland.

"We should be there in approximately ten minutes, judging by the map." Flynn pointed down a small road. The car was quiet again as they drove past a large field of grapevines. Their sweetness perfumed the air, lingering in the car as they drove with the windows down.

Grant made a sharp right, the car inching its way over rough gravel in front of a large school. A large iron fence wrapped around the school with a chain link that kept the gates shut. A few infected roamed the grounds.

But it was nothing they couldn't handle.

"Lily, come with me. Grant, stay here. Your gun might

draw unwanted attention," Flynn said. He and Lily slid out of the car.

"Stay with Grant," she told Sammy. Her lips pressed against the top of her daughter's head before she closed the car door. "Keep her safe," she said to Grant. She leaned lower, poking her head through the open driver's window to leave kiss him. As she pulled away, her lips tingled, wanting more.

He winked as he nodded, then rolled up the window.

One-by-one, Lily and Flynn made their way through a dozen infected scattered around the front of the school. They sliced and stabbed, her knives and his sword leaving trails of blood along the grass and cement walkway.

After ten minutes, the infected laid finally dead on the ground. No movement came from the woods around them. The soccer field beside the school was empty and over-grown, but nothing moved. Silence filled the air around them.

Flynn locked eyes with Lily. "Are you alright, Sweetheart?"

She nodded. "You?"

Flynn closed the gap between them. His broad shoulders lined up with her vision before she raised her head. Warmth bloomed in her chest as his eyes twinkled in the sunlight. He bent down, sweeping his lips against hers. The smell of sweat and spice lingered in the air, cocooning them from the woods and everything else.

Lily closed her eyes, her body, her mind, losing herself to the moment. The heat of the summer sun warmed her shoulders as his kiss heated her blood.

Flynn stepped back, his gaze flickering to the car for a moment before returning to her. "Never better." He winked before slipping his sword back in its scabbard.

Lily couldn't hide her smile as they returned to the car.

Her fingers itched to touch him. "The fence isn't too high. Maybe nine feet. Do we climb?"

"I think I can pick the lock," Flynn said. "If not, we can try to climb. I thought about maybe running the car through the front gate, but it might knock one of the gates off its hinge. They might not have the parts to fix it inside, and I'm not about to ruin a surefire way of keeping the infected out."

"Sounds like you thought of everything." Lily gazed up at him, watching the corner of his lip flicker into a smile before they reached the car.

Grant and Sammy climbed out and stretched their limbs. Grant yawned, covering his mouth with the back of his broad hand. Sammy stared up at him and watched, yawning herself and placing her hand over her mouth in the exact same way. Grant laughed, smiling down at Sammy with a shine of happiness lighting in his eyes.

Lily's heart skipped a beat, then hammered like a drum in her chest.

"Your joints bothering you, old man?" Flynn teased.

"I'm five years older than you. Stuff it," Grant said.

"Stuff what?" Sammy asked.

"Nothing, sweetie," Lily said.

"Do you have a lockpick kit?" Flynn asked Grant as he opened the trunk of the car and began rummaging through their bags.

"No, do you have anything small, like one of those hairpins?" he asked Lily.

She pulled one out from under her ponytail, some short wisps of hair falling and clinging to the sweat on the back of her neck. She handed it off to Flynn. "Keep an eye out," he said as he kneeled and started fidgeting with the lock on the school gate.

"Aye aye, captain," Lily said. She held both knives clenched tight in her fists. Her gaze scanned the woods around them. Some bushes rustled in the far distance, but she wasn't sure if they were infected or forest animals so she made sure she kept aware.

Sammy giggled in delight as she played with a clump of dandelions by the edge of a nearby tree. The yellow flowers were being picked one by one and stuffed into a bright bouquet.

"I remember when my dad told me those were just weeds." Grant's rough voice trickled over her like a waterfall, his shadow casting over Lily's short frame as he stood beside her. "I used to think they were flowers. I picked some for my sister once, but my dad threw them outside. Said there were weeds."

"Your dad sounds a bit rough around the edges."

Grant chuckled. "He was, but he was a good guy. He cared about us. Can't ask for anything more than that from a parent."

Lily said nothing, letting the silence fill the air between them as Sammy rushed back and forth between dandelion patches.

"It's nice out here," Grant said. "I missed being around trees. The smell...it takes me back. Reminds me of when things were happier. When the world made sense."

"Why the trees?" she asked.

"I grew up in the Poconos, in a trailer park with a big lake on one side and trees everywhere. The forests remind me of before the war. The desert...The dryness made me feel like a mummy. Like I might crumble into the sand and get swept up in a sandstorm. But the forest, these trees...it's never dry here. The air's wet. And it's peaceful."

"Did you grow up around here?" she asked.

"Not too far, actually. Farther northeast in Pennsylvania. First in the trailer park. When I was fifteen, we finally moved into a duplex. Except for Afghanistan, I always lived in the same five-mile radius. Grew up with the same people. Went to school. After I had graduated high school, I enlisted and signed up for the Marines. My dad was a Marine. My younger brother joined after me. It ran in our family. When I came back, I went to work in a factory. Been there for almost six years before all this happened."

"Do you know what happened to your family? You know, after the infection spread?" Her gaze skimmed the perimeter of the forest, though her attention focused on Grant's story. Finally, he was opening up to her.

She scanned once more before glancing at him.

No movement. No infected.

"My parents died years ago. My brother was deployed to Kuwait. No idea what happened to him. No calls. No mail. My sister…she ran off with her boyfriend when all of this happened. Just left a note saying she was leaving with him. I was tracking them until last week…I found them."

A pregnant pause lingered in the air around them, like a thunderstorm threatening rain. Grant's eyes glazed over, as though he was replaying a bad memory in his head.

"Almost half of her body was eaten. She was trapped in his car. Infected. The seat belt was still buckled. I don't know how it happened. I just saw her. Knew it was her. That cheap ring he gave her was still on her finger. Half her face was bitten off, but I knew it was her… I shot her. And moved on."

Lily stared at Grant like she was seeing him for the first time. He didn't flinch. He never moved a muscle as he spoke, but the glimmer in his eye was a window to the mountain of pain he tried to tamp down. He bottled his feelings inside of him, but what would happen if he bottled up too much? Would he explode?

Lily knew almost nothing about post-traumatic stress disorder, but a flicker of nervousness told her that Grant had it. He might not let on. He might not be afraid of gunfire, and he hadn't screamed from nightmares in the middle of the night but something haunted him so deep it rooted in his bones.

"I'm sorry." What else could she say?

"Got it," Flynn said from behind them. The loud clanking of chain against metal rattled around them. The chain links clattered to one side of the fence.

Flynn pushed open the gate just enough for the Sunbird to drive through. Grant took the wheel and steered the car inside, parking it so the car faced the gate. Best route of escape if there was an emergency. Once everyone was inside, Flynn locked the gate.

They stared out past the fence, then back up at the school. The building towered over their small group, casting them in shadow as the sunlight faded. No noises came from inside. No sounds came from beyond the gate.

For now, their world was quiet, and that scared them.

CHAPTER 8

*L*ily grabbed a bag from the car with some clothes, food, and medicine packed inside. "Who knows what we'll find once we get inside, and the sun's starting to set already."

Flynn smiled at her, while Grant simply nodded, his attention focused on the front door. The group shifted into a tighter formation. Sammy hovered in front of her mother, who had two hands protectively on the little girl's shoulders, ready to shove Sammy out of harm's way at a moment's notice. The men locked eyes and Grant nodded again.

"I'll go first." Grant's boots thudded against the concrete steps. He pulled out his gun, flicked off the safety, and nudged the door open with the barrel of his pistol.

Nothing.

He tapped the barrel of his gun against the door, creating a grating noise that filled the air.

Nothing.

He launched himself behind the door, shifting left, right, left. "Clear."

"Whatever happens, stick together," Flynn ordered as he

drew his sword and followed Grant. Lily saw his head turn back to be sure nothing was behind him before disappearing down the hall.

Lily guided Sammy forward, almost pushing the little girl inside. One-by-one, Flynn and Grant opened each classroom and office door they passed. Still, no movement.

Colorful, handmade posters advertised a student council election. Some lockers were left open, the smells of rotting sandwiches and stale gym clothes wafting every few feet down the hallway. Flies buzzed in and out of cracks in the windows, hovering near the heaping trashcans loaded with old garbage.

A low moan echoed down the hallway, freezing the group where they stood. Heads whipped around, trying to find the source of the sound. A loud banging against a locker jolted fear down their spines, their senses heightening to full alertness.

"Mommy," Sammy whimpered. She shoved her head into her mother's hip and trembled. Her little hands dug into the skin of Lily's hip as Lily reached down and placed a hand on the top of her daughter's messy hair.

Another loud bang echoed down the hallway, but no infected came out to meet them.

Flynn grasped his sword tighter and slinked down the hall. Locks of hair swished around the collar of his shirt as he glanced from side-to-side.

"Stay back." He tapped on one set of lockers. Nothing. He tapped on another. Another loud bang and a moan followed. "Someone trapped one in here," he said. "But there's no lock."

He tapped another door. A loud screeching mixed with the moans and hungry gurgles of an infected trapped inside the locker. Flynn yanked on the handle and stepped back, pointing his sword upward.

An infected stumbled out, impaling itself onto Flynn's sword. With a quick, upward thrust, Flynn sliced its chest clean in two. A red mess of guts spewed out along the tile floor, leaking into the locker and down the infected's body. Its arms flailed, trying to move closer to Flynn.

He kicked the infected off his blade and with another quick jab, stabbed it through an eyeball. It slumped to the ground, finally dead.

"Well, that was easy," Flynn smiled. He continued walking down the hallway, tapping on lockers to see if any more infected came out. The only sounds were silence and his occasional bang against the metal.

"Freeze!" shouted a voice behind them. "Drop your weapons. Now!"

They turned, staring at two men and one woman carrying guns pointed directly at them.

Flynn's cutlass fell to the ground with a clatter. Grant flipped the safety on his gun and placed it beside him. Lily pulled the knife out of its holster, then the knife in her boot, laying both beside her feet. Both hands wrapped around her daughter, shielding Sammy behind her.

"Now we're unarmed." Flynn's hand rose in the air above his head. "We have a little girl with us. Don't shoot."

"You don't fucking tell us what to do." The youngest in their group, a bird-like teenager in an oversized band t-shirt, bounced on the balls of his feet. His companions gave him wary glances.

His nerves were getting the better of him.

"Relax," the woman beside him said. "They're unarmed. Lower your gun and go check them for more weapons."

The young man nodded and laid his rifle against a wall, relief washing over his face. He stepped closer toward them, his expression slipping into a glower.

"Is anyone else with you?" he asked.

Lily eyed him up and down. He couldn't be much older than eighteen. Maybe he had been a student in this school once upon a time. "It's just the four of us."

Grant grumbled as the boy began patting him down with his awkward, clunky hands. "Watch the goods," Grant snapped as the boy's hands crept higher up his legs.

"You're not in any position to give orders, pal," the boy barked.

"Pal?" Grant smirked. "I don't think so, kid."

The boy sneered and finished patting down Grant's torso and arms before moving onto Lily. "You touch her in any way we don't like, and I swear to God, kid, you won't live long enough to see a girl touch your dick," Grant said.

"Oh yeah? What makes you think I haven't done that already?" the boy asked.

The man with the gun tried not to laugh, but a faint chuckle echoed down the hall. "Shut up, Will."

"Well, your hands keep shaking like you've never touched any girl besides your mom," Flynn prodded. "And you keep staring at our woman like she's the first you've ever seen. Like a confused little boy."

"Shut up!" Will's hands roamed up and down Lily's legs, careful not to get too close to the apex of her thighs. His hands moved to her back, then her arms. "Sorry," he grumbled as his hands roamed over her stomach. He hesitated as his hands hovered an inch above her breasts.

"Touch them and those men will follow through on their threats. I can promise you that." She glared at Will, her eyes challenging him to back off. After a few seconds, he stepped away and leaned lower toward Sammy.

Lily pushed Sammy out of Will's reach. "You touch my daughter and I'll cut off your fucking balls and feed them to the next infected I find."

He glanced back to his group, the confusion on his face

leaving him standing there while half a dozen sets of eyes watched him.

"You can leave the little girl. Check the next one," the woman said.

Will slithered between Lily and Grant, careful to step around the infected's corpse as he strode over to Flynn. "Don't try anything funny," he warned, trying to sound tough.

Flynn smirked. "Sure thing, kid. Can you please make this quick so we can move along already?" Will patted down Flynn and nodded when he finished.

"Check their bag, too." The woman instructed.

Will yanked open the duffle bag, rummaging through the contents. "Clothes. Food. Water. A first aid kit. No weapons."

"Grab it." She waved him to come back.

Hoisting the bag over his shoulder, Will turned to go back to his group.

Grant smacked him upside the head like a pissed-off parent as the kid walked past. "You better learn to be more respectful to a lady, even if the world's gone to shit."

"Yes, sir," Will grumbled, rubbing the back of his head. The woman's eyebrow quirked as she nodded at Will to pick up his gun. He grabbed it but didn't point it this time.

"What are you doing here?" she asked.

"We needed shelter for a little while. We thought the school was safe. We didn't know anyone was home." Grant lowered his arms and crossed them over his chest.

"Where are you from?" The woman's gaze flickered to Grant's bulging biceps, lingering over him and she traced him up and down.

Jealousy pinched the back of Lily's neck like a mosquito bite. Her grip tightened on Sammy's shoulders.

"Does it matter anymore?" Flynn replied.

"I suppose not," she answered. "I'm Marissa. This is Sanjay. And Will." She lowered her gun, flicking on the safety. "Put your weapons away. Let's talk."

Sanjay said nothing as he lowered his gun in good faith. The tall, Indian man glared at them as he watched the group pick up their weapons and sheath them in their holsters. He noticed Sammy cower behind her mother, staring up at him like he was the giant in Jack and the Beanstalk. He stepped forward and crouched down onto his knees. Marissa and Will stared at him like he had lost his mind.

"I won't hurt you, princess," he said. "I had a neighbor who looked just like you. She had red hair, too, like Ariel from *The Little Mermaid*. We have books and toys in the library if you want to play with them."

Sammy stared at Sanjay, then up at her mother, her lips pressed tight, but her eyes gleaming with curiosity.

"Hold up," Marissa said. "We don't know these guys. You want them sleeping with the rest of us tonight? No way."

"How many of you are there?" Lily asked, pressing Sammy closer to her leg, her hand rubbing her daughter's messy hair.

"Eleven," Marissa answered.

"Did any of you know each other before all of this?" Grant asked.

"Some of us. Did you?" Marissa asked.

"No," Lily said. "Sammy's my daughter. I'm Lily. We met Flynn and Grant just a couple of days ago."

"I met the three of them on the road," Grant added.

"Alright. I don't want to talk right now. It's almost dark. We'll set you guys up in the gym for now. Keep you guys locked in. You try any funny business, and we'll shoot every one of you." Marissa's eyes flashed with a warning. This mama bear was protecting her group no matter what cost. The petite African American woman stood tall, holding her gun in front of her like a shield—a reminder not to get too close.

"We won't try anything. But, if anything happens to my daughter, this place will go down in flames. Remember the movie, *Carrie*?" Lily quirked an eyebrow at Marissa. This mama bear wasn't going to back down either.

Marissa smirked. "We don't hurt kids. Just don't try anything stupid. The locker rooms are still set up with water for showers. You'll be comfortable enough there for tonight. Tomorrow, we talk."

Lily scooped Sammy up in her arms. Her little body clung to Lily as her fingers dug into her mom's skin. The poor thing was terrified.

Lily pressed a gentle kiss to Sammy's forehead as the group followed Marissa. Sanjay and Will walked behind Grant and Flynn.

"No funny business," Will reminded them.

"You got it, kiddo." Flynn smirked.

"Smartass," Sanjay murmured.

"Better a smartass than a dumbass," Grant added.

Sanjay laughed, the sound echoing down the hall, bouncing off the walls. "I might start to like this guy." He nudged Will, nodding toward Grant. The scrawny teenager rolled his eyes.

"The gym's in here," Marissa pointed past a set of heavy, metal double doors. "Sorry, but I need any guns you have," she stared pointedly at Grant. "Safety precaution. You can keep the sword and knives. We just can't have you making noise and drawing the zombies closer to us."

"You think I'm dumb enough to try and bring infected here?" Grant asked.

"I sure as hell hope not, or we're going to throw you out on your ass in the middle of a zombie horde," Will said.

Grant rolled his eyes. "This kid's got one hell of a mouth on him."

"Pot calling the kettle," Flynn murmured.

"Give her the gun." Lily's tone was final as she walked past Marissa and into the gym. Sammy clung to her mother's shoulder as she watched Grant hand over his gun and follow them inside.

Flynn glanced at the door, then back to Marissa. "We need our bag. We need food and clothes."

Marissa shrugged and tossed the bag ten feet inside the gym. "There."

Flynn shuffled his feet, his knuckles blanching as the door slammed shut behind him. The scrape of metal against the door handles grated on Lily's nerves, a shiver sliding up her back as a lock clicked into place. They were trapped, and at the mercy of total strangers.

"At least the sun hasn't set yet. We can check this place out without roaming around in the dark." Lily placed Sammy on her feet and strolled around the large gym. The benches had been pulled out, and banners of crimson and navy boasted the slogan, "Go Cougars!" across the gym walls. A large, blue cat was painted over the wood in the center of the basketball court. A crate of sports equipment was pushed off to the side of the gym, a small bag of tennis balls threatening to spill out over the edge of the cart.

Grant followed her while Flynn kept an eye on Sammy. He picked up the little girl in his strong arms and walked with her up the bleachers, watching Lily and Grant roam around the room.

They checked around corners and behind doors. The coach's office door swung open with a gentle push. No sign of anything, living, or dead, or undead. No moans. No sounds. They checked the locker rooms but no sign of life anywhere.

Lily pressed a hand against the bathroom wall, the tile cool beneath her warm hands. She breathed a sigh of relief. "Maybe we can get some easy sleep tonight." No infected had any way of getting into the gym unless they learned to climb and break through twelve-foot-high windows.

"You think the water works in here?" Grant asked. His heavy voice echoed around the tiled bathroom walls.

"There's only one way to find out." She twisted a faucet inside one of the standing showers. There was a sputtering, a gurgling, and then cool water sprinkled from the rusty showerhead. "We have water!"

"It nice to see you smile, Sugar." He wrapped his arms around her waist and held her close to his chest.

Lily sunk deeper into his embrace, watching some of the water flow before shutting off the shower. A bubble of happiness spread through her chest. Maybe this was a good omen. Maybe this place wouldn't be so bad after all.

"It's nice to have a reason to smile again," she said.

"I never thought I'd be so thankful for a cold shower in my life," he teased.

She giggled. "We should tell Flynn. And we should probably get cleaned up before the sun goes down. It'll be too dark to see in here soon."

"You're right, but let's find a way to get sweaty before we clean up." The huskiness in his voice sent a shiver down to her toes. He kissed her cheek before releasing her.

"But Sammy's still awake. Wait until she goes to bed."

His eyebrow quirked in amusement, a smirk tugging at the edge of his lip. "What's going on in that dirty mind of yours? I was talking about playing a game of basketball." His smirk broke into a full-on grin as Lily's jaw slipped, her cheeks staining themselves red in embarrassment.

Grant laughed and walked away. Lily followed like a love-struck puppy, annoyed but awed by him.

Finally, his lighter side was coming out to play.

"Who's up for a game of horse?" Grant asked, striding toward the cart of sports equipment. He pushed aside a well-worn baseball glove. His large hands wrapped around a basketball.

Lily's stomach churned as she wondered what those thick fingers would feel like on her body.

"What's horse?" Sammy's voice squeaking with excitement. She jumped off the bleachers and rushed down, eager to finally play a game.

While Grant crouched down and tried to show Sammy how to throw a basketball, Flynn strode over to Lily. "Are you alright, Sweetheart? You look a little pink."

"I'm fine," she gushed, as he stepped closer into her personal space. "Just a bit flustered I guess. Those people out there, locking us inside. I know why they did it, but I hate feeling out of control."

"Do you?" Flynn asked. Their gazes locked, his blue eyes dancing like shadows in firelight. "Sometimes losing control isn't such a bad thing."

She bit her bottom lip.

A soft growling sound ripped from his throat before a basketball slammed into his knee, shaking him out what whatever fantasy he had been dreaming.

"Throw it back," Grant said.

"Mommy, come play!" Sammy shouted. Her carefree grin sparkled in the fading sunlight.

Lily's heart pounded in her chest as she watched Sammy spin and toss a ball over her head, missing the basketball hoop by a dozen feet, but still giggling in excitement.

Her daughter's smile kept her going. Cold showers kept her going. It was the little things.

"Come on." Flynn hustled toward the court with a broad grin on his face. Happiness and sunshine filled the gym for a little while. The four of them tossed a basketball around, acting like they were playing in a park instead of being trapped inside a locked gym while infected roamed the woods outside and strangers kept them caged like circus animals. For a little while, they felt human again.

"We should go get that shower now." Lily rummaged through their bag for clothes "Let's go, Sammy."

Sammy huffed and rolled her eyes at her mother. "If I have to," she sighed, giving in to the fact that she was going to have to shower sometime before dinner.

Flynn and Grant grabbed clothes and headed toward the men's locker room.

After quick showers, and a fuss from Sammy as Lily fought with her and her mess of tangled hair, the four of them met back on the basketball court.

Grant rummaged through the bag, pulling out three bottles of water, and half a dozen chocolate and peanut butter protein bars. "Eat up." He strolled up to the bleachers and laid out across the top, watching the sunset through the high windows.

Flynn sat with one arm draped over his knee, watching the same sunset slice through the open window, casting a fiery orange light across the painted cement walls. He chomped on a protein bar, losing himself in thought as the light on the wall rose higher and higher before disappearing altogether and giving way to the night.

Sammy grumbled as she nibbled on half a protein bar before yawning. Her head drooped on her mother's arm, drowsiness weighing her down like a deflating balloon.

"I think someone's tired out and ready for bed." Lily's heart stretched like happy in her chest as Sammy slept against her.

Flynn carried Sammy to the coach's office. A hoodie hung on the back of a desk chair. A blanket with the school's emblem was rolled up in a ball on a shelf. Flynn laid Sammy on the floor near the door.

Lily rolled up the jacket as a pillow, carefully lifting her daughter's head and resting it underneath. She laid the blanket over Sammy, watching her baby girl's pink lips open, the tip of her tongue lolling out. Her eyelashes fluttered and her whole body seemed to rise and fall with her even breathing.

"Sound asleep," Flynn whispered, rising carefully on his feet and creeping out of the door. Lily placed a gentle kiss on her daughter's forehead before following him. She closed the door with a soft click.

<h1 style="text-align:center">Chapter 9</h1>

"Tired?" Flynn asked as Lily strolled toward the bleachers where Grant sat.

"No. Actually, I'm wide awake." She sat on the bottom bleacher. She watched Grant laying out a rainbow parachute along the gym floor like a makeshift, plastic-lined blanket.

Lily inhaled slowly, trying to let the fresh summer air relax her. But she couldn't relax. Her body coiled, wound up like a tight spring.

"Good. I think we're safe enough here. We don't need to sleep in shifts tonight," he said.

"We all need a full night's sleep. Those bastards better leave us alone." Grant said as he sat down a few feet from Lily and nodded toward the gym door. "I keep getting the feeling they're watching us, but I never see anyone through the windows."

"I think we're all a little paranoid. On edge. Jumpy," Lily said. A sudden chill swept through the air, and she shivered, clutching her arms and rubbing them for warmth.

"Chilly?" Flynn frowned as he eased himself beside her. His arms reached for her, shifting her body closer to him.

His body heat penetrated through her clothes and warmed wherever he touched. "I forgot how cold it gets at night."

"We'll keep you warm, Sugar." Grant's voice purred as he stepped down the bleachers to sit on the other side of her.

"Oh?" she said, curiosity peeking through the chill. A small pool of warmth began to bubble in her lower belly. "And how do you plan on doing that?" A ghost of a smile tugged at her lips. If only she were better at playing coy, at acting sexy…

"Well, how about this for a start." Grant snaked his hand up the back of her neck, fingers tangling in her damp hair. He tilted her head upward, her lips tingling as she waited. He lowered his head, his lips hovering. He paused, letting her savor the moment, the anticipation of his lips on hers. His breath teased her, hot and wet. Then he closed the gap, his kiss warming her body.

Flynn's fingers teased the skin of her thigh, moving in small circles, slowly creeping up her leg.

"Grant," she murmured, "Flynn. What are we doing?"

"Keeping you warm, Sugar," Grant answered, slipping his rough palm up her thigh.

"But…us? Three of us?" Her head swam with satisfaction, exhaustion, and confusion. Two men? How could this be happening?

"Sweetheart, we both care about you. We want to keep you safe. And we both want you, all of you. This might be the best compromise we could come up with. Do you want just one of us?"

Flynn's soft voice sent a chilling panic over her. She glanced back and forth at the two of them. "No. No, I…I want both of you. It's selfish. I know, it's really selfish of me. But—"

"Then it's settled," Grant said.

"But, what about jealousy and that sort of thing?" There was a lingering pause, her question hanging in the air.

"We'll get over it," Flynn answered. "Yes, Sweetheart. Sometimes jealous will rear its ugly head, but that's a fact of life. That's just the way it is. Grant and I are only human, after all. But we both want you, any way we can have you. I'd rather share you than not have you at all."

"Same here,'" Grant added, his hand tracing over her trim waist. "I'd rather share you than not have any of you, Sugar." He planted a gentle kiss on her shoulder, the stubble on his cheeks scratching her skin. He reached underneath her chin, capturing her lips against his.

Sparks burned in her belly, a tingling sensation spreading down to the tips of her toes. Her blood heated as his tongue poked out, sliding between the seam of her lips, penetrating her, opening her to him.

Lily sunk deeper into his kiss, her mind swimming in a dizzying fog. She held onto his arm, her fingertips clutching strong muscle.

Flynn pressed his hard body against her back, his hands roaming over her skin. His rough fingertips skimmed across her arms, over her stomach, over the fabric of her shorts. Heat sizzled through her when his fingers reached the bare skin of her thighs.

A haze settled over Lily's mind like a veil. This much heat and testosterone could drive a woman mad with need. She wanted to lose herself to the madness.

Her hand reached around, tracing the inner seam of Flynn's jeans while her other hand released Grant's arm and moved south, cupping his bulging erection through the denim. "I want you," she whispered, breaking the kiss.

Opening her eyes, she glanced over her shoulder to Flynn. "I want both of you."

Grant's arms slipped under her bent knees as he lifted her in the air as easily as Lily held Sammy. She carried her a few feet over, sitting her down on the cool parachute. The flimsy fabric tickled the backs of her legs.

Flynn met them on the parachute, bending low and capturing Lily's lips with his own. A hungry growl ripped from his throat, shaking her to her core. Heat penetrated her skin, piercing her down to the bone.

Grant's lips traced her collarbone and shoulder, his soft touch teasing her as he stroked the bottom edge of her shirt, his knuckles brushing over her stomach.

Lily's blood prickled with heat, awareness tingling between her thighs. Her mind swam in a haze as Flynn's tongue sank deeper into her mouth, slipping through her lips and dancing with her tongue. The taste of him, hot and spicy with a hint of mint, overwhelmed her senses.

Grant's hands raked higher over her stomach, his rough fingertips pressing firm lines over her skin as he lifted the fabric inch by inch. He broke their kiss and pulled the shirt off her, dropping it on the floor. With a small pop, Flynn unclasped her bra and yanked it from her shoulders. Her breasts spilled out, her nipples puckering in the sudden rush of cool air around her.

"Beautiful," Grant murmured. His large hand covered one of her heavy breasts. Pale flesh spilled out from between his fingers, his warm palm tickling her tight nipple.

Pleasure buzzed in her chest, pulsing through her as Grant's hand massaged her. "Oh," she whimpered. Her head lolled back as pleasure consumed her.

Flynn bent his head lower, capturing her free nipple between his soft lips, the tip of his tongue teasing her. He groaned as she wiggled under their grasp. She leaned back, the edge of the bleacher pressing into her shoulder blades. She gasped at the discomfort as the metal edge pressed deeper into her skin.

"Floor," Grant murmured as he released her breast.

Flynn leaned back and glanced up at him. Nodding to Grant, he scooped Lily up into his arms.

Grant walked over to the equipment cart, pulling out a rainbow parachute and laying it out on the ground. Flynn laid Lily down, her body encased in a sea of bright color.

"Gorgeous." Grant knelt beside her. His hand tangled in her hair as he kissed her, his tongue gliding inside of her, in and out, slowly seducing her mouth. He grasped her hands in his, pushing them above her head and holding them in place as his lips teased her.

Flynn knelt between her legs and unbuttoned her shorts. He tugged the fabric down her long legs, pulling off her boots and socks with them. Cool summer air tickled the damp curls between her legs. Her blood heated as Grant's kiss grew hungrier. She could smell her sex in the summer air around them.

Flynn's firm hands slid up her inner thighs, pulling them further apart the higher he went. He paused, his fingers hovering inches from her pussy. His fingertips brushed against her pussy lips, spreading her open like a flower.

She mewled against Grant's lips as his tongue sank further inside her mouth. His hand released her hair, sliding down her collarbone, tracing a steady path to her breasts. She moaned as the rough pad of his thumb slipped over her tight nipple. Pleasure sparked in her chest as she wiggled her hips, begging Flynn for more.

His tongue pressed against the sensitive bud of her clit. Lily jumped, moaning into Grant's mouth as Flynn's tongue pressed firmer against her, creating wet designs over her clit. She shuddered under their touch.

Grant's hand gripped her wrists tighter, stretching her out as her back arched into the pleasure from Flynn's mouth. White-hot stars burst behind her eyes as she whimpered. Flynn's finger slipped into her damp opening, stretching her just a little bit. His tongue lapped at her clit as his finger began to thrust in and out of her in small circles.

Lily cried out against Grant's mouth as his fingers pinched her nipple, a small shock of pain mixing with the building pressure between her legs. Her heels dug into the parachute laid out under her like a blanket.

Flynn slipped a second finger inside her and growled against her clit. "God, you're so wet for us, Sweetheart." His lips moved against her pussy as he spoke, sending wicked shivers racing up and down her spine.

"God, yes," she whimpered, as Grant broke their kiss.

"Do you want Flynn to fuck you?" Grant's rough voice slid over her senses like a feather, tickling and teasing her.

"Yes," she begged.

"Do you want Grant to fuck you?" Flynn asked between her thighs.

"Yes," she moaned. Flynn's tongue circled her clit again as his fingers pumped harder inside her, stretching her further. "I want both of you," she moaned.

"Good," Grant smirked above her.

Flynn knelt between her legs, tugging his shirt off. Grant followed suit, stripping above her and keeping firm eye contact. His eyes hypnotized her, keeping her gaze glued to him. Inch-by-inch, he lifted his shirt, revealing hard and lean muscle beneath tanned skin. He yanked the shirt over his head, revealing a "USMC" tattoo in Old English font stamped over a scrolling ribbon on his left bicep. His hands slipped to his belt and jingled it open. She heard the same noises coming from between her legs, but she couldn't tear her gaze away from Grant.

He slid his pants and briefs down his lean legs. His thick erection bobbed out and his balls hung heavy and tight between strong thighs. A drop of pre-cum oozed from the tip of his stiff cock.

"Grant," she whimpered.

Lily yelped in surprise as Flynn's firm hands gripped her ankles, lifting her legs in the air. He wrapped her legs around his trim hips, positioning himself above her.

Lily glanced down. His cock hovered between her legs, hard and ready for her. She bit her lip, wondering if he'd stretched her enough with just his fingers. It had been years…

"Oh!" she gasped, closing her eyes as the thick head of Flynn's cock pushed into her wet cunt. "Flynn," she moaned.

"That's it, Sweetheart. Take it all in. God, you're so tight." Flynn gritted his teeth, panting above her to keep control.

Grant grasped Lily's hands and raised them above her head, pinning them in place. Her body stretched beneath Flynn's like a virgin sacrifice on an altar. "That's it, Sugar. Take it nice and deep." Grant purred in her ear. "Feel him stretching out that pussy. Feel your cunt squeeze on his cock."

Lily moaned as Flynn sunk deeper inside her, his groin pressing against her sensitized clit. He paused for a second, his breathing deep and steady before sliding himself from her. He pushed back in with a stronger force, her hips jerking with his movements. Slowly he fucked her, pumping his thick cock in and out of her tight hole.

"That's it, Lily. Take it. Take every long, thick inch of it," Grant whispered in her ear. His hand traced over her throat, down her collarbone, reaching for her breast. He squeezed, the sensitive flesh tingling beneath his hot palm.

"Oh God," Lily moaned. Her back arched. An orgasm crested inside her, higher and higher. She felt it peak, ready to wash over her and drown her like a tidal wave. "Oh, God. Flynn! Flynn!"

Grant's lips captured hers, eating her words and moans of pleasure. Lily's body shook as her orgasm broke like a thousand pieces of glass sparkling in the moonlight. Hot pleasure pulsed through her as she spasmed, her body squeezing Flynn's cock.

"Oh, God. Yes," Flynn groaned. He ground his hips against her one last time as his cock throbbed and pulsed, filling her pussy with his cum. "God, Sweetheart," he groaned, his cock jerking deep inside her.

Her pussy squeezed him as her orgasm died down, wringing him for every drop. "God," she whimpered as Grant's lips slipped away from hers.

"Wow, you're a screamer." Grant smirked down at her. "Now, let's see what I can do."

Flynn pushed himself away from Lily, lying beside her. Grant knelt between her damp thighs. He gripped Lily's weak legs and wrapped her ankles around his neck. He slipped the underside of his cock along her clit, rubbing her juices onto him.

Aftershocks ripped through every inch of Lily's body, waking nerves she thought had fallen asleep in exhaustion. "Grant," she murmured.

Grant stared down at her, watching her expression change as he slid the head of his cock inside her. Her eyes widened in shock as sensation bubbled inside her belly.

"Grant," Lily moaned again. She arched her back as he sunk in deeper...deeper...deeper than Flynn had reached. A dull ache spread throughout her cunt as his long cock nestled deep in her wet pussy. "Grant," she gasped as his hips pressed against her thighs, finally stopping.

"Good girl, Sugar. Take all of me," he groaned. His hand

reached down between them, his fingers teasing her clit as inch-by-inch, he slid out from her.

Flynn rested his weight on his arm, his free hand reaching over and cupping her breast. He squeezed, testing the weight in his hand for a moment before dipping his head lower. His tongue circled her nipple, his lips pressing firmly and sucking her into his mouth.

"Fuck," Lily moaned, her pussy clamping down on Grant's cock.

"Damn, she likes when you do that," Grant groaned.

Flynn sucked harder on her nipple as Grant's hips began to thrust in and out, in a hard, punishing rhythm.

Lily trembled under Grant's thrusts. Flynn's mouth seemed to be the only thing keeping her from shooting off into space. Hot pleasure burst throughout her like small bombs exploding until she couldn't think. "Grant," she shuddered, her orgasm surprising her as it sped toward her.

"Grant!" Lily shouted. Flynn pulled his lips from her breast, kissing her with a fierce hunger. His fingers pinched her damp nipple as Grant's thrusts picked up speed. Lily shouted into Flynn's mouth as her orgasm blinded her, bringing her out of reality and into a world where only pleasure existed.

Only the three of them existed.

Flynn broke their kiss and Lily whimpered, her mind foggy, her body trembling as Grant's thrust continued her aftershocks.

"I have an idea," Grant said, releasing her legs and sliding them down. He slipped his long cock from between her aching thighs and leaned backward. "Lily, turn around on all fours."

Flynn rose and knelt in front of Lily as she obeyed. Her limbs shook under her weight, the cold floor seeping through the parachute fabric and cooling her hands and knees. Cold air tickled the sensitive spot between her legs.

Grant gripped her hips, his fingertips digging into the soft flesh. The head of his cock pressed against her opening as inch-by-inch, he slid back inside her heat.

"God, yes, Sugar," he groaned.

Flynn knelt in front of her, his cock hardening again as it bobbed inches from her kiss-bruised lips. "Taste me." He reached for her. His fingers tangled in her damp locks of hair.

Lily opened her mouth as Flynn's hips thrust forward, the head of his cock slipping against her tongue. She closed her lips over him, tasting him fully, traces of her juices still stuck to him. Her tongue wrapped around him, teasing his cock.

Grant slipped his cock several inches from her before thrusting deep inside again. Lily's body jerked, pushing her head further down Flynn's cock. She slid back a few inches before Grant thrust again, moving her forward. She rocked backward and forward between them, trapped with two thick, hard cocks invading her body. She moaned, her lips vibrating against Flynn's smooth flesh as Grant's thrusts quickened their pace.

Grant's hand slipped around her hips, his fingers searching for her sensitive clit. She moaned on Flynn's cock as Grant's fingers hit home. "Oh, God," she choked on Flynn's cock.

Grant's thrusts moved faster, stroking her inner walls and building up her orgasm.

Her lips tightened around Flynn as she rocked back and forth.

"Oh, God, Sweetheart," Flynn groaned, his fingers tightening in her hair. His cock pulsed in her mouth, jets of hot cum leaking onto her tongue, salty and sweet.

Lily swallowed, trying to keep her body focused as

Grant's fingers moved faster. She moaned, jerking under his assault on her clit as pleasure burst throughout her, consuming her like fire.

Lily whimpered as another orgasm ripped through her. Flynn's cock slipped from between her lips and her arms gave way. Hot bolts of lightning shot through her, hard and fierce and so amazing she nearly forgot to breathe.

Somewhere above her, she heard Grant— heard him grunt and moan her name. His long cock swelled and jerked as her cunt squeezed him, milking him for his cum. His fingers dug harder into the soft flesh of her hips and the swell of her ass.

Lily gasped for breath, her mind whirling as Grant's cock slipped from her limp body. Flynn's hands rubbed her shoulders, her back, pressing soft kisses on her shoulder blades.

"Sugar, you're amazing," Grant murmured, pulling her body against his.

Lily's mind whirled, trying to figure out where she was and what was happening.

Grant.

Flynn.

Sex.

Wow.

Breathe.

Exhaustion and afterglow flooded her brain.

Flynn shifted beside her, lifting her arms and tugging a shirt over her head. He carefully spread her legs apart and wiped her clean with a corner of the parachute before shimmying a pair of dry panties and shorts up her legs, buttoning them in place.

Grant's hand moved over her, kissing her and nuzzling her, relaxing her body as sleep welcomed her.

"You're both amazing," she managed to murmur.

She heard both men chuckle and start to whisper sweet

nothings to her as she drifted off to sleep. She wondered for a moment why she felt so different, like her guard had fallen. She knew it was because of these men—her men—and for the first time since she saw an infected, she felt safe. Safe, secure, and satisfied.

CHAPTER 9

"Morning," a rough voice whispered in Lily's ear. Warm breath tickled her sensitive skin.

A flutter of awareness tingled in her belly like a dozen escaped butterflies.

Flynn. Grant.

Every touch, every feeling from last night returned to her, and happiness flooded her system like an endorphin rush. Her muscles ached with every slow movement as she rolled over and opened her eyes.

Flynn's face hovered inches from hers. He placed a scratchy kiss on her cheek, some of his stubble rubbing against her skin.

The same stubble that felt wicked against her thighs last night. "Morning," she said, tilting her head to try and hide some of her morning breath. She eased herself into a sitting position. The muscles in her waist and hips tightened.

She groaned a little as her aching muscles protested, stretching and screaming from exhaustion. "I should go check on Sammy." She yawned, her arms rising above her head, tugging at her aching shoulder muscles.

"She's sound asleep," Flynn said with a smile. "I checked on her a few minutes before you woke up."

"Thank you." A happy, fluttery feeling blossomed in Lily's belly. They really did care about Sammy.

"Can you hand me the bag?" she asked Flynn. She watched him stand, still shirtless. Muscles along his back bunched and tensed as he leaned down. He strode across the room, bag in hand, with a satisfied grin. His eyes twinkled in the morning light, a sparkling blue like a brilliant summer sky.

"Thanks." She rummaged through the bag until her fingers wrapped around the bottle of pills. She pulled out a half-empty bottle of water from one of the side compartments. She popped three pills and took a long swig of water to wash them down. "Thank God for aspirin."

Beside her, Grant yawned and stretched his arms out. "Morning already?" he asked, his eyes blinking open as he sat up.

"Nah, you still need your beauty sleep." Flynn grabbed a shirt in their bag and tossed it at Grant. It landed over his head and forced him to sit up. Both men slipped on shirts while Lily stood on shaky legs.

She wondered how Sammy had slept through the night. She stepped over toward the office door across the gym and pressed her ear to the door. A soft, mewling noise came from inside.

Sammy was snoring.

Lily's her heart fluttering and her belly tightening. Warmth and love filled her chest at the small, funny sound. She tugged on the doorknob and found her daughter where she'd left her, sound asleep on the office floor. A little trail of dribble dripped down Sammy's cheek, dampening the jacket under her head.

"Sammy? Sweetie, time to wake up," she crooned. She sat beside her daughter and carefully nudged her awake.

Sammy yawned, rubbing the sleepiness from her eyes. She slowly opened her eyes, blinking up at her mother. She grabbed a corner of the blanket and tugged it up over her head, hiding from view. "No," she said.

"No?" Lily smiled. "You don't want to get up for me?"

"No," Sammy said again, shaking her head under the blanket. A corner of the sheet rose over Sammy's foot.

"So, I can't get you to wake up?" Lily said.

"No," the four-year-old repeated in her high-pitched, happy voice.

"Not even if I do this?" Lily tickled her daughter's foot.

Sammy shrieked with laughter, the giggling sounds echoing around the office. "Mommy, stop." Little limbs flailed around as the blanket slipped off her.

"But, it's in the mommy handbook. Moms are allowed to tickle daughters," she teased.

"No, no, there is no handbook!" Sammy laughed, even after Lily stopped tickling her.

"Yes, there is. It's rule number one." Lily pulled her still giggling daughter onto her lap and kissed her forehead. "How about we get some breakfast?"

Sammy nodded and hopped off her mother's lap. She bolted into the gym.

"Morning, Sammy."

"Morning, baby girl."

Grant and Flynn's voices melded together in a harmony of tender affection.

A ball of warmth heated Lily's chest. Both men cared for her and Sammy. It was evident, even in their voices, even when she wasn't there to see it. They had nothing to prove to Lily. Their affection toward Sammy was infectious and genuine.

Lily's heart thudded as she stood and walked back into the gym, watching both men smile down at her daughter like she was their own.

A pinch tugged at her heart. Flynn had lost his daughter. Grant had lost his sister. Yet somehow, here they were—smiling at her daughter like she was their whole world. Maybe she was. What else did they have besides each other now?

A loud metal rattling sounded outside the gym door. Chains clattered against the handles. Marissa and another teenager with bright red hair came into the room, guns in hand, but not aimed at their group this time. "Sleep well?" Marissa chimed, a small smile adding to her attempt at friendliness.

"Yeah, thanks." Grant stretched out his shoulder as Sammy jumped up onto his back for a piggyback ride he'd just promised.

"Good. We need to talk," Marissa said. "Jonathan wants to meet with you. All of you. Grab your bag." She nodded to the duffle bag on the floor and stood aside.

The teenage boy walked outside the gym door and hovered, waiting to escort them. His fingertips drummed against the gun, but his fingers stayed far from the trigger. Wide eyes darted between Flynn and Grant like he was watching a tennis match. "This way," he murmured, so quietly they could barely hear him.

Flynn followed the boy out of the gym, Grant and Sammy in the middle, with Lily and Marissa pulling up the rear.

"Mind me asking how you have running water?" Lily asked, glancing over her shoulder to Marissa, who kept her gun pointed sideways. Not a threat, but a reminder of who was in charge.

Marissa smiled. "Sorry, can't answer any questions just

yet. Jonathan needs to make sure you all check out before we can tell you anything about us. Those are the rules."

"I take it he's the one in charge then?" Lily asked.

"Sort of. We're more of a democracy, but everyone goes to Jonathan for leadership. Guidance. Advice. Just a shoulder to cry on sometimes. He's good at reading people. He was the school's psychologist before the world went to H E double hockey sticks."

Lily said nothing as she followed the line down the hall like they were a kindergarten class taking a trip to the bathrooms. Line leader in tow, gun in hand, and quiet as a church mouse.

Sammy bounced on Grant's back, oblivious to the tension building between the adults.

Soon they turned into the cafeteria, where chairs and tables were shoved to one side of the room.

An older gentleman with Einstein-like hair sat in a chair while a younger man sat on a table. The young man smiled while the old man waved his hands, telling a story. The young man's laughter filled the room before fading as he caught a glimpse of the group coming toward them. "Hey Marissa," he called across the room, nodding his head toward them.

She nodded back and continued to be the caboose of their sad little train, trudging their way across the large cafeteria. "I brought company."

"We brought company," said the teenager in the front of the line. A small scowl tugged across his lips as a flash of annoyance lit up his face like lightning.

"Whatever." She shrugged.

The teenager stopped short a dozen feet from the old man. "Jonathan, we brought them in from the gym. They were the ones who killed the walker in the hallway."

"Walker? What is this, a damn TV show?" Grant grumbled.

Jonathan's loud laugh boomed from deep in his belly, almost frightening, almost a relief. "Well, it sounds better than zombies, I'd reckon. Why don't you four take a load off and sit by me," he offered.

"Roman," he said to the teenage boy. "Go get a bag of M&Ms from my stash in the office. For the little one." He placed his hands on his knees as he watched the four newcomers sit across from him, their eyes darting around the room.

When Grant set Sammy on her feet, she ran to her mother and launched herself into Lily's lap. She pressed her head close to her mother's chest. Lily's arms wrapped tight around her daughter.

"No one here will hurt you." The old man frowned, shifting in his seat.

The girl's discomfort was obvious, but she restrained herself. Sammy didn't cry, but her fear mingled with the tension humming in the air like electric waves. Her small body trembled like a frightened kitten as she turned her head into her mother's chest.

"What're your names?" he asked.

"I'm Flynn. That's Grant, and Lily, and her daughter, Sammy." Flynn thumbed down the line as he introduced each one of them.

"How do you know each other?" Jonathan hunched forward studying each one of them as if he could somehow peek into their soul.

His pale blue eyes studied them with intense curiosity. Her head swiveled behind her. Marissa stared at them from a corner, her gun still in her hands, pointed downwards.

Jonathan must have decided they were not a threat. For now.

"We met on the road. I came across Lily and Sammy on a supply run. We were on our way to…somewhere when we came across Grant. He saved Lily's life."

"Where were you going?" Jonathan asked.

Flynn sighed. "Well, we were on our way to a refugee camp I'd heard about. It's not too far from here, but it would take a few more days for us to reach it. We decided to come in here and rest for the night. We didn't know this place was already taken. No cars. No lights inside. No noise. We thought it might have been abandoned when the infection started."

Jonathan shook his head. "No. Just the opposite. When the fever spread, we stayed here. It seemed safe. A few of us who were in the school decided to stay. The rest ran home to their families. We haven't seen any of them since. A couple of others joined us here and there. Some ventured out on their own after a while. But, enough about us. You said Grant saved Lily." Jonathan stared at Grant with that piercing curiosity in his eyes. "Tell me what happened."

"She was attacked. I stopped it." Grant crossed one ankle over his knee and leaned back in his chair. His eyes hardened as he eyed Jonathan.

"Well, the devil's in the details. Elaborate for me, please," Jonathan said.

"Some men were trying to rape me," Lily began.

"Lily," Flynn hissed.

"No," she snapped, "We need to be honest about what happened. No half-truths."

Jonathan shifted in his chair, giving her his full attention. "Go on."

"I was in a store collecting supplies. Flynn and Sammy were just outside getting gas. I didn't check to see if anyone else was already inside. It was quiet so I thought it was empty. Three men ambushed me and locked the door. They dragged me into the back room, but Grant came in through the back door. He shot them. We left after that."

"Well, there was a bit more to it than that. Some infected came up and cornered us before we could get to the car." Flynn said.

"Infected? And you're making fun of us for calling them walkers?" Marissa teased from the back.

"What happened to the men inside?" Jonathan's eyes hardened to an icy blue as his brows furrowed together, trying to piece together their story.

"We killed them," Lily said.

Grant winced.

Flynn ran a hand through his hair and glanced at the wall, a chair, the sun-bleached American flag against the wall. Anything to avoid seeing the expression on Jonathan's face. Surely this would get them thrown out of the school without their supplies. At best.

"Good," Jonathan leaned back in his seat. "You're resourceful. You did what you had to survive. Understandable. I doubt any of us would have done any different. But have you killed anyone else?"

Flynn and Lily shook their heads. Grant stayed still as a statue, his body tensing in his chair. A vein thumped in the side of his neck.

"Did you?" Jonathan asked again, staring directly at Grant.

"I was in Iraq. I don't talk about it. And it's none of your damned business, old man," he growled, his foot shaking and tapping to a rhythm none of them could hear.

"After the infection, after the world fell apart, did you kill anyone else?" Jonathan asked.

"No. No one that was still a person anyway. Alright? Happy now?" Grant spat.

"Yes. How long have you four been traveling together?" he asked, turning back toward Flynn.

"Just a few days," Flynn said.

"So, you don't know one another very well?" he asked.

Lily's blush gave them away as heat crept up her neck, dying her cheeks a bright pink. Grant and Flynn's gaze flickered to her for a moment.

"Ah, I see. So, which one of them is it?" Jonathan asked, his gaze landing on Lily.

His knowing smile made Lily blush harder. "Both," she whispered, her flesh now a dark crimson as she stared at the top of Sammy's head, too embarrassed to look anyone in the eye.

Jonathan laughed again. "Well, good for you. It's nice to have companionship in these hard times. I'm not judging you. Please, don't think I'm judging you. If anything, I'm envious. I lost my wife to the infection. Nothing's been the same since." A gloomy veil fell over him and the weight of the world pressed his body deeper into his chair.

"I'm sorry," Lily said.

"So am I." He sighed and heaved himself out of the chair. "But she's still with me. Somewhere out there. Some days I swear I can still feel her in the same room. If I close my eyes, I can see her laughing. Sometimes I almost hear it."

A cool shiver trickled down Lily's spine like icy water. She could only imagine the pain Jonathan endured when his wife passed away. Dying from this outbreak, this disease, this horror… Lily's stomach twisted like a wet rag, wringing out every ounce of sympathy she had. She couldn't imagine…

"Mommy," Sammy curled up closer to her mother, "can I go play?"

"Not yet, sweetie. We can play soon. But, first, the adults have to talk."

"But all you do is talk." Sammy sighed and slumped her head against her mother. "I'm bored."

A little puff of air against her chest let Lily know how exhausted and tired Sammy really was. And she couldn't blame her. No breakfast. No toys. Nothing to entertain her while this man interrogated them.

"Want me to take her to the library when Roman gets back?" Marissa asked. "We have some toys in there."

"Can one of us go with you?" Lily asked. "No offense, but I don't know you. You don't know us. I'm not leaving my child alone with a stranger. I don't know what's in this school. We found one infected in here already. How do you know there aren't any more lurking around that just haven't found you yet?"

"She's got a good point," Jonathan interrupted as Marissa opened her mouth to respond. "Lily, why don't you go with your daughter? I'd like to continue talking to these two. We might have a few jobs for you all if we think you'll fit in alright here."

"And if we don't fit in?" Grant asked.

"I think you'll fit in just fine," Jonathan said. "But, that's not entirely up for me to decide. We're a democracy here."

"Found them!" Roman shouted as he jogged into the room with a bag of M&Ms in hand. "Man, you know how to hide your good stuff."

Jonathan chuckled. "Thanks. You can give them to Sammy here."

Roman carefully trod over to Sammy. He stared at the smiling four-year-old like she was an angry puppy that might snap at him. He held his hand out far from the rest of his body and shook the bag at her like a dog treat. "Here you go. Go ahead, take it." He offered her an awkward smile, his eyes widening in near panic.

"Thank you," Sammy said as she took the candy from him and held it up to her mother to open.

"Thank you, Roman. And you too, Jonathan." Lily said. "That was very sweet of you." She opened a small corner of the brown bag and handed it to her daughter, who popped a red candy in her mouth and sighed like she had never eaten chocolate before.

"You can both come with me," Marissa said from across the room.

Lily tucked Sammy's small hand into her own and led the four-year-old behind her as she followed Marissa down a few winding hallways.

"I thought you could use a break." She offered Lily a friendly smile. "Jonathan's interrogations can be exhausting. And you and Sammy don't seem like a threat. No offense."

"None taken," Lily mumbled. "But what about the men?"

"Jonathan will ask them some more questions. Make sure they're sane, that they'll gel well with the rest of us and that they're willing to pitch in. We don't take in mooches."

"Pitch in how?" she asked.

"We all do different jobs to keep this place running. Most of the adults group up and go on supply runs every few days. He might see how they can help and if they have any specialized skills we could use. There's always plenty of work to go around. More people means more supply runs. And you guys brought a car, so that'll go a long way to help. Right now, we have a falling apart minivan and a broken-down school bus out back. It'll help to have a good car like yours."

"Flynn's kind of a mechanic. At least, I know he works on cars. He fixed the one we brought with us," Lily said.

"Good. Maybe he can get the bus in the back running again."

Marissa opened a door, leading to a small children's library. The room was well kept, the wooden bookshelves gleaming in the morning sun that peeked through the windows. A garden mural was painted in the corner along a wall with an adult-sized chair set up for story time. A small corner was filled with toys, but most of the room was lined with children's books.

"Do you have a copy of *Harry Potter* in here? I was reading it to Sammy before we left my mother's house and I forgot to pack it." Lily rested Sammy on her feet.

The little girl wandered over to a box of LEGO, the stack of dolls completely ignored.

"That's my girl." A small bubble of pride swelled in her chest.

"Yeah, I think we still have some of them in here. 823.914R797 if I remember correctly," Marissa said.

Lily stopped in her tracks, whipping around to face the woman. "What?"

"It's the Dewey Decimal number for those books. They were popular with the kids," Marissa said. "I was the librarian here. You know, back when this was still a school."

"Oh," Lily said. "That must have been nice."

What else could she say? It was so easy to forget that the woman holding a gun in her hands once had a normal life too.

"I used to be an assistant for a funeral home and a waitress on the weekends," she said, searching for some common ground with the only other woman she'd seen since the world ended.

"I used to waitress in college," Marissa said. "While I put myself through grad school. Olive Garden. God, I miss their breadsticks."

"I loved those," Lily smiled. "With some of that alfredo sauce on the side? Those were the best snack."

"Yeah. Suddenly I'm not looking forward to Ramen and beef jerky for lunch," Marissa grimaced.

"Shame we don't have any wine. Anything tastes good after a few bottles."

"So, my curiosity is getting the better of me and I have to ask." Marissa sat on top of a wobbly kids' table. "Flynn. Grant. Both of them. How did that happen?" She shifted her hips and settled into place, watching Lily with an odd sort of fascination.

"Um, well, I'm not sure. It just did." Her blush crept up the back of her neck like a bad feeling.

"Oh, come on. Stuff like that doesn't just happen. Are they bisexual? Is one of them gay? Are you three committed, or is it just a fun time?" Marissa pressed.

"We're committed…I think. I mean, we haven't said it, but I think it's just understood. And no, they're not bisexual. Or homosexual. Just…really sexual." She bit her lip. The feeling of their skin pressed against her, the sore and stretched feeling as they filled her lingered in her mind.

Marissa laughed, her voice drifting around the room like a ghost of something happy.

The sound set Lily on edge. Hearing laughter was so rare that it was like hearing a gunshot at night. It left her with an uneasy feeling in her stomach, worry swirling in her veins. With no one around her for over a month except her daughter, she lost her comfort around people.

"Well, lucky you. I'd keep a tight leash on them. We have a girl here who's a little hot under the collar if you know what I mean. A few teenage boys and some old men…There are slim pickings around here. Just hope those men of yours don't have wandering dicks," Marissa warned.

Lily shook her head. "No. They're not like that."

"You sure?" Marissa asked, crossing her arms. Her eyebrow quirked up, challenging Lily. "You haven't known them for very long. They could have been serial cheaters or polygamists or asshole frat boys in their past lives for all you know."

Lily shrugged. "Are any of us still what we were in our past lives?"

Marissa froze, pondering Lily's question. Her shoulders slumped. Defeated, she said nothing. Lily was right, even if she didn't want to be.

"What do you think Jonathan will make them do?" Lily asked, changing the subject.

"I'm not sure. Everyone here who's old enough goes on supply runs. If they can't do much else, he'll have them clean or maybe help cook. I'm sure Jonathan will find something for them to do."

"And what do you do, besides help with the welcoming committee?" Lily asked.

"I also head the decorating committee, the student council, and I'm prom queen."

Lily laughed, the sound still giving her a weird feeling. But it felt good to laugh again. She missed laughter. "Think we'll fit in here?" Lily asked.

"Mommy, look! A house!" Sammy shouted from across the room, showing her mom a disjointed sort of cube with LEGO windows on all four sides and no door.

"Wow, great job! That is so good, sweetie. I love it." Lily smiled at her daughter as Sammy began to build something else. She faced Marissa, who was watching the little girl with a smile of her own.

"Yeah," Marissa said. "I think you'll all fit in just fine."

CHAPTER 10

"This will be your room. It has a sort of broom closet attached, which should work out just fine for Sammy."

Jonathan opened the door like a bellhop leading them into a hotel room.

Desks had been pushed aside and stacked on top of one another in a corner by the windows. Even though the windows were ten feet above the ground, something about the barricade between them and the outside world was comforting. Two mattresses were pressed together with mismatched sheets on each. A cot was tucked into Sammy's small room, along with a pile of toys.

"Thanks." Grant entered the room. His eyes darted around every corner. He walked across the room, pushing open the door to Sammy's room. He nodded to Flynn who entered behind, followed by Lily, who carried Sammy in her arms.

"We need some people to go on a supply run today," Jonathan said. "Grant. Lily. I want you both out there. And

Flynn, can you try to get that bus out back up and running? It'll come in handy for bigger things we can't haul back in a minivan."

"With what parts?" Flynn asked.

"We have a shop room out back by the gym. There should be plenty of spare parts out there. And it's fenced in so no one's been stealing anything out of there, at least as far as we can tell. No one's been dumb enough to climb that fence."

"Or they haven't gotten caught," Grant mumbled.

"What about Sammy?" Lily asked. "She's not going out there and I'm not leaving her with strangers I don't know."

"I can take her," Flynn offered. "There should be some small stuff in the garage to entertain herself. I used to take Hope down to the garage with me sometimes. She loved messing with my tools."

Flynn's smile didn't reach his eyes. He appeared haunted by the ghost of his daughter. His eyes glanced at Sammy with wistful happiness. Maybe Sammy reminded him a bit of Hope.

Grant grunted. "I don't think Lily should go."

"Why?" Lily asked, setting Sammy on her feet.

The four-year-old yawned with boredom as the adults talked. She waddled off to play with the new toys in the corner.

"Because Sammy needs you. You shouldn't be putting yourself in danger when there are plenty of people here who can go instead," he said.

"We can all chip in. I want to help," Lily said.

Grant shook his head. "It's too dangerous."

"I can protect myself." Her voice rose higher as anger crept into her bones.

"You can, but accidents happen. It's not worth the risk." Grant crossed his arms and glared at her.

"And you're not going to say anything?" Lily said to Flynn.

"Lily, this is not my fight. This is between the two of you." Flynn turned to Sammy. "Hey, Sammy, want to check out the garage. There is a lot of cool stuff to play with there. Have you ever used a monkey wrench?"

Sammy giggled and jumped to her feet, rushing over to him. "A monkey wrench? But monkeys don't use wrenches."

Flynn laughed and hoisted the little girl onto his shoulders. "You two sort this out on your own." He shot them both a pointed look and turned to Jonathan. "So, where's the garage?"

"I'll show you," he said. "The group's heading out in two hours for the run. I don't care what you two decide but at least one of you is going."

"No problem," Lily said.

"One of us will be going," Grant huffed. His gaze pierced through Lily like a lance.

The door closed with a sharp click, leaving the two of them alone.

"Who the fuck do you think you are, telling me what to do?" Lily shouted. Anger boiled under her skin, bubbling over and out of her mouth as she stared at him.

"You want to put your life at risk? The rest of us can go. Flynn and I can go. You're a mother. Your daughter needs you," he shouted back at her.

"I know she needs me, but these people are helping us. They're giving us a place to stay. They're giving us food. If we're going to stay, we all have to pull our weight around here."

"Right, and you can find a way to help here. Inside. Where it's safe. There's no reason for you to go and put yourself in danger."

"I can take care of myself. I can fight. I can protect myself," she yelled.

"And what if there's horde out there? Or what if you get ambushed again? Last time I checked, you needed my help with just three humans. What if a swarm of a hundred infected comes up and takes you by surprise? Think you can fight off a hundred of them? I've seen them swarm. It happens. Don't roll your eyes."

"Those men took my weapons and they had guns. Infected can't fight with weapons, and you damned well know that. It's not the same."

"Right. And those men could have let you go. If an infected gets you, you're dead. There's no talking your way out of it to let them keep you alive. You're not going and that's final," he shouted.

"You don't get to tell me what I fucking do. If I want to go on a fucking run, I'll go. You can run your mouth all you want, but it's my choice. No one tells me what to do, you asshole!" Her fists clenched at her sides, her fingernails digging into her palms.

"You think this is a game? What the hell are you trying to prove? You might get killed out there!" Grant's eyes hardened like bright amber gemstones. "Think about Sammy. What would happen to her if you got hurt? Yeah, she'd have us to look out for her, but that's a shit replacement for her mother and you know it. You're all she has in this world and she needs you."

"Don't tell me what to do," she snarled.

"Fuck," Grant growled, running a rough hand through his hair.

His brown eyes flashed and he was on her in an instant. The sound of shredding clothing filled the room as his mouth fell on hers.

Lily's slap across Grant's cheek echoed around the room

before his lips touched hers, silencing her protests. "Shut up," he whispered against her mouth, his hands fisting in her hair to hold her steady.

A whimper escaped Lily's throat, heat pulsing between her thighs. Hot, needy and so ready. "Fuck me," she murmured against his mouth, tasting his hot breath on her tongue.

Anger still simmered, feeding into the fire that he stoked deep in her belly. Her blood pulsed hot in her veins as need pierced through her brain. The world around her faded away as she clung to him.

He gripped the remains of her shirt and slid it off her shoulders. The flimsy fabric dropped to the floor around her feet. His hands groped, sliding around her waist and pulling her lean body against him.

His hard muscle moved like lava against her skin, hot and fluid. Lily's hands reached for him, shaking as she held onto the hem of his shirt and lifted it higher, revealing inch by inch of thick, tight muscle to her hungry gaze. Her lips slid against his, her tongue slipping between the seam of his lips, penetrating him, tasting him.

Grant's fingers slid through her thick curls, keeping her still. His tongue pushed hers back into her mouth, invading her. Their tongues danced together, tasting one another. Their bodies pressed together, sweat-slicked flesh squeezed close. His scent seeped into her, the smell of man and earth and sex perfuming the air.

Lily spread her legs wider, his thigh slipping between hers. Heat poured from between her legs, warming him. "Fuck," he growled against her lips before his tongue traced over her jawline, drinking in her sweetness.

Her hand reached lower, cupping his erection through the fly of his jeans. He growled, thrusting into her hand.

The sound tugged at Lily's lower belly. Her panties stuck,

damp and slick between the folds of her lips. She ground herself harder against the tense muscles of his thigh. Pleasure heated between her legs, burning hotter.

"Fuck," he murmured against the delicate skin of her neck. His tongue slipped out, licking a path down her collarbone to her throat.

Lily leaned back, letting herself feel his hot tongue dancing over her skin. She unbuckled the belt around his jeans and inched his zipper down until it couldn't go any further. She dipped her hand below his waistband and held onto him.

"God," she whimpered, feeling his heaviness in her palm, thick and hard. He twitched in her hand, his body responding to her grip. Lily dropped to her knees in front of him.

"Sugar," Grant warned as she slid his pants down around his calves.

Lily opened her mouth, her tongue flicking over the head of his hard cock. Grant's groan above her encouraged her to move deeper. Her lips wrapped around the tip of his cock as she licked a drop of pre-cum that oozed from him.

Grant hissed, fisting her hair and holding her head still as his hips moved forward. His cock slid deeper into her mouth, gliding until it hit the back of her throat.

Lily choked a little but fought to keep her gag reflexes under control. Her hand reached up, her fingertips digging into his thighs, hard and solid like marble. She sunk lower, sliding her tongue around to taste him.

"Oh, fuck, Sugar," Grant groaned, his eyes closing. His head lolled to the side as his hips moved in a slow rhythm. His cock thrust in and out of her mouth, fucking her, giving her a taste of what was to come.

He pulled back, his fingers entwined in her hair, holding

her steady. His cock slipped between her lips with a soft "pop."

Grant sank to his knees. "Lay down." He released her hair and pushed Lily onto her back.

He fumbled with the small buttons on her denim shorts. He popped them open, one by one before slipping her shorts and panties down her long legs and tugging them over her boots. Unbuckling the holster along her hip, Grant let the sides of the belt fall to the floor beside her.

His large hands reached for her full breasts, his fingers rubbing her nipples into tight pearls. He leaned over her body, the smell of him overpowering her like an aphrodisiac. She could get drunk off the smell. Grass. Gunpowder. Sex. Man. All of it.

Lily whimpered as his head dipped to her breast, catching one of the tight buds between his lips. Pleasure sparked in her chest, desire burning with every touch.

His tongue flicked out, circling her nipple before moving to the other one. "Fuck, you're incredible," he murmured before his tongue began sliding along her tit.

Lily's heart hammered so loud, it echoed in her brain. Heat overwhelmed her, licking her skin and boiling her blood. It was as hot as hell, but she felt like she was in heaven. "Grant," she whimpered.

"I love hearing you moan my name," he growled. He pulled his head back with a smile that dripped male satisfaction across his face. His body slid down hers, his lips tracing small kisses along her abdomen, and then her groin. Grant's firm hands gripped her thighs, pulling them apart before dipping his head between her legs.

Lily saw a flash of his blond hair before pleasure overpowered her. She closed her eyes, her body trembling as his tongue flicked over her clit. She laid back, indulging in the wicked sensations between her legs, dampness seeping from her entrance. Her legs spread further, welcoming the lashing from his evil tongue.

The tip of his tongue licked and poked around her wet folds, circling over her clit. His lips sucked the tiny bud into his mouth. He slid two fingers inside her wet cunt. Her pussy sucked his finger in deeper until his knuckles stopped him from going any further.

A fiery heat spread from her thighs, sending waves throughout the rest of her body. Lily screamed, shaking as an orgasm built higher and higher, almost ready to erupt.

"You're so ready, Sugar," he growled from between her thighs.

Lily whimpered, too dumbstruck from pleasure to speak. Her throat tightened and she blinked her eyes open. The sensations between her legs had stopped.

Grant's grip around her arms shocked her. He lifted her body with ease, flipping her onto her belly. She rested her weight on her forearms, staring down at the tiled floor. The floor that used to once be part of a classroom.

Grant's hand released her arms once she had settled herself. They gripped her hips, his rough fingers digging into the soft flesh. The head of his cock pressed against her, teasing her wet opening with a dirty promise of what was about to come.

"Please," she whimpered, backing up against him. The head of his cock pressed harder against her opening, but still didn't penetrate her. "Grant," she begged.

He thrust deep inside her, her pussy stretching wide to accommodate his girth. He slid his cock out an inch before pistoning his hips back into her, ramming balls deep inside her dripping cunt.

Shock, pain, and pleasure drowned Lily as she quivered on the floor, while Grant fucked her like a madman on a mission. In and out in hard, fast thrusts.

Grant had turned into a mindless fucking machine, hell-bent on coming deep inside her. He grunted above her, drops of sweat dripping onto her lower back.

Lily's fingertips slid lower, touching her sensitive clit. "Grant," she moaned. Her fingers rubbed her sensitized clit in small circles as an orgasm built back up again, soaring higher and higher, threatening to burst.

Grant's hand fell hard on Lily's ass as her wet fingers slipped over the tight bud. "Fuck, Grant!" Lily screamed as an orgasm rocketed through her, sending her into space. Pleasure burst like breaking glass. Waves of it washed over her, consuming her.

"Lily. Oh fuck, Lily!" Grant groaned before his body stilled. His hips jerked hard against her one last time before hot cum shot deep into her pussy. Her cunt squeezed him, milking his cock for every drop of cum as her orgasm began to ebb away in smaller and smaller waves.

Grant shook over her body, panting as he fought to catch his breath. His cock softened, slipping from her dripping hole. He rolled off to the side, pulling Lily into his chest as he laid against the cool tiled floor. "God, you're incredible, Sugar."

Lily cuddled up closer to him. She shivered a little as the heat drained from her limbs. Her body sunk against his, soaking in their afterglow as Grant traced his fingertips in small designs over her skin.

"I'm still going." Her voice drifted away like dandelion puffs in the wind.

"Only if I'm going with you," Grant said, a steely edge hardening his voice. "I won't stop you from going. But, only if I go, too. Or Flynn. One of us. We can't just sit back and wonder what's happening with you out there alone."

Lily stretched, twisting her body around to face him. Her leg rose over his, the heat from her thighs spilling out between them. Cum dripped from between her legs. "Alright. I can agree with that."

She leaned up and gave Grant a soft kiss.

He rewarded her with a smile. "We should get going soon. They're going to be leaving in a little while and we need to dress. If I can feel my legs, that is."

Lily giggled, sitting up to watch him. A beam of sunlight sliced through the window, warming them as he stared back at her. A twinkle in his eye, one that hadn't been there before, shimmered in the light.

"We should go," Grant said.

Lily nodded, watching him slowly stand and dress. She knew they should go, but she wanted to stay on that dirty floor with him for a long, long time.

She hoisted herself off the floor and slipped back into her clothes, changing her shirt for one he hadn't ripped. She combed her fingers through her tangles, but nothing could hide the giddy grin smeared across her face.

Grant and Lily strutted down the hall, a distinct afterglow radiating between the two of them. Their flushed faces were still varying shades of red and pink and their lips were bruised, swollen and tender to the touch.

But they smiled like fools.

"I think the front entrance is down this way," Grant pointed.

Taking her small hand in his, he led her down a hallway filled with sun-bleached posters and dingy lockers. They wandered past trophy cabinets and empty classrooms, some of which now doubled as bedrooms or lounges. A few were still arranged with desks. Fresh chalk smeared across some of the blackboards.

Lily's heart warmed a little. Something familiar in this chaos. Something good for Sammy to cling to in this mess. Sammy could start going to school, like a normal child in a normal world. She could have an education.

They stood in front of the double doors they had entered through yesterday, small slits of the outside world shining through the tiny windows.

"They should be outside," Grant said. He opened one of the doors and moved out into the bright sunlight, shielding his eyes with his hand as he glanced around. "Let's check the back." He led Lily down the steps and they walked around toward the side of the school.

Jonathan stood in the back courtyard. Flynn hunched over the hood of the car. Even though she couldn't see his face, Lily would recognize his perfect ass anywhere. Her smile widened as she and Grant walked over to the bus.

"Mommy," Sammy shouted. "Look. I have a tool!" Sammy held a screwdriver in the air with a goofy grin.

Lily laughed. "That's great, sweetie. Did Flynn show you how to use it?" Sammy rushed over to her mother. Lily scooped her up in her arms, carrying her a few more feet toward Flynn.

"It'll take a few days. But I think I can get this running with the parts we have here." Flynn rubbed his hands on his jeans, smearing some grease on the denim.

"Good. Let us know if you need anything. We're all here to pitch in." Jonathan patted Flynn on the back before turning to Grant. "So, have you two made a decision?"

"We both go." Grant frowned. He might have been unhappy about her decision, but at least he respected it.

"Glad to hear it. They're just about ready to go. They should be over by the minivan. You listen to Marissa. She's got a good head on her shoulders." Jonathan patted Lily on the shoulder before walking away.

"I'll be at the car in a few minutes," she nodded to Grant.

He nodded back, glancing at Flynn. He shoved his hands in his pockets and walked away to give them some privacy.

"Sammy, why don't you go play with your tool. Just stay near Flynn, ok?"

Sammy nodded before wandering off and digging in the dirt with the screwdriver.

Lily frowned. "Flynn?"

"Yeah." He continued to stare over the hood of the bus, avoiding her gaze.

"Can we talk?" she asked.

"About what?"

"About what just happened in there? About Grant?"

She hesitated.

His hands stopped moving and his shoulders slouched.

With a heavy sigh, he stood and faced her. A smudge of grease stuck to his cheek, his dark brows creased. His eyes glistened almost yellow in the sunlight.

She bit her lip, her body perking up to attention. Her nipples stretched against the thin cotton of her shirt, and she saw his gaze peek before snapping back to attention. She'd just had the ride of her life and her body wanted more? She never thought of herself as insatiable... *Guess these men brought out a new side of me.*

"What do you have to say about it?" he growled, crossing his arms and leaning against the hood.

"Well, I mean...I didn't plan...It just sort of happened." She shrugged.

"Okay." He shrugged back.

"I guess, I'm sorry. Maybe we should have talked about it. I mean, you, me, we're all, I don't know. This whole thing has me tangled up in knots. I don't know what I'm doing. I don't want anyone to get hurt, but I—"

"Lily, stop," he said. "Stop apologizing. Maybe we should

talk about what's going on, yeah. But you have no reason to apologize."

"But, I thought you were angry at me?" she stammered.

"No, I'm not angry. I just wish we had discussed this sooner. I don't plan on being involved every time you want to fuck him. If you two want some time to yourselves, that's fine. So long as he shows me the same courtesy." He smiled, his brilliantly white teeth catching the sunlight and blinding her for a moment.

"Courtesy?"

Flynn smirked for a moment before his hands wrapped behind her. One hand tugged on her ponytail, tilting her head upward, the other slid around her waist and pulled her eager body against him. His mouth pressed against her bruised lips, his tongue sweeping out to taste her.

She groaned, her hands clinging to his waist to keep her balance. The strong muscles under his shirt strained beneath her fingertips.

Slowly, with long, deep strokes, his tongue invaded her mouth. The taste of dark chocolate, berries, and something uniquely him filled her, invaded all of her senses. Her head spun as his body moved against her, grinding her petite frame against him. Her blood swirled with desire, spiking higher with every eager thrust of his tongue.

All too soon, he broke their kiss, his chest rising and falling hard against hers. "Tonight, I want you. Alone. I have some wicked ideas playing in my head that I think you'll enjoy." His smirk was back.

His smile and his words shot a cold shiver down her spine. The night couldn't come fast enough. "But, what about Sammy?" Lily asked with an airy whisper.

"I'm sure Grant can watch her for a few hours. Or we can find someone else to keep an eye on her. Half the camp already loves that kid."

"Okay. Tonight, then."

With a smile, she pulled herself from his arms and moved toward the car. She hadn't stepped foot outside the gate and already she was eager to be back in his arms. She caught Grant's gaze, his eyes glittering. He smirked, glanced over her shoulder, and nodded to Flynn from across the yard.

Lily hoped this supply run would be over soon. Since the infection, she'd never been so excited for night to come.

CHAPTER 11

Grant and Lily climbed into the Honda Odyssey minivan along with Marissa, Will, and a middle-aged woman named Virginia.

"Either of you ever shot a gun before," Will asked, turning in the front passenger seat to face them.

Grant nodded. Lily shook her head.

"Don't worry babe. We'll teach you."

"You better watch who you're calling babe, kid." Grant growled from the back of the minivan, his arm wrapping protectively around Lily's shoulders. "Have some respect."

"Sorry man," Will shrugged, shrinking a bit in his seat as he swiveled back around.

Marissa moved the car between chunks of fallen branches and some broken-down cars. "It's a short ride, only about ten minutes up the road."

"Where are we going this time?" Virginia pulled a revolver from her holster and loaded the barrels.

"The police station. See if we can clean out whatever's left in the armory," Marissa answered.

"And if there's nothing there? We're running low on bullets," Will said.

"Then we check out the gun store in town. See what's left and hope it wasn't emptied already."

"You didn't clear out the gun store yet?" Grant asked.

"No," Marissa said. "We haven't made a lot of runs. Gas is tough to come by, and the closest gun shop is an hour's drive away. The nearest station is five miles down the road, and it's almost dry. We're trying not to waste what we've got."

"Why not siphon gas from the cars on the road?" Lily suggested.

Grant beamed down at her. "That's my girl." He placed a warm kiss on the top of her head.

"We don't have the right equipment," Will said.

"Do you have a clear hose and a gas tank?" Grant asked.

"I think I saw a hose in the garage. And we have plenty of gas tanks. Why?" Marissa asked.

Grant shrugged. "Because I can show you the good old-fashioned way of doing it."

"How?" Virginia asked with wide-eyed surprise. "We don't have a pump."

"You don't need one if you have functioning lungs and enough sense not to swallow."

"Never heard a man say that before," Marissa smirked.

Grant laughed. "See, it's tough to get the hose into the tank, but once you do, you just suck it up the hose and stop before it reaches your mouth, then pour it into the tank. It takes a while but it's possible. Makes your lungs burn a little, though."

Virginia pursed her lips together as she swiveled forward in her seat.

"The police station is just up ahead. Lily, can you grab the duffle bags from the back?" Marissa asked.

Lily grabbed the empty bags by her feet as Marissa pulled up to a patch of grass and parked. Marissa turned in her seat to face everyone. "Now, remember, we need to be quiet. Will, grab the bolt cutters. We might need it. You guys all armed?"

Her gaze spanned over every one of them as they nodded to her.

"Good," she said. "Remember, we all look out for each other. We all get back safely. Got it?"

Grant glanced out the windows, checking as much of the perimeter as he could see. The coast was clear, so they hustled out of the van.

Marissa waved and they moved closer to the front doors of the police station. She climbed the steps, tapping on the door with the barrel of her handgun. Silence.

She nodded at Will, who walked up the steps with the bolt cutters in hand. He jiggled the door handle, but it didn't budge. "I can't open this. Let's go around back."

Their shoes rustled in the grass as they walked around the back of the building. Still no infected in sight. No people in sight.

Lily breathed a small sigh of relief. Maybe they would catch a break.

Will trod up to the back entrance and banged the bolt cutters against the metal doors. Three quick knocks. Silence filled the air as they waited. Still no noise from inside.

"Come on," he said. After a moment of struggling with the bolt cutters, he broke through the chain holding the back doors together. The loud clink of metal on metal filled the air around them.

Grant checked the perimeter for any motion. No rustling. No movement. No sound. The emptiness sent a shiver racing up and down Lily's spine.

Will pushed one of the doors open. The dark room loomed in front of them like an endless, black tunnel. No noise. Nothing rushed toward them or crept out into the daylight.

Marissa held her gun in front of her as she walked up the steps. She pulled a flashlight out of her back pocket and followed the beam of light into the station. She disappeared into the darkness.

Grant followed in second, then Lily. They walked around the sunlit room. Flies buzzed by one of the chairs, the sound churning Lily's stomach. A corpse sat at the desk chair, bloodstains splattered against the cement wall behind it. A gruesome, fly-covered stump sat where the man's head should have been. A rifle laid on the floor next to him, discarded and dusty.

"He won't be needing this anymore," Grant said. He stooped down to check that the weapon was unloaded, and stuffed it into one of the duffle bags. "Let's keep moving."

"You stole a dead man's rifle?" Virginia's eyebrows crinkled in disgust.

"He's not going to use it. We might need it. This rifle could be life or death to someone in the school. So yeah, we're taking it." Grant ignored Virginia's hard stare as he strolled past her.

"Let's keep going. We need to find the armory," Lily said, breaking up some of the tension.

Virginia shot one last appalled look over her shoulder before moving closer to Will.

"You alright?" Lily stepped closer to Grant as the group walked past them.

He shrugged. "They're sheltered. They don't know what has to be done to survive out here."

"Bingo," Marissa shouted from across the room. A few rifles, a dozen handguns, and dozens of boxes of bullets were locked up through a caged door. "Will, where are the bolt cutters?" He handed it to her, and they all stepped back, watching her snap the lock handle clean in half. "Pack up everything and let's get out of here."

The little librarian hustled inside and began cramming handguns and boxes of bullets into her bag. Will followed suit and started to pack up. Virginia watched them, her eyes shifting as though she couldn't make up her mind to join in or leave them work. "This is stealing," she mumbled.

"You paid taxes, right?" Marissa rolled her eyes as she crammed a Glock into the bag. "Well, these were paid for with good old taxpayer dollars. So have at it!"

Grant shrugged past Lily, cramming the rifles into his long bag along with some boxes of bullets.

Lily glared at Virginia once more before moving to help him. In minutes, they'd emptied the armory.

"Anything else in here we can use?" Grant asked as they walked out of the caged room.

"I don't think so. We have the guns. It's just paperwork. There might be some food or water in the kitchen," Lily suggested.

"We'll go check it out," Marissa said, nodding to Will and Virginia. "We'll meet you by the car. Load up the guns." She handed her bag to Lily and moved to the kitchen. Will handed his bag off to Grant before following Marissa into the kitchen. Virginia stared down at the floor as she shuffled behind Will.

"Let's go," Grant said, moving past the desks to the front door. With a turn of the bolt, the front door opened, leading right to the minivan. He opened the trunk, piling their bags into the back. He closed it with a loud *thunk* and checked to see if anything heard the sound.

Silence.

"It's spooky how quiet it is out here," Lily said. "There were always infected roaming around my mom's house. I would hear them all the time, especially at night. The dark seemed to magnify the sound. It was like all I could hear was the moaning. It never stopped until we got out of there."

"I miss the quiet," Grant said. "I used to go fishing out on a lake near my house every Sunday morning. Before the sunrise, when it was still dark outside, I'd go out on my boat and fish on the lake and watch the sun come up. I liked watching the sky turn colors. And it was different every time. It started out dark blue to orange, then red and pink, then almost white before it turned sky blue." His wistful, nostalgic expression, the fine lines around his eyes crinkling with unshed tears, the hard line between his tight lips— Grant's sorrow almost moved Lily to tears.

A rustling in the grass attracted their attention. Lily spun on her heel, her knife in her hand. "We should get moving. We still have to hit the gun shop," Marissa said, opening the driver's door.

"Maybe if someone hadn't held us up back at the school," Virginia said, glaring at Lily like she was the whore of Babylon.

Lily rolled her eyes and hopped into the back row of the car, Grant sliding in beside her. Will sat in the front seat, closing the door behind him. Virginia kept glaring.

Grant's hand reached over, brushing the top of Lily's hand before engulfing it with his own.

"Unnatural," Virginia murmured before sitting into one of the middle row seats and sliding their door shut.

"Oh, shut up, you judgmental vulture," Grant snapped at the woman.

Her mouth hung open in shock as Marissa pulled away from the station, driving in the direction of the only gun shop in town.

"Don't talk to my mother like that," Will snapped, shifting in the front seat to glare daggers at Grant.

"I'll talk to her with more respect when she treats my girl-friend with more respect," Grant shouted back.

"Whose girlfriend is she exactly?" Virginia smirked. "Yours or Flynn's?"

"Both," Lily snapped, her brows creasing into a hard line. Blood boiled beneath her skin, her stomach jumping and threatening to leave her body and rip Virginia apart.

The car screeched to a sudden halt in the middle of a blacktop road.

"All of you, shut the fuck up. Grant, be nicer to people here. Virginia, it's none of your damned business who Lily's fucking or how many guys she's dating or anything. Now, if you don't play nice, keep your mouths shut, and pretend to like each other, I'm going to turn this car back around, and the four of you can tell Jonathan exactly why we're low on ammo and supplies from this run. And you can tell him why we wasted gas. Got it?"

The small woman's voice packed a loud punch, weighing the group down in their seats. They all slumped like children who had been caught spilling glue on the carpet and pulling each other's hair. Even Grant's shoulders sunk a little in fear of the tiny librarian.

"Yes," they all murmured.

Marissa nodded and drove the car back along the road.

The five-minute drive to the gun shop was silent.

Marissa steered the car into the dirty parking lot littered with food wrappers, dead leaves, and papers for missing persons, all of which were months old. The metal gun shop sign reflected some of the dimming light as the sun began to slowly set over the dead town.

One by one, they hustled out of the car, each of them checking their weapons before walking up to the open shop doors that squeaked in the wind.

Grant made a move to go through.

"No, I'll go," Will said, puffing out his chest.

Grant stopped and let Will move inside. Both men kept their guns pointed in front of them. The rest of the group paused, waiting. Silence.

"Oh shit!" Will yelled from deep inside the store.

"William!" Virginia shouted, rushing inside, her gun pointed down with the safety still on.

"Damn," Grant murmured, raising his gun in front of him and following Virginia inside. Her piercing scream sent Marissa and Lily dashing inside behind Grant.

Will kicked hard against an infected that wrapped its gnarled arms around his leg. He raised his gun. The monster's mouth gaped wide, leaning toward Will's calf.

Pop!

The monster's head fell to the side, half of its mouth blown to bits across the floor.

"Mom!" Will shouted out, his head whipping around.

Virginia held one of the infected away from her with the end of a rifle. The monster swung its arms, trying to latch onto Virginia. With another loud bang, the infected fell in a crumpled heap to the floor, finally dead.

"Oh God," Virginia cried, tears streaking down her face. The gun fell as her arms shook, then the rest of her body trembled

Grant dashed across the room to her, holding her up in his arms before she collapsed next to the infected's corpse.

"It's alright Virginia. We're all here. Are there any more of them?" Grant asked, walking around the counter, as he held the shaking woman.

"William," she sobbed.

"Mom," Will rushed over to her, his eyes gleaming with worry.

"William," she cried, a smile breaking through the terror

on her face. Her expression was like watching glass crack. "My boy! Oh, thank God, my boy!"

Will hugged his mother in an awkward embrace, the woman still trembling like a leaf in Grant's arms.

Grant sized up Will, but even with a growing boy's strength, he would have been too weak to carry Virginia back to the car.

"Lily, Marissa, clean out what you can," Grant instructed. "I'm going to take her back to the van. Will, come with me. You're going to guard her until we're done in here." He strolled out of the store, mother and son staring at one another with a small gush of relief.

"Hand me a bag, would you?" Marissa asked.

Lily handed Marissa a duffle bag before moving across the store to load up on ammo. She wasn't sure what types of guns they had, what sort of magazines went with what, or the difference between the bullets besides how many came in a pack…She needed to catch up on her weapons knowledge, and she'd have to learn fast. "I think maybe we should set up some sort of gun range in the gym."

"Why? That's just a waste of ammo." Marissa stuffed a silencer into her bag as she glanced over at Lily.

"To practice," Lily answered. "I could write down everything I know about guns on an index card and have plenty of room to spare. I bet most of us don't know as much as we think we do and it never hurts to know more. And we'd waste more ammo missing our targets if we actually needed to use them. Besides, we need to learn to protect ourselves. If there's an invasion—"

"The school's not going to be invaded." Marissa's sharp voice pierced through Lily's gut, but she kept talking.

"Better safe than sorry in these times. I think you know that," Lily said.

"Talk to Jonathan. That's not my call. But I don't see why we should waste ammo practicing," Marissa replied.

"Because we'll waste plenty of ammo missing our targets if we don't practice," Lily snapped. "And we run the risk of losing more than a few bullets if we're not prepared."

"Maybe. Like I said, talk to Jonathan. That's not my call," she said. "Do you think pepper spray will work against an infected?" She held up a pink pepper sprayer shaped like a small pistol.

Lily chuckled. "I'd rather not get close enough to find out."

"Everything alright?" Grant said, dropping a duffle bag from his shoulder and loading up a few rifles that hung up on the walls.

"Yeah, we're good. Almost finished over here," Lily said. She grabbed a couple of packages of earplugs and stuffed them in the bag before zipping it shut. "I'm going to go drop this off at the car. This bag's full."

She lifted the bag with two hands, waddling a little as she carried the heavy duffle bag back to the minivan.

Virginia was sitting shotgun, the door open. Will was crouched under the driver's seat, tugging on a few wires.

"Is everything alright here?" Lily asked.

Virginia gasped as Will's head jerked up, slamming into the steering wheel.

"Just peachy," he glowered.

"What were you doing?" she asked.

"One of the wires was dangling down low," he said. "I was checking it."

Lily frowned but said nothing. lifted the handle of the trunk and heaved the bag into the back. As she shut the door, Marissa and Grant joined her, both carrying heavy bags stuffed full of weapons, ammo, and odd accessories.

"We should head back," Marissa said. "I don't want to have to put the headlights on when we're driving back."

"Looks like we caught a break," Will said as he climbed into the back of the minivan.

Lily followed Flynn, eying him with caution as she sat in the row behind him. She turned in her seat to see Grant lift the duffle bags like they were nothing more than a small bag of flour. His muscles strained against the tight fabric of his shirt, a small glimmer of sweat trickling down his chest, dampening a thick line down the middle of his shirt, stopping just above his hard abs.

Her fingers twitched, remembering the feel of his hard body beneath her fingertips. Her body tightened like a bowstring, eager and ready to touch him again.

He slammed the trunk shut, jerking her from her delicious daydream before he climbed into the back seat beside her. The scent of sweat, earth, and something spicy clung to his skin, taunting her as they pulled away from the shop back toward the school.

Though the car was silent, Lily's blood hummed with excitement. Soon they would be back in the school, back to Flynn and Sammy, back to safety.

CHAPTER 12

Sanjay sat on the front steps of the school with a sharpened pipe in hand, waiting for the group. The car lights flashed once across the grass, signaling their return.

Over Marissa's shoulder, Lily watched him jump from the steps to unlock the gate and push it open so they could drive through. Once the car cleared the gate, he rushed to close and lock it again.

Two infected roamed toward them, their slow steps and guttural moans echoing around them as Marissa killed the car engine. The infected wandered up to the locked gate, sticking their hands through the iron bars to get at Sanjay.

He scowled and lifted the pipe in his hand like a Greek warrior. The tip of the pipe surged through the first infected's head before the body crumpled to the round. A small trail of congealed blood and purple goop followed the pipe's path. He quickly dispatched the second infected.

The moaning around them stopped.

Lily hopped out of the car. "Have you seen Sammy?" she asked.

"Your little girl? Yeah, she was playing with Flynn and Carly in the garage. It's off to the side a bit, just around the corner. That whole area's fenced off." Sanjay helped Virginia lift one of the heavier duffle bags from the trunk.

"We need to get the bags inside first. You can find them after we bring these to the armory," Marissa instructed.

Grant nodded, moving back toward the trunk. He lifted one of the bags and shoved it onto his shoulder.

Lily gripped a smaller bag with both hands and did the same.

He walked while she waddled toward the armory. Despite his half a dozen offers to help her, Lily insisted on carrying the heavy bag herself. By the time they reached the armory, she thought her shoulders might pop out of their sockets. She dropped the bag inside with a sigh of relief.

"Let's go find Sammy and Flynn," she panted.

Grant eased his bag down against a wall. He said nothing as he followed her out to the back garage.

Following Sanjay's instructions, they rounded the corner of the school along a fenced-in area.

Sammy sat near a tree, using a wrench to try and dig up a pile of dirt.

"Hi, sweetie," Lily said, crouching down a few feet from Sammy.

"Mommy!" Sammy jumped to her feet. The little bundle of excitement rushed into her mother's arms, burying her bushy head into the crux of her mother's neck. Her tiny arms barely reached around her mother's shoulders.

Lily lifted her up rested her baby girl on her hips as made their way across the yard toward Flynn.

Flynn stood, his head flung back in laughter as a young woman in her late teens stood in front of him with a gleaming white grin and sparkling emerald eyes. Her hand reached out and touched Flynn's arm as her curtain of black hair whipped behind her in the wind.

Jealousy bubbled in Lily's gut as Flynn continue talking to her.

The woman's tight tank top and Daisy Duke shorts gnawed at the back of Lily's mind. When the woman bent over to ask Flynn something about a mechanical part under the hood of the bus, Lily saw red.

"Can you hold her for a second?" Lily passed Sammy off to Grant.

The amused glint in Grant's eye did nothing to sway her pissy mood.

"Hey, Flynn," she called over. She offered a sticky sweet smile dripping with warning.

He turned, his grin widening when he saw her. He opened his arms out to her for a welcoming hug.

She one-upped him and jumped into his open embrace, her legs wrapping around his waist. She planted a possessive, deep kiss on his lips, marking her territory.

"Glad to see you're back. It's getting dark out. I was starting to get a little worried," he said.

"Oh, were you? You didn't look worried a second ago," she teased, watching her barb slide into place.

A flicker of guilt dampened his face.

"Besides, you know I can take care of myself." She bit the tip of her tongue. She wanted to be petty, catty even and say that she had Grant to protect her, but putting Flynn and Grant against one another was a recipe for disaster and heartache.

"Who's your new friend?" Lily asked. She unwrapped her legs from Flynn's hips and hopped down beside him, wrapping around his waist.

"Lily, this is Carly." Flynn nodded toward the other woman. "Carly, meet my girlfriend, Lily."

Carly straightened up, a stunned look slapped across her face. "Nice to meet you," she said through her teeth.

"Same here. I'm Lily. I see you've met my daughter, Sammy. And that's Grant, my other boyfriend," she said, a not-so-subtle ring of possessiveness sounding out at the word *boyfriend*.

Carly's eyebrow quirked "Oh?" Her head swiveled back and forth between Grant and Flynn, then back to Lily. "Okay, then?"

Grant walked up beside them. "I'm going to go watch Sammy for a bit, Sugar. You and Flynn have some catching up to do." He leaned his head lower, capturing her lips on his. Warmth blossomed in Lily's cheeks as Grant's lips stirred a warmth bubbling in her belly. Flynn's fingers gripped her hips, digging into her skin as Grant kissed her inches from Flynn's lips.

Grant broke their kiss and nodded to Carly.

"Nice to meet you," he said before turning back toward the school, Sammy bouncing along in his arms.

"Oh," Carly said, her lips falling into a hard line. "I see. Well, I'll see you around." She waved as she walked past them toward the school.

Once Carly circled around the corner, Lily spoke. "I see you made a friend. She certainly seemed friendly with you."

His eyebrow quirked in surprise. "Jealous, Sweetheart?"

Lily's smile slipped a little. "Who, me? Never."

"Sure, whatever you say. Now, how about we go back inside and enjoy our time alone."

His arms slipped around her small waist and pressed her body close to his chest. Heat radiated from him, warming the summer air around her.

"Let's get inside before it's too dark out here. I want to spend as much time with you as I can before we have to go back to the others."

His lips fell on hers in a gentle sweep before he moved away from her. Taking her small hand in his, he walked with her toward the front of the school.

"Where are we going?" she asked as he pushed open the front door.

Keeping her hand in his, he led her up to the second floor and down a hallway. "Someplace private. I discovered this room earlier today, while you were away," he said.

Flynn twisted a doorknob to an unused classroom and pulled her inside. The setting sunlight lit the tops of the desks bright orange. Streaks of twisted shadows from the nearby trees left ghastly marks over the desks and floor.

"Most of the rooms around here need cleaning, or they're occupied," Flynn said, shutting the door and closing the shade behind him. He turned to her with a heart-melting smile.

"Alone at last."

Lily's pulse quickened as he stepped closer and closed the gap between them. His large hand fisted in her hair, holding her head in place as his lips crashed over hers.

Finally.

Sweetness flooded her mouth. Mint and something dark and spicy lingered on her tongue as he slipped between her lips. She body coiled tight against him as her hands wound around his trim waist. Fingertips dug into flesh as her mind whirled like she'd drunk too much wine. She couldn't feel the floor and the room began to spin around her.

Flynn broke their kiss and bent down, lifting her up and carried her over to the teacher's desk. He sat her down in the middle and pushed off a stack of papers and a pen holder. Pens and pencils clattered to the floor as the papers whooshed around them like confetti.

His rough hands gripped her knees, spreading her legs

open. He stepped between them, his hard gaze piercing through her.

Lily froze, excitement racing. Her heart hammered like a tribal drum, so loud it rang through her brain. Need slipped into every fiber of her as the summer heat and Flynn's warm scent wafted like an aphrodisiac. Her body hummed like a tight string piano string, ready to be plucked.

"Flynn," she moaned as he pushed her shoulder back.

"Lie back, Sweetheart. I want to take my time with you tonight." His wicked smile transformed into a sinful smirk as he hovered above her.

"You're gorgeous." His fingertip traced along Lily's jawline and down the long column of her neck.

Small shots of pleasure spread where he touched.

"Kiss me," she said.

Flynn bent over her, his strong body overpowering hers as he pressed her harder into the desk. His lips trapped hers in a long, lazy kiss. His tongue flicked out over her lower lip, asking for an invitation.

She parted her lips and his tongue slid in, tasting her, devouring her as his hand wound in her hair.

Lily moaned, her hips wiggling against the edge of the desk. Flynn's hips slipped between her thighs, her shorts pressing against the hot denim of his jeans. He brushed against the thin fabric of her t-shirt.

She reached up for him, her hands holding onto the strong muscles of his back as if he might disappear at any moment.

"Flynn," she whimpered against his mouth.

His hand fisted in her hair, holding her steady as his lips traced a slow path down her jawline. His stubble scratched her skin. The faint beard burn heated her blood to near boiling as his lips teased the column of her neck. A wicked tickling sensation spread down her chest as he nibbled a sensitive spot along her collarbone.

"You taste so sweet," he growled against her flesh. His finger fumbled with the button of her shorts before tugging them down her thighs.

He stepped away, gliding the fabric down her knees and lean calves. He smirked down at her as he dropped her shorts on the floor.

The curls between her legs glistened with moisture. Her body flushed with heat as the sun and her arousal warmed her skin. Streaks of bright orange sunset mixed with the pink blush of her skin.

He unlaced her boots, tugging them off her feet and tossing them aside before reaching up for her shirt. His fingers fisted the thin fabric, inching it up higher to reveal her rounded belly with a jagged stretch mark. Higher to the underside of her rounded breasts. He paused before groaning and lifting it up over her head, revealing her naked body to his hungry gaze.

Lily shimmied, her body humming like a live wire, waiting for his touch. Her blood thrummed with need as desire pooled between her legs.

Empty.

Achy.

She needed him like she needed air.

"Touch me," she whispered.

Flynn's helpless groan peaked her excitement and a fresh wave of arousal dampened the junction between her thighs.

His face shifting in pain as he fought to keep control. He bent forward, his head dipping to her chest. His warm tongue flicked out between his soft lips and sucked a nipple into his mouth.

Pleasure bolted through Lily's chest, her back arching toward him, trying to get closer. She shivered as the rough pads of his fingertips slid along the outside of her thigh, moving steadily higher.

"Flynn," she whimpered. Her hands fisted the dark locks of his hair as his hands reached closer to the course of her ache. "Please."

His fingertips brushed over her clit, pleasure sparking through her. White hot spots danced behind her eyes. Her hips bucked toward his hand, needing more.

His fingers quickened their pace, teasing her clit in small, fast circles. He slipped a finger inside her heat, stretching her as his thumb worked over the nub of her clit.

"Flynn!" Her hips bucked again, fucking his fingers in small, quick thrusts.

"Sensitive tonight, aren't you?" He released her nipple and smirked above her.

He worked her pussy with his finger as he fisted his shirt with his free hand, tugging it up and over, the fabric dangling around his one shoulder. He fumbled with his belt buckle, unzipping his pants and kicking them down around his knees. His swollen cock hung heavy between his legs. The swollen tip glistened with drops of pre-cum as it strained toward her like it had a mind of its own. He slipped his finger from her pussy with a small sucking sound before lifting it to his mouth.

Lily watched in dizzy amazement as his finger disappeared between his lips, tasting her. His eyes closed like he was sucking on candy before sliding his finger from between those soft lips.

"God, you're so hot for me, Sweetheart." He smirked down at her before falling to his knees between her spread thighs. "I need more of you."

Lily shouted as his tongue lapped at her clit. Bolts of pleasure rocketed through her like someone had lit a match near a crate of fireworks. She thrashed against the desk and his mouth explored her hot sex. A vibration filled her mind, pleasure stroking higher and higher as an orgasm began to rise over her.

Flynn reached up with one arm, pinning her hips down as she squirmed, trying to get closer and yet move further from the pleasure overwhelming her.

"Flynn," she moaned, his name turning into one long, guttural sound as the wave continued to rise.

His tongue flicked faster over the small bud of her clit, letting the wave crest over her, threatening her.

"Flynn!" Her orgasm broke, drowning her in hot pleasure that brought her out of reality and into a world of her own. Her voice rang louder than a school bell as she shook on top of the desk, gasping for air in the still summer night. Heat pricked at her flushed skin, her chest rising and falling with each heavy pant.

"Flynn," she moaned, her head lolling to the side in exhaustion as he pulled away from her with one last lick.

She watched him rise between her legs with a satisfied smirk as he licked his lips. She followed his gaze as his stare traced over her curves. Her mind swirled in a sex drunk haze, almost too dizzy to notice his rough grip on her ankles as he lifted her legs in the air. He leaned forward, wrapping her ankles around his neck. The head of his cock nudged at her wet entrance, waking nerve cells that had fallen asleep from exhaustion moments ago.

"I've wanted you to myself for a long time, Sweetheart," he murmured. Bending forward, he gripped his cock in his hand as he held himself steady. He slipped the head of his cock into her damp pussy, stretching her.

"Oh, God!" She squeezed her eyes shut as his cock slipped deeper inch by thick, wonderful inch. He stretched her sore pussy.

Her body sucked him deeper like she couldn't get enough of him. Hunger and need bubbled in her lower belly.

His sunk fully inside her.

She could feel him watching her as she closed her eyes, her body writhing underneath him. Pleasure sparked between her legs as he slipped a few inches from her before thrusting back to fill her again. Her body jerked against the warm desk, her breasts bouncing with each slow, steady thrust of his cock.

"Look at me," he growled above her.

Flynn swimming into view as she blinked her eyes open. His brow furrowed in concentration, that smile slipping a little as his hips slowed, grinding against her.

"I'm going to watch you come. And you're going to watch me. I want you to know who's doing this to you. Who's fucking you? Who's making you feel so fucking good you won't be able to walk straight tonight? You're mine." His hips jerked back before slamming into her.

"Flynn!" she shouted, his cock stretching her further, sliding in even deeper. Heat kissed her skin as the fiery orange light consumed them.

He dropped her legs beside him, wrapping them around his hips as he leaned lower, capturing her hands in his and lacing their fingers together. He lifted her hands over her head, her arms stretching and back arching to him.

"You're mine, Sweetheart." His lips pressed against her in a demanding, soul-branding kiss.

She moaned against his mouth before he pulled back. He watched her reaction as his hips began to thrust in slow, steady movements. He teased her, the muscles in his groin pressing against her clit with each slow thrust.

Pleasure spiked higher, her body trapped beneath him. Her gaze slid up over his muscled chest, his broad shoulders, the thick cord of his neck and finally on those wicked blue eyes, almost silver in the light. His teeth flashed between those soft pink lips.

The muscles of his groin pressed against her sensitive clit, creating a sinful friction with each slow, steady thrust. Pleasure spiked higher and higher with each jerk of his hips.

"Flynn," she whimpered, her pleasure building up slowly, like the overture of an incredible show. "Please. More."

His lips curled into a cocky smirk as his hips pistoned faster into her. His restraint shattered as he pumped himself into her body like a madman, the desk beneath them shaking as he jerked it back inch by inch, moving with it. Her body swayed with each heavy thrust, her pants mixing with his groans.

"Flynn!" Her pleasure shot from her like a rocket out of a cannon. Sensations exploded over her, drowning her as she trembled beneath him, her fingers trapped between his, her body arching up for him, offering her pleasure up to him.

"Fuck, yes, Lily," he groaned, his hips hammering a bit faster before he stilled.

"Fuck!" he roared. The masculine edge in his voice left her pussy quivering in aftershocks around his spasming cock.

"God. Lily." he murmured, his forehead resting in the crux of her neck. His fingers released hers.

"Yeah," she panted beneath him.

She lowered her hands, resting them along the tight muscles of his back. Her fingers traced up and down the sinewy contours of his shoulders.

Sex, sweat, and summer breezes lingered in the air around them as Lily smiled. Even in hell, she'd found her own personal heaven.

$\mathcal{L}$ily stretched her sore muscles in the lukewarm shower, the water washing away Flynn and Grant's scents from her skin. The grime and grittiness from yesterday's supply run with Flynn and Sanjay slipped down the drain. A week of work around the school left her feeling safe, yes, but also sore. Though the ache in her muscles lingered, a happy little reminder of her ménage with her men last night.

She hoped that today they would give her a chance to rest a bit.

Her body hummed with awareness, and she slid a bar of soap across her belly, raising her hand to lather her upper stomach and breasts in suds. Her nipples puckered. From her movements or from her memories of her men, Lily didn't know.

She stepped back under the stream of water, rinsing herself off one last time. Once the bubbles were gone and her skin felt clean, she shut off the water. A scratchy towel hung on a hook beside her shower. She swept her hair up in a tight knot at the back of her head and toweled off.

It felt wonderful to be clean.

She hummed to herself, realizing that she had been smiling like a fool since she woke up in Flynn's arms with Grant nuzzled against her chest, his leg thrown over both of them. Strength. Security. It rolled over her from the moment she woke until the moment she fell asleep in their arms again. She felt safer than she had even before the outbreak.

In the madness of the world, she found happiness. Her daughter was safe and protected in these walls. Her men would do stop at nothing to keep her and Sammy safe. And somehow, Lily felt a strange feeling toward both of them. Love? Maybe. She'd never been in love.

"Morning," Marissa chirped as she stepped into the locker room. "I thought I heard you. Were you humming?"

Lily blushed, clutching the towel a bit tighter around her. The air cooled as the steam wafted out of the open locker room door.

"Yeah, sorry," she murmured.

"No, it's alright. Don't apologize," Marissa rushed, "I haven't heard anyone humming in so long. I almost forgot it existed."

"Oh," Lily said.

"I haven't hummed in ages. I never liked my singing voice. My mom was an amateur opera singer. She used to say my voice could never compare with hers. She sounded like an angel when she sang," Marissa sighed.

"And she sounded like a bitch when she talked," Lily added.

Marissa smiled. "Maybe. She never liked my singing."

"I bet she was jealous. You probably sounded better than her, and she didn't want to be upstaged," Lily said.

Marissa shrugged. "Guess I'll never know for sure."

"I'm going to go get changed. See you at breakfast." Lily

grabbed her clothes from the floor and walking into the changing rooms.

She finished toweling off the droplets on her legs and hips and shoved on some underwear, shorts, and a tank top. The bra she found was a bit too small, her cleavage bulging out the top.

"Great," she murmured. She unhooked the bra and stuffed it back into the bag. Her nipples poked through the tight tank top. At least she would have Flynn and Grant's full attention this morning.

She strolled out of the locker room, carrying her towel and bag with her and dropping them back in her room before heading to the cafeteria for breakfast. Flynn and Grant had taken Sammy with them to give her a chance to wash up and relax for a moment.

How thoughtful.

"Lily!" a woman's voice echoed down the hall behind her.

Lily pivoted on her heels.

Carly jogged down the hallway, her breasts bouncing in her top like she was in an episode of Baywatch.

"Hi, I'm glad I caught you." Carly rested a hand on Lil's shoulder, taking a small puff of air to catch her breath. "Whoa, ran a bit too fast."

Lily's fists clenched and unclenched at her sides, wondering what Carly wanted. "Carly, are you alright?"

"Yeah. Yeah, thanks." Carly inhaled a long, deep breath, standing up straighter and letting go of Lily's shoulder. "Sorry. Asthma. Anyway, I think we got off on the wrong foot. I wanted to talk to you and apologize for what happened in the yard last week. You know, with Flynn? I didn't know you were with Flynn too. I mean, it's not normal... Well, two guys... I mean, who would have guessed there were three of you?"

Carly's face flushed a deeper shade of pink as she tried to speak.

"Anyway, I'm sorry. No harm, no foul. I'll keep my hands off. I don't want any trouble. And, well, with everything else out there, boy trouble is the last thing we all need to be fighting over. Friends?" Carly stuck her hand out, waiting for Lily to take it.

"Um, sure. Friends." Lily gripped Carly's hand and shook it once before dropping it. "Anyway, I'm going to go grab breakfast."

"Great. Mind if I join you?"

"Sure," she shrugged and continued walking down the hallway.

Lily opened the double doors leading into the cafeteria, Carly following behind her.

A cocktail of happiness and excitement swirled in her belly as she saw her men and Sammy sitting at a table. Sammy sat in Grant's lap as she munched on a piece of toast. Flynn and Grant chatted with a couple of women a few years older than Lily. She strolled over to the small set up of food, placed her allotted rations on her plate, and joined them.

"Morning," she chirped.

"Good morning." Flynn's gaze dropped instantly to the two mounds stretching the top of her shirt. "Wow, it's a very good morning so far."

"Yeah, it is." Grant smirked beside her as his gaze lowered to her chest.

She smiled, shaking her head.

"Hi," she waved to the women at the table. A woman with a curtain of jet black hair sat beside Flynn. Her exotic eyes and creamy skin hinted at a touch of Asian in her heritage. The woman sitting beside Grant was clearly Irish. Her fiery red hair shone brightly in the sunlight, her freckles dotting her nose and cheeks, with green eyes that twinkled with mischief.

"Hi," they said in unison.

"I'm Alexa," the Asian woman said with a soft smile. "This is my wife, Colleen."

"Hi, I'm Lily. Nice to meet you," she nodded at them.

"Mommy, I don't like Spam," Sammy said, wrinkling her nose in disgust as she sniffed at the seared salted meat product.

Lily couldn't blame her for that one. "Did you try it?" she asked.

"No," Sammy said. "It smells funny."

"But it tastes good." Lily cut off a piece of her Spam and biting into it. She chewed, forcing herself not to gag from the saltiness. Immediately after swallowing, she gulped down some water.

Sammy glanced at her mother, then the grayish-pink cube on her plate.

"Try a little piece," Lily goaded. "If you don't like it, I won't make you eat it, but you should always try new things."

"If you try it, I'll give you the crust I pulled off my toast," Flynn said.

"You don't like crust?" Grant asked.

Flynn made a squished face.

"Nope, but Hope loved the crusts, just like Sammy." A wistful sadness clouded over his eyes for a moment. He smiled, his expression catching the gloominess and brushing it away. "Try some. I bet you'll like it. It's like tasty ham."

"I like ham," Sammy said. She speared a piece of cut-up Spam, lifted the fork to her mouth, and bit down on the offending meat. She chewed for a moment. Then her eyes closed, a large smile spreading across her face.

"Yum!" She speared another piece with her fork and popped it into her mouth.

They all let out a soft chuckle. "See, I told you," Flynn said, sliding his toast crusts onto Sammy's plate.

"Mom," a small voice piped from behind Lily.

She swiveled in her seat, staring down.

A young boy, about eight-years-old than Sammy, was staring at Colleen. His bright blond hair stood up at odd angles, his brown eyes twinkled with youth and excitement. "Can I go play in the library?" he asked.

"What's the magic word?" Colleen replied with a small smile.

"Please." He grinned.

She sighed. "Alright, but only the library."

"Mommy, can I go too?" Sammy asked in a rush of excitement. "I want to play."

"After you finish your breakfast, you can go play in the library," Lily said.

Sammy shoved the last three small cubes of Spam into her mouth before rushing off behind the boy.

"Cute kid," Grant said, watching them hurry through the doors.

"Thanks. That's Rob." Alexa smiled from her cup of water.

"We adopted him when he was two months old. His mother..." Colleen trailed off.

"His biological mother died of a drug overdose. He became a ward of the state. We were looking to adopt, and we just fell in love with him," Alexa sighed with love-struck eyes.

"Who would have thought you could go through love at first sight twice?" Colleen asked, her hand reaching across the table to hold Alexa's hand. She squeezed, the two women locking eyes over the table.

A gooey warmth spread across Lily's stomach. It was nice to see people madly in love.

"That's sweet," Flynn said. "Not the case for us, though. This one tried to kill me." He nodded toward Lily with a grin and a twinkle in his bright blue eyes. Grant and the women laughed.

"You chased me and broke into my house with a sword," Lily said.

"Well, you shouldn't have run from me," he said. "And, besides, Sammy thought I was a prince, what with my big sword, bursting in to save the day."

"Men and their swords," Alexa mumbled.

"At least that's one thing we don't have to worry about," Colleen added.

Lily chuckled. "Try having two to worry about," she smirked before taking a sip of water.

Colleen and Alexa's gaze wandered from Grant to Flynn, back to Grant, and ended on Lily. "Two?" Alexa asked.

"Yeah, we're both with her," Grant said, wrapping his arm around her shoulder.

Warmth trickled from Lily's shoulder downward, spreading throughout her body. She reached over the table and held onto Flynn's hand as she leaned against Grant's chest.

A fuzzy feeling spread over her chest.

Happiness.

That's what she felt.

"How did you all meet?" Alexa asked, her eyebrow quirking up as she sipped her drink, eyeing the threesome next to her.

"Well, you know how I met Flynn," Lily smiled. "Grant saved my life. I was locked in a gas station when three men attacked me. He busted through the back door and, well—"

"We've all had to do things we're not proud of to survive. The world's gone mad after all," Grant shrugged.

"I know," Alexa frowned.

"Babe?" Colleen asked. "Are you alright?"

Alexa shook her head. "There's nothing wrong with being honest in times like this. I've killed people, too."

Colleen's head hung down as she stared at their entwined hands.

Alexa squeezed Colleen's hand in hers. "They deserve to know. Jonathan already knows."

Colleen sighed. "If you think that's best."

Alexa nodded. "I killed two people who tried to steal our supplies. One of them put a gun to our son's head. Anyone—" Alexa froze, her eyes squinting as a sudden burst of anger vibrated the air around them. "Anyone who tries to hurt my family—anyone who tries to kill them—they won't make it out alive." Alexa growled through gritted teeth.

"No one is going to hurt us, babe." Colleen placed a calming hand on Alexa's forearm. "We're safe here."

"Are we?" Alexa bit out. "For how long? We've been here for four weeks. Can you say you feel safe now? What happens when another group comes and tries to steal our home? What then?"

"Then we'll stay and fight," Flynn said. "But this world is bad enough without worrying about those kinds of what-ifs, and I'm tired of playing that game." He scowled, his brows furrowing together like a dark brown caterpillar.

"I'm sorry." Colleen's apologetic smile tugged at Lily's heartstrings.

"Don't be," Lily replied. "We'd all do anything in our power to protect our families. Now more than ever."

"There you are!" Jonathan walked over to them with puffy red cheeks as if he'd jogged all over the building to find them. Marissa strode beside him. "I was hoping I could convince two of you to go on another supply run today if that's alright."

"What for?" Grant asked.

"We need some more medicine," Jonathan replied. "What we have at the nurse's station is running low. Just a bunch of aspirin and Band-Aids mostly. A couple of antacids. We need everything. Anything you can get your hands on."

"Perhaps we should go," Flynn said, nodding to Grant. "Lily will have the opportunity to stay here and watch Sammy this time. We'll rotate runs."

"Fine with me," Jonathan said. "Raj and Sanjay want to leave as soon as you've all finished breakfast."

"We're done." Grant slid his empty plate across the table with an ear-rattling screech.

"Good," Jonathan said before walking away from them.

"Raj?" Lily turned toward Colleen and Alexa.

Alexa coughed. "Sanjay and Raj. They're brothers. They've been staying at this school even longer than we have. Nice guys, but they keep to themselves for the most part. I've heard them talk about their sister, Preeti. I think she became infected, but I'm not sure. They don't like to talk about themselves."

"Sanjay's a nice enough guy. He's friendly. Polite. Holds up his end of a conversation."

Colleen frowned. "Raj is a bit more of a mystery. He's one of those guys who can do everything, but you don't know how."

"What do you mean?" Flynn asked, leaning forward.

A small, queasy feeling tossed in Lily's stomach like a rough storm out at sea.

"I mean, he's been the closest thing we have here to a doctor. He's a good handyman. A good cook. He volunteers for extra shifts for kitchen duty and laundry duty. But he doesn't talk about himself if he even talks at all. He'll ask questions about other people, try to get to know them. But no one knows anything about him."

"They're a strange pair," Alexa added.

"But you trust them?" Lily asked. "I just want to be sure, if Grant and Flynn are both going out there with them."

Alexa and Colleen both shrugged. "I guess so. They're both quiet guys, sure, but they pull their weight around here. And then some. So, yeah, I'd trust them."

"We should get going." Flynn stood, the chair leg scraping over the linoleum floor.

Grant rose from his seat, towering over Lily.

She strained her neck to look up at him, her eyes roaming over every hard line and curve of his body. She imagined running her tongue over every inch.

Maybe when he got back.

He bent low to slide his fingers into her hair, his lips capturing hers in a rough but tender kiss. All too soon, he broke away from her and left the table.

Flynn strode over to her, standing beside her.

"I promise we'll be back soon, Sweetheart." The rough side of his finger pressed under her chin, keeping her head lifted. He dipped low, capturing her lips against his. Once. Twice. After the third kiss, he pulled back.

Her lips tingled, her body thrumming with excitement and, if she had to admit it, fear. Fear they might not come back. Fear that something could happen to them out there and she'd be powerless to stop it.

She mentally stomped down on those horrible thoughts before her fear grew and overwhelmed her.

"I'll see you when you get back."

Flynn smiled at her, his eyes twinkling with emotion before he followed Grant toward the door.

A cauldron of emotions bubbled in her chest. Happiness. Fear. Worry. Excitement. Lust. They pulsed through her veins like a heavy potion, just as much a part of her as her own blood. She couldn't live without these two men.

"I love you."

Her voice rang around the cafeteria.

All the background noise faded away, leaving a heavy silence in the air. Every pair of eyes stared at Lily, watching her sink further into her seat. Heat crept up her cheeks, and the silence lingered.

"Love you too, Sugar." A smile broke over Grant's face. He tried to say stoic, but the excitement burst through. He was almost glowing as he watched her smile back.

Flynn blinked at her, his eyes widening to the size of silver dollars as he stared at her. In four quick steps, he closed the distance between them. His lips brushed against hers again.

Heavy awareness spread throughout her body, sparks tickling the tips of her fingers and toes. Warmth spread from her lower belly, easing her body into the kiss.

"I love you too, Sweetheart. We'll see you soon." Flynn released her, striding back over toward Grant.

Both men grinned like fools. Grant reached over and clapped Flynn on the shoulder. Their cheeriness spread like an infection and soon the whole cafeteria was smiling to some degree or another.

Lily's heart thudded in her chest.

It was wonderful to see people smiling again.

Carly spun on her heel and gave Lily two thumbs up and a cheery smile before spinning back around toward the door as she, Grant, Flynn, Sanjay, and Raj, left the cafeteria.

Lily laughed, noticing that while Carly was looking at her, Sanjay was glancing over his shoulder, his gaze stuck on Carly. Something akin to lust sparked in his honey brown eyes. Maybe Carly and Sanjay would have a successful hunting trip after all.

CHAPTER 14

*L*ily leaned on her elbow, eyeing Colleen and Alexa's clasped hands resting on the tabletop as they talked about their son. Their smiles were infectious, and the butterflies in Lily's stomach left a giddy airiness around her. Floating on a cloud must feel like this.

"Hey, ladies," Marissa said, as she strode over toward them. "Where are the kids?"

"In the library," Lily said.

The library. Such a safe and normal place for children to be.

Another wave of happiness rolled over Lily, knowing that Sammy was playing in a library. What better place for a child than to be surrounded by books? Maybe they could stay here. What were the chances that the refugee camp would be any better? If it even existed...

"Let's go check on them," Colleen suggested, bursting Lily's thought bubble.

The four women left the cafeteria and walked down the hallway to the library. From behind the closed door, the tinkling of children's laughter filled the air, warming a small spot in Lily's chest.

Her daughter was huddled close to Rob, the two of them playing with a couple of Transformer toys.

"No, Optimus Prime. You can't stop me." Rob hammered the action figure's feet into the floor like it was stomping down an entire city. "I. Am. Invincible!"

"I will stop you!" Sammy shrieked. Her toy dive-bombed and met Rob's toy mid-air, the two of them smashing the toys in an epic battle to save the world.

Lily's smile stretched from ear-to-ear. Her daughter's laughter, the sheer joy on her face, struck Lily through the heart like Cupid's arrow. Sammy's happiness made everything seem right with the world.

If only Grant and Flynn were there to see it too.

"Hi, guys," Marissa said, walking over to them. "What're you playing?"

"Transformer battle!" Rob shouted in excitement, pounding the toy in his hand into some blocks they piled together as a makeshift city. "Take that, Empire State Building."

"But now you just hurt all the people in the building," Alexa said as she walked toward them. She crossed her arms, eying her son with amusement.

"No, I didn't. They all ran away from the city. It's empty now," he said.

"Well, that's good. You don't want anyone to get hurt." Colleen pulled out a child-sized chair and sat down, her knees level with her chest.

"Do you guys want to go for a walk around the school? Check it out?" Lily suggested. A walk and the chance to explore the school might be good for them.

"Yeah," the children said in unison, jumping to their feet like eager frogs.

Sammy grabbed her mother's hand, almost pulling her toward the library door. "I'm going on an adventure!" she shrieked excitedly.

"Alright there, Bilbo." Marissa chuckled and she led them out of the library.

Lily led her daughter down the hallway accompanied by Marissa. Colleen, Alexa, and Rob trailed a few feet behind them. The small train of people wound their way up the stairs to the third floor, admiring the art studios that were up there, as well as some of the classrooms that weren't in use.

The women chatted as the kids ran around, exploring the rooms and letting off some morning energy.

"They'll sleep well tonight," Colleen smiled. "They need to play more."

"We should start up a gym time for them. It wouldn't hurt the rest of us to get a bit more exercise too." Marissa poked the tiny pudge of her stomach.

"Oh, please." Lily stuck her tongue out. "You should see the stretch marks I got from Sammy. They're a heck of a lot harder to lose than the baby weight."

"Right," Colleen said. "You don't look like you've ever had kids. You're so tiny." Her voice filled with enough sarcasm that she and Lily laughed like old friends.

"Hey, guys. The music room is on the second floor." Marissa called out as Sammy ran up and down the hallway, Rob chasing after her, trying to tag her. "Want to go check it out?"

"Yeah!" Rob shouted and ran over toward the stairway, Sammy trailing on his heels.

"Remember, we have to stick together," Colleen said.

The small group wound their way to the second floor, stopping in front of a closed door. Marissa twisted the doorknob slowly, letting the tension build and their excitement bubble over before flinging the door open.

Sammy and Rob burst into the music room, set up with stands and instruments, most of them nestled away in their cases.

"I think we can let them play around in here on their own," Alexa said. "I don't think we need to listen to their concert."

"Good idea," Lily said.

She stepped inside the room as Sammy plopped her small frame on a piano bench, staring at the secondhand piano in wonder.

"We'll be right outside if you need us," she shouted to Sammy and Rob. Lost in their amazement of the noisy instruments surrounding them, they said nothing. Lily shrugged and closed the door.

Just as the door clicked shut, a small burst of noise came from the piano, followed by the heavy pounding of drums. The soundproof room was enough to keep the sound from attracting unwanted attention from outside, but inside the noise could still trigger a strong headache.

"There's a teachers' lounge at the end of the hallway." Marissa nodded as she showed them to a door marked "private" just across the hallway. The dusty smell of old leather and stale bread wafted around them.

Colleen and Alexa sat down on a couch, stretching out and smiling.

"I could get used to this place," Alexa said as she rested her head on Colleen's shoulder. Colleen placed a small kiss on the top of her wife's head.

A flutter tickled Lily's belly. Flynn and Grant both kissed her like that. And she'd seen that soft affection in their eyes.

She sunk into an overstuffed leather recliner, the fabric swallowing her until she felt trapped in the cushion. "Who has furniture like this in a teacher's lounge? I thought there would just be more cafeteria chairs?" Lily wiggled herself out of the chair's clutches just enough to sit comfortably.

"Those were a donation from a teacher who retired three years ago. Mrs. Winston. Sweet woman. She taught art, but couldn't draw a stick figure to save her life. I never understood how she got that job," Marissa said.

"So, what was it like being a librarian?" Lily asked.

"It was great, especially working with the kids. They were so excited to come in and read. I used to have story time for the younger kids once a week. That was the best." She grabbed a bottle of water from the counter and twisted open the top before taking a long sip.

"Yeah, kids are pretty awesome. I used to teach piano at home," Colleen said.

"And you sold Avon. And babysat the neighbor's kids. And joined the PTA. And volunteered for the Pets for Patrons group. And—" Alexa teased.

"Alright, I get it." Colleen nudged Alexa with her elbow. "I like to be busy. And she doesn't talk about it much, but Alexa used to be a cop. That's how we met."

"Best speeding ticket ever."

"The only time I got off with just a warning," Colleen said.

"And the first time you got off." Alexa winked.

Colleen's face flushed a dark rose while the other women laughed.

"Anyway, speaking of piano, I could give Sammy some lessons. She seemed to rush over to that piano without even looking at any other instrument," Colleen offered.

"I've always wanted her to have music lessons," Lily said.

"Well, good. We'll set up a set time for me to meet with her every day and she can learn," Colleen said.

"We have enough supplies here, why not teach them something more than music?" Marissa suggested.

"Like homeschooling?" Alexa asked.

"Yeah, why not? It'll keep them out of trouble, and you never know. They might learn something that could come in handy. We don't know what's going to happen in the future. They might need an education."

"I'm in," Lily said. "Some routine and stability might do the kids some good."

Colleen and Alexa nodded in agreement.

Marissa leaned against the counter, twisting the cap back on her water bottle. "Good. We can suggest it to Jonathan. I think he'd agree as long as it doesn't interfere with runs and chores around this place."

A small silence hung in the air like muggy dampness. "I'd kill for a bottle of wine right about now," Alexa said.

Lily moaned. "Wine and a nice slice of cheesecake."

"With whipped cream and chocolate chips," Marissa added.

"This is starting to sound like an episode of *The Golden Girls*," Colleen said.

"I love that show!" Lily exclaimed, a bit louder than she'd meant to. She blushed as the other women giggled. "I grew up watching that show. I used to watch it with my mom in her home before..."

The excited fire in Lily's belly died like someone had dumped ice water on her. Her mother was gone. She would never get to watch that show with her again. A small pain punched through Lily's chest, remembering just how much she'd lost so quickly. Everyone lost someone or something when the world went to hell.

"I wonder when the group will be back from the supply run." Alexa switched subjects, the mood shifting to something darker, like a storm on the horizon. If they let their thoughts wander down that dark path, who knew if they'd come back out.

"I heard some people don't come back from those runs," Lily frowned.

"Yeah, we've lost Mitchell and David a few weeks back," Colleen said.

"Will told us what happened. He was with both of them. The poor kid saw his dad get bit by a zombie. He said David begged him to take him back in the van with them, that he didn't want to die in some warehouse." Marissa shivered. "Will said yes and made David turn around to get his backpack off the ground and shot him in the back of the head."

"Wow," Colleen muttered.

"David was Will's father," Marissa said, glancing at Colleen and Alexa for a moment before shifting her gaze back to Lily.

The table froze like time had stopped. Seconds ticked by as they gazed at one another.

"Poor Will." Lily's squeaky voice sounded foreign and unwelcome to her ears. "That's why he was so worried about his mother on our last run."

"What happened?" Alexa asked. She leaned forward and draped her hand over Colleen's lap.

"Virginia was almost attacked by an infected when we went into a gun shop. Will had a near panic attack. Even when she was sitting in the van, perfectly alright, he seemed shaky, on the verge of an anxiety attack or something. That kid, he's too young for this."

"We all are. No one is cut out for this kind of world," Colleen mumbled.

"And you mentioned someone named Mitchell? What happened to him?" Lily asked.

Alex and Colleen turned their gazes to Marissa.

Tears sprung to Marissa's eyes. She left the room, clutching her arms and rubbing her arms like she was trying to keep warm despite the summer weather around them.

Heartache tugged at Lily's chest like a fish caught on a hook. Clearly, Mitchell had meant something to her. Poor Marissa.

"Mitchell was her boyfriend," Colleen said just above a whisper. "He came to get her not long after the infection spread in this area. They decided to stay here. He was bitten the day before we got here on the same trip as David. Will and Virginia said an infected caught him by surprise when he tried to reach David. Snuck up from behind him and knocked him over. Will said it bit his ankle almost clean in half."

"Marissa was a wreck, poor thing," Alexa murmured, tucking herself tighter into Colleen's chest.

"Yeah, nothing hurts as much as losing someone you love." Lily sighed and she pushed herself out of the seat and stood. "Maybe we should check on the kids."

Lily left to find Marissa.

She found her with her nose pressed to the glass of the music room door. Her eyes glistened with tears as she watched the children wreak havoc on the instruments without a care in the world. Lily could see them, too. Their small, smiling faces bright pink and cheery, like they were playing with new toys on Christmas morning.

"I always wanted a family," Marissa's voice crackled in the air like breaking glass. "I guess that'll never happen…"

A small pinch in Lily's chest ached with sympathy. This poor woman had been through hell too.

"You never know. Don't lose hope." Lily placed her arm on the young woman's shoulder, giving it a gentle squeeze. "I found someone. Two someones in fact. The world's a funny place."

"This doesn't seem so funny." Marissa sighed as she opened the door and ended their brief conversation. "Come on kids, time to go back to the first floor."

The children stopped hammering their chubby fingers on the instruments and groaned in protest.

"Please, just five more minutes," Sammy whined.

"Maybe we can come back tomorrow if you're good. We have some chores we have to do first," Lily said, holding out her hand for Sammy.

The little girl took it with a bit of reluctance and let her mother guide her out into the hallway. Rob followed behind them with a frown as Colleen and Alexa strolled out from the lounge.

"This way," Marissa said, walking down the hallway.

"But there's a stairway right here that's closer to the kitchen," Colleen thumbed the set of double doors behind her.

"Jonathan doesn't want anyone going down that part of the first floor," Marissa said. "This way."

"I think we want to see what's down this way," Alexa said, turning toward the double door, pulling out a knife from her boot. "After all, if no one has anything to hide…"

She opened the doors and looked around. She disappeared down the staircase, followed by Colleen and Rob.

Lily darted her gaze between the doors and Marissa. "They have a point. I'm not keeping my family here if I don't know what's under my roof. If there's nothing to hide, then we're okay."

She hoisted Sammy in her arms and followed Alexa and Colleen through the doors. Behind her, Lily heard Marissa's stomping footsteps and a heavy sigh. "Jonathan won't be happy about this."

The group stepped down the stairs a bit slower than normal, trying to examine their surroundings. Although this staircase appeared just like the others, the unfamiliar territory was scary.

And, if Jonathan had made that section of the floor off limits, that only doubled their concern.

"Do you know why he won't let people down that part of the first floor?" Alexa asked from the front of the group.

"No idea," Marissa shouted down from the staircase above her. "He just pulled some beast stunt from *Beauty and the Beast*. That section is forbidden. He's been a real leader here since the infection broke out. Picked up the slack for all of us. I don't question him."

"I like the beast," Sammy muttered against her mom's neck.

Lily smiled, her heart hammering in her chest. Nerves tickled her belly. She gripped Sammy tighter in her arms as they wound their way to the first floor.

No noises came from behind the doors. The only sounds were their footsteps on the dusty cement floor and their steady breaths.

Alexa pushed open one of the doors and moved backward, blocking Rob. A streak of sunlight brightened the dim stairwell. No noise. No movement.

"Clear," Alexa said, jumping into the first-floor hallway. Her gaze darted left, then right, then left again. "Nothing's here."

The rest of the group slowly inched their way into the hallway. This section of the hall looked like the others. Lockers were mostly closed, some half open with books spilling onto the floor. Posters for student council offices littered the hallway, some of the tape losing its tackiness and scattering posters face down on the floor.

"Curiouser and curiouser," Marissa mumbled.

They moved down the hallway toward the kitchen, turning a sharp corner.

A low moan echoed around them.

Fear thickened in the air, making it hard to breathe. The

group's gaze shifted in unison. A metal door with the sign "Boiler Room: Maintenance Personnel Only" was shut tight beside them. The moaning echoed from behind the door and beneath their feet.

"Infected," Lily whispered. Sammy tucked her head against her mother's neck, slamming her eyes shut.

"Well, now we know why he didn't want us here," Alexa murmured. She stepped closer, her knife in one hand, the other reached for the lock. She nudged it, testing it. The door stayed shut. "It's locked," she said. "They're not getting out."

"But who locked them in there?" Colleen asked.

"I don't know. But, I plan on asking Jonathan what the hell is going on and why he didn't tell us," Alexa snarled as she stomped toward the kitchen.

"No, wait," Marissa rushed forward, jumping in front of Alexa with her arms outstretched. "Wait, please, let me talk to him. Tonight. I don't want everyone else hearing this. It might start a panic." Her wild eyes widened, like an animal trapped in a cage.

"Maybe we should be panicking," Colleen said. "There are infected under the same roof as our children."

"Please," Marissa stomped her foot, lowering her arms. "I'm sure Jonathan has a perfectly good explanation. And besides, you saw the door was locked. They can't get to us. We're safe. Please, let me talk to him." Her eyes glistened as she pleaded with the women. "This is the only thing I have left. I can't lose my home too."

"Alright." Lily's voice rang in the hallway like a bell. "We'll let you talk to Jonathan. But we want an answer. A good answer. Understood?"

Alexa brushed past her, followed by Colleen and Rob as Marissa stared at the door.

Low moans echoed around them, a bit louder. Maybe the dead heard their conversation. Their moans rang in Lily's ears like the church bells by her old house. But, her old house and those church bells were gone. Everything else was gone.

Lily walked away from Marissa, hoping, praying that Jonathan had a good enough explanation.

"The supply group is back," Marissa shouted down the hallway toward Lily. "I can hear them outside."

Lily stopped, a small smile fighting its way to the corner of her lips. "Ready to go see Grant and Flynn?" she asked her daughter.

The little girl shot her head up, her splotchy, pink eyes shining, her smile brightening the small hallway. "Yeah!"

"Let's go!" Lily grinned s Sammy bounced in her arms and they headed to the front doors.

CHAPTER 15

The car rumbled through the open gate, gravel crunching beneath the tires. Raj huffed as he pushed the iron gate closed and locked it into place.

Sammy sat on the front steps while Lily roamed around the inside of the gate with a pole in hand. Lily jabbed the sharp end upward, puncturing an infected's skull through the eye socket before its corpse sunk to the ground. She heard movement from the car, the trunk popping open, but through the tinted windows, she could see nothing.

Sammy bounced on the balls of her feet, standing on the steps. The little girl and her mother watched, holding their breaths.

Carly stepped out of the back seat and slung two bags over her shoulder. Sanjay unfolded himself from the cramped back seat behind her, following closely. His eyes stayed glued to Carly's hips as they swayed back and forth. He hauled out three large bags, swinging them over his shoulders. They strolled up the steps past Sammy and walked inside.

Lily stared ahead, watching the car, her heart fluttering as nerves sent small shocks throughout her system, reminding her to breathe.

The driver's door opened and Grant stepped out. His gaze skimmed over the school, smiling when it landed on Sammy, who rushed toward him with a bright smile.

Relief fluttered in Lily's chest like a bird. Grant was safe.

He bent, lifting the little girl and spinning her around. "Hey, baby girl!"

Lily heard the joy in his voice, even from across the front yard. She stepped closer to the car and further from the gate.

Grant glanced over Sammy's shoulder and beamed a stomach-churning smile at Lily. Happiness buzzed the air around them like fireflies.

Grant's eyes twinkled for a moment before the light slipped away, his gaze falling toward the spear in her hand.

Lily heard another car door open and close. Flynn strolled around the hood of the car, his grin wide, revealing glowing white teeth.

"Hey Sweetheart," he said, walking toward her, the air growing hotter with each step he took. His warm smile left Lily's insides fluttering. He wrapped an arm around her waist and pulled her body close to his before his lips brushed hers in an inferno of a kiss.

"Hey," she panted as he released her.

Grant placed Sammy on her feet and she rushed over to Flynn to give him a small bear hug around his legs while Lily tilted her head up, meeting Grant's lips in another deep kiss.

Kisses that felt as natural as a wife kissing her husband as he walked in from a day of work. A feeling of normalcy in an otherwise weird situation.

"We missed you both."

"We missed you too, Sugar," Grant said.

"How was the run?" she asked.

"Great," Flynn said, lifting Sammy in his arms and resting her against his hip. "We found a pharmacy nearby that was nearly untouched, so we stocked up."

"Plus, we got some T-O-Y-S for Sammy." Grant winked.

"T-O-Y-S? Mommy, what's T-O-Y-S?" Sammy asked.

"You want to show her?" Grant asked Flynn.

Flynn nodded, setting the little girl down on her bouncing feet.

Grant pulled out a couple of boxes.

Sammy's excited shriek left Lily cringing, looking over her shoulder to see if the noise attracted any unwanted attention.

"LEGO!" Sammy shouted. "Thank you, thank you, thank you, Daddy!" She flung her arms around Grant's legs before she happily yanked the box from Grant's grasp.

"Daddy?" he mouthed in confusion, glancing between Lily and Flynn.

Sammy broke free from Grant's legs and hurried over to Flynn, her small arms wrapping around his thighs in a tight hug. "Thank you too, Daddy."

Her sweet voice lifted their spirits a bit.

"Sammy," Lily said. "Who said that Grant or Flynn was your dad?"

"Rob did. He said that he has two mommies and I have a Mommy and two daddies. So, my family's bigger." Sammy tugged at the glue that kept the cardboard box sealed shut.

"Oh?" Lily said.

"Yeah. Grant and Flynn are my dads, and you're my mom." The four-year-old continued to fumble over the edges of the box while the adults stared at her with wide eyes and open mouths.

"Okay, then," Grant said, before bursting into a radiant smile.

Lily's smile followed, relief flooding through her as though some sort of damn had broken free inside her heart.

Grant hadn't run away at the word. In fact, he seemed thrilled by it. This usually aloof and dark man glowed with happiness that brightened his eyes in a way that made Lily's heart melt like butter on a hot summer sidewalk.

"I've missed being a dad," Flynn said, a sadness tingeing his smile. His hand reached down, patting Sammy on the head with warm affection. His eyes watered a little.

Lily wondered if he was remembering Hope, his daughter, the one he lost too soon. Could he see some of Hope in Sammy?

She froze in place as Grant moved beside Flynn and embraced him in a tight hug. Not the one-armed "bro" hug Lily had seen men give to friends and family. No, this hug lifted Flynn's spirits. Flynn's arms wrapped around Grant, holding onto him for support as a few tears leaked from Flynn's eyes.

"I'm alright," Flynn said, his voice crackling slightly like breaking ice. He rubbed away the last of his tears, inhaling a long, shaky breath. Grant stepped back and gave him some breathing room.

Lily realized her mouth was hanging open as both men began to stare at her. "What, huh?" Lily mumbled. Confusion mouthed as the men glanced at one another.

Grant shrugged. "Flynn saved my life out there today." He said it so easily, so casually, that Lily let out of a puff of air like an empty laugh.

Flynn punched Grant on the arm. "We agreed not to tell her," Flynn growled.

"Not tell me what? What happened out there?" Panic squeezed Lily's throat as the men exchanged guilty glances between them.

Grant was the first to break the silence. "The ceiling in

the pharmacy was starting to cave in. When we were there, it started to rain and the ceiling crumbled. Chunks fell out before half the roof collapsed."

"Grant," Flynn groaned, his eyes squinting shut like it pained him to hear it.

"There was a horde of infected," Grant continued. "They cornered me. The others fled back to the car when the roof caved. Flynn could have gone with them and left me there, but he came back. He saved me from, what, twenty infected?"

Flynn nodded, some of the color slipping from his face. "I wasn't just going to leave you there."

"But, you could have. God knows you'd have enough reason to want me out of the picture." Grant's gaze flickered to Lily for a moment before returning to Flynn.

"Yeah, well, like it or not you've grown on me, old man. We're a family, the four of us. Rob said so." Even though his skin was still a ghastly gray, Flynn smiled and some light humor reached his eyes.

"Right. We'll work out our jealousy, Sugar." Grant slid an arm around Lily's waist and pulled her in closer to him. He placed a scruffy kiss on her cheek, making the butterflies in her belly tingle. "But we're both here for you. We're not going anywhere."

Flynn stepped forward, closing the gap between them. His hand reached under Lily's chin, tilting her head upward. His lips pressed against hers, a gentle, soft reminder that he would be there for her. As he pulled back, his hand tilted her head slightly toward Grant.

Grant's lips captured hers in another gentle reminder. All too soon, he released her, his hand fell from her waist as his lips pulled away.

"So, did anything happen while we were gone?" Flynn asked.

Lily's stomach iced over as the thought of infected in the boiler room bubbled to the surface of her mind. She shrugged as she calculated whether to let her men know about the monsters living under their roof.

"Hi, guys." Marissa hurried toward them with a perky smile. "How was the trip?"

"Good." Grant shrugged before kicking a rock against the ground.

"Successful," Flynn added.

"Well, that's good. It's getting dark. Want me to take Sammy inside?" Marissa offered.

Lily nodded, and Marissa lifted the little girl who was happy to show off her new toy.

"So, what happened while we were gone?" Grant asked again, his smile slipping from his face.

"Well, some of us decided to start up a homeschool program for the kids. We think it'll be good for them. Give them a basic education. Keep them grounded," Lily said.

The memory of the zombies on the first floor nagged at her, but this didn't seem like the time to tell them. The men looked tired, worn down, even. They needed sleep, and who could sleep peacefully with a horde of zombies in the basement, even if they were tightly locked away?

Flynn and Grant glanced between one another, silently exchanging words. Grant shook his head and crossed his arms. "Told you this would happen," he said.

"What would happen?" she asked.

"That you'd get too attached to this place," Flynn replied.

"So? What's wrong with this place?" Lily asked.

Grant sighed. "Well, this was just supposed to be a place to stop and sleep for the night, remember?"

"Well, yeah, but—"

"But we've been here for over a week now. And even

though this building is fenced in, it's inevitable that another group will find this place and want it for themselves," Flynn said.

"But, we're—"

"And we have supplies. But how long will they hold up? These fences aren't sturdy, especially against a horde or a group of people smart enough to drive right through the front gate," Grant added.

"Now that's just—"

"And, I don't appreciate Jonathan calling all the shots around here," Flynn frowned. "Who put him in charge? And why? The man seems to spend most of the day sitting on his ass and barking orders."

"Jesus, Mary, and Joseph, would you two let me talk?" Lily shouted. Her small boom of a voice echoed around them, sending a few birds squawking and flying from the trees nearby.

"Keep your voice down," Grant said.

Heat burned on the back of Lily's neck. "Don't you tell me to keep my fucking voice down when you talk over me like I'm a goddamned child!"

"Seriously, Lily. Can we discuss this inside?" Flynn pointed over her shoulder.

Thirty yards away, an infected roamed over toward them, stumbling in the overgrown brush on the edge of the trees.

Lily threw her hands up in the air, an exasperated grunt straining from her throat. "Oh, Jesus Christ, I'm getting so sick of these things." With that, she stomped inside, Flynn trailing behind her.

Grant picked up the discarded pipe and strolled over toward the fence to handle the infected.

"Come on, Lily. You know this wasn't what we planned," Flynn said.

"What *we* planned? A month ago, I didn't even know you.

Now you think you can just barge into my life and start ordering me around? Hell, no!"

Flynn pinched the bridge of his nose, frowning down at her with such condescending disappointment that Lily wanted to slap that look right off his face.

Her fingers tingled in anticipation.

Grant jogged down the hallway to meet up with them. "Lily, you left your mother's house because it was best for Sammy. How does staying trapped inside this school like sitting ducks protect her?" Grant asked.

"We're not sitting ducks. We're fenced in. We have people. We have supplies. We have guns. We're safe here. And Sammy needs a normal life," she said.

"She's never going to have a normal life. None of us will anymore. She'll adapt. But you have to let her," Flynn said.

"You don't understand. You're not trying to raise a child in this hellhole," she snapped.

Flynn winced, and guilt kicked her in the stomach like an angry donkey.

Hope. His daughter…

Lily wished she could take back her words. "I'm sorry," she said, "I didn't mean…"

"I love Sammy, too. You know?" Flynn mumbled.

Lily stumbled on her feet for a moment, bowled over by his words. He loved her daughter.

"We both do. She's got this one already wrapped around her finger." Grant nudged Flynn in the arm, trying to lighten the mood.

A small smile flickered on Flynn's face. "True. Though you're equally guilty of that, old man."

"Lily, we're all in this together," Grant said, stepping between her and Flynn. "We're a team. We all want what's best for Sammy."

Lily sighed and began to walk away from the men.

"I'll think about it," she called over her shoulder, leaving them standing alone in the hallway like lost puppies.

She stomped around the hallway, looking for Marissa, or Colleen, or Alexa. She found Marissa sitting in an empty classroom, reading a tattered copy of *Little Women*.

"I loved this book when I was a kid," she said. "It made life seem simple and happy and pretty. Everything the world isn't right now." She slid a bookmark into place and closed it, glancing up at Lily.

"We had a fight," Lily said.

"Figured it would happen at some point," Marissa said. "What about?"

"They want to leave," Lily said. "Go find that refugee camp and take Sammy and me with them. I don't want Sammy to leave here. She can have some schooling. She'll have structure and people to watch out for her, and we don't even know for sure if this camp exists—"

"Sounds like you already made up your mind," Marissa said. "Did they get spooked by the infected in the boiler room?"

Lily shook her head. "No. In fact, I was so floored by them just telling me that we're leaving that I forgot to mention the infected living under our roof."

"Huh. Living." Marissa scowled at the irony.

"It sounds like they want to leave. What if they leave without us?"

"We all know that they won't just leave you here. They're crazy about you and Sammy. They'd bop you on the head with a club, haul you up over their shoulders like cavemen, and drag you out of here before they'd leave you behind."

Lily laughed. "That's never going to happen, and don't go giving them any ideas."

"Hell, no. I want you to stick around. All of you." Marissa said. "It's almost time for dinner. Ready to go?"

Lily nodded and waited for Marissa to tuck the book back into her pocket. The two women walked with their heads close together, chatting about cavemen and stupid boys.

CHAPTER 16

*L*ily and Marissa carried their dinner trays over to Grant, Flynn, and Sammy. The women glanced up at one another, their eyes locking before their gazes turned down to the food. Canned pasta with meatballs and a slice of overripe watermelon from someone's front garden that Carly had found on their supply run.

A feast fit for kings, at least in this hellhole.

"So, are we going to talk about what happened?" Grant asked Lily.

She shrugged. "I don't know what there is to talk about. We're not leaving. I'm not uprooting Sammy. And I'm not having this discussion in front of her either."

Sammy bounced up and down beside Flynn. Her feet swung under the chair as she speared a small meatball onto her fork. Her short attention span seemed glued to the food.

"It's not safe here, Sweetheart." Flynn's hand reached across the table to squeeze hers. His rough fingertips traced tiny circles over her skin. A familiar warmth blossomed in Lily's belly at his touch, smoothing some of the more jagged edges of her nerves.

"It's safe," Sammy piped up as the meatball fell off her fork. "There are only monsters in the basement. Mommy said they're locked in."

"Sammy!" Lily gasped.

Everyone at the table froze and stared at the little girl in horror.

Sammy stared up at the adults with wide eyes before she went back to eating her pasta. "Sorry," she mumbled.

"Sammy, what do you mean there are monsters in the basement?" Grant tried to keep a calm voice. He leaned over the table and tried to soften the expression on his face, though a vein began to throb in his neck. He managed a cross between a grimace and a Joker smile.

"There are monsters in the basement. They're behind a door. Mommy said they can't hurt us. But I could hear them talking." The little girl bit into a giant meatball and chewed, watching her plate.

"There. Are. Infected. In. The. School." Flynn spat out each word like a poisonous dart. "And you want to stay here?" he growled, his voice staying low. His grip on Lily's hand tightened. "Are you crazy?"

"Oh, yes, Flynn. Clearly, I've lost my sanity and want to put us in as much danger as possible. Maybe I'll run over the gate with our car and blast mariachi music from the speakers. See how big of a horde I can draw here." She rolled her eyes and yanked her arm out of his grip.

"Why the fuck are they in here?" Grant spat.

"Language," Marissa snapped, nodding her head toward Sammy.

"Marissa," Flynn hummed. "Do you know something about this?"

She shrugged her shoulders, avoiding his blazing stare. "I knew they were there. Jonathan said we couldn't get rid of them. If we shot at them, we'd probably hit something and cause an explosion. And if we just let them out, God knows what would happen."

The men exchanged wary glances.

"They're behind a reinforced, steel door. They're not getting out. We're safer here than we are anywhere else," Marissa continued.

"Except the refugee camp," Grant barked.

Lily rolled her eyes. "You two and this Goddamn refugee camp. We don't know if it even exists."

"I think the three of you should go discuss this somewhere else," Marissa chimed in, pointing down at Sammy behind the little girl's back.

Sammy continued chomping away at her food, oblivious that the conversation had taken a turn for the worse.

"I agree," Lily said, rising from her chair.

"I'll watch her," Marissa offered.

"Thanks," Flynn grumbled. He stood and walked out of the cafeteria while Grant and Lily trailed behind, rushing through the heavy metal doors.

The trio hustled down the hallway, anger radiating in the air around them. It hummed like an electric live wire. Flynn stopped in front of the auditorium doors, flinging them wide open. Plenty of open space. Lots of room for yelling. No one else around to hear them. It was Perfect.

Flynn marched down the middle aisle, up to the front of the stage, and sat on the edge.

Lily followed him, running the last few feet, jumping onto the short stage beside Flynn.

"You jerks." She stomped her foot beside Flynn and glared at both men. Her deadly gaze followed Grant as he hustled up to the front of the stage. "You don't get to fight with me in front of Sammy. You don't get to tell me where we're going or how to live."

"Lily, stop it," Flynn huffed beside her, one leg rising to

rest on the edge of the stage. He looked up at her, his brow furrowed in a mixture of worry, pity, and, worst of all, condescension.

Her blood was near boiling with rage. She wanted to punch something and scream until her lungs gave out.

"Fuck you," she spat, her anger rising higher.

"Fuck you back!" Grant shouted at her. "You think you get to drag us into this mess? Huh? Make us fucking fall in love with you and that little girl and then let you put your lives, our lives, at risk without letting us have a say?"

"You can have a say. You can say all you want, but you don't get to tell me what to do or where we're going to live. That's *my* choice!"

"I'm so sick of having this discussion." Flynn groaned, rubbing his temples.

"Then, stop talking," Grant said. His eyes blazed with anger and heat and a need to clear the air between the three of them.

Lily growled, anger and heat rising inside her. She needed a release. She needed to break the tension. "Fuck me," she said, her eyes meeting Grant's in a heady challenge.

"What?" Flynn said, glancing up at her.

Anger and power poured from her body as she crouched beside Flynn, pressing him further backward. "Fuck me," she purred, a wicked smirk on her face.

"What the fuck, Lily?" Grant stepped onto the stage to sit beside her.

Lily rolled over, lust glazing over her eyes. She tugged on the hem of his shirt, pulling him closer until his lips hovered an inch above hers.

"I'm tired of talking. Fuck me."

Grant's lips crashed down onto her, heat sizzling through his touch. The taste of oranges and smoke danced on her tongue and his lips moved against hers in a wicked tango.

Everywhere his fingers pressed, Lily's skin burned with need. His hands groped, reaching for every inch of her.

Flynn's hands fiddled with the buttons of Lily's shorts while Grant's hands glided along her belly, raising her shirt higher.

Heat pooled between Lily's thighs. Her heartbeat thumped so loud she could hear it ringing in her skull. The musky smell of sweat and need mingled in the damp summer air. Anger still thrummed under the surface.

She kissed back harder, her hand sinking into Grant's hair, dragging him closer to the warmth of her body. With her back rested against Flynn's hard chest, so much heat engulfed her that she thought she might burst into flames.

Flynn's hands tugged her shorts lower on her hips, the small wisp of lace panties sticking out from her shorts like a naughty invitation. His fingers traced over the delicate fabric. He tugged on the lace, tearing it over her hip, and gripped the edge of her shorts, sliding them down to her knees, baring her naked flesh to their hungry gazes.

Lily mewled against Grant's lips. Her hips bucked against Flynn's hand as he spread her thighs wider, her shorts slipping past her knees, trapping her lower limbs together. Cool air tickled her pussy. Shivers raced through her, her nipples puckering against the soft fabric of her shirt.

Grant reached for her, his large hand closed over her breast and he squeezed. His thumbs slid over her stiff nipples, tugging at them and giving them a soft pinch.

Lily moaned, arching into his hand as the small pain mixed with overwhelming pleasure. Her mind began to fade away, her senses taking over as the men played a wicked duet with her body.

Flynn's fingers slipped between the slick folds of her lips, his finger sliding over her clit, rubbing over it in soft small circles. His head bent down, capturing a hard nipple through her shirt. His tongue reached for her, licking as his lips sucked. He released her breast, a small damp spot spread over the fabric.

Lily bucked harder against Flynn's hand, pleasure spiking and sparking like small fireworks somewhere just outside her mind. She was slipping into another dimension. Pleasure built higher, bringing her closer to space, away from reality.

Grant broke their kiss. He reached up and yanked her shirt over her head, tossing it somewhere across the stage. His hand dropped lower, his large palm encasing her heavy breast.

"Perfect," he murmured before his lips met the long column of her neck.

Grant's tongue flicked over the sensitive spot where her neck met her collarbone, and she moaned, wiggling against Flynn's hand as sensation from her clit mingled with the tickling feeling at her neck. Her body begged for more. Needing more.

Flynn slid one finger deep inside her, only stopping once his knuckles met her entrance. "You're so wet for us, Sweet-heart," he murmured in her ear.

Her pussy squeezed, trying to suck Flynn's finger in deeper. She needed one of them, both of them, filling her and stretching her again. She needed the fullness only their bodies could give her.

"Please," she begged. Her hips rose and fell as she fucked his hand, trying to bring her climax closer.

"Not yet, Sugar." Grant's dark voice echoed on the edge of her reality. His lips released her neck as his hands pressed onto her shoulders, laying her onto her back against the summer warmed wood.

Flynn stood, sliding off the small stage, stripping his shirt as he went. Thick cords of muscle glistened with a sheen of sweat in the summer heat.

Lily moaned at the sight of him. Grant's hands traced small designs over her collarbone as he watched her.

Flynn's rough hands grabbed Lily's knees and tugged her forward until her thighs dangled off the edge of the raised stage. He knelt on the tile floor, pulling off her shorts. He dropped them and wet scrap of lace beside him.

His rough hands spread her thighs open, cold air tickling her again.

"Please," she moaned. She didn't know what she wanted. But she knew she needed something. Anything to get rid of this aching need.

Flynn's head dipped between her legs, his stubble scratching along her inner thigh. His hot breath blew onto the dampness around her clit.

Lily moaned, her hips bucking, trying to reach for him.

"Please!" Her cry sounded foreign in her ears. Silence roared like a train whistle in her brain. She waited, anticipation pulsing through her body.

Flynn's hot tongue licked her clit, sucking on her sweetness, and she screamed as hot pleasure shot through her like lightning.

He leaned back, giving her body a moment of relief before he lowered his head again for another taste. She whimpered as his tongue slipped between her folds, two fingers sliding deep inside her greedy pussy.

"Flynn," she whimpered, trying to move her hips faster.

He fucked her with his fingers, slowly at first, and his free hand took hold of her hip, pinning her down to the edge of the stage. Her legs dangled, helpless to his wicked attack.

Grant kneeled beside her head, watching them. He tugged his t-shirt up over his arms, dropping it to the floor with the rest of Lily's clothes. He stripped out of his pants, pushing them down to his knees before kicking them off. His hard cock hovered a few inches over Lily's lips.

She leaned up, grabbing onto his shaft, and took his cock-head into her mouth. Her tongue swirled over the hot tip, a droplet of salty pre-cum oozing from him.

"Fuck, Sugar," he groaned.

He reached down, lifting her head higher and holding it in place. His muscles tightened as she sucked him in deeper, half his cock sliding in and out of her mouth in a fast, pumping pace. She kept in time with Flynn's fingers, still fucking her dripping pussy.

Flynn slipped his fingers from her with a soft, sucking sound. He rose between her legs and took hold of her calves, lifting them until her ankles wrapped around the back of his neck. He leaned forward, feeding the head of his cock into her hungry opening.

Lily moaned on Grant's cock as she felt Flynn slowly sink into her, inch by thick inch. Both men filled her, stretching her holes as Grant slid deeper into the back of her throat.

White, hot pleasure consumed her as both men began to move inside her, stretching, emptying, and filling her again. Her ankles locked around Flynn's neck as his cock pushed deeper inside her, bottoming out of her. The head of his cock slid in harder, a dull ache building in her lower belly. Harder. More. She couldn't get enough. Mindless need drove her as her hips bucked against his.

Her tongue moved in fast licks over the underside of Grant's cock and his hand tightened in her hair, sending a small pain over her scalp. She moaned in response.

Both men grunted somewhere above her as her eyes closed, her body sinking into the pleasure they gave her. Grant's fingers pinched her nipple, shooting pleasure from her chest down to the apex of her thighs where Flynn fucked her faster.

Lily's body soared higher, her orgasm teetering on the

edge of exploding. Grant's hips picked up speed, matching Flynn thrust for thrust. Full. Empty. Full.

Lily's head swam on the brink of a world-shattering orgasm.

Flynn's hand danced over her clit, rolling it between the rough pads of his fingers, as Lily choked on Grant's cock, pleasure consuming her like hellfire. Heat and ecstasy and music burst through her, shaking her very being. Her pussy spasmed around Flynn's cock while she cried out on Grant's.

She whimpered as her orgasm ebbed away like the tide, her mind swimming in a sex-drunk haze as her body grew limp with exhaustion. Her head sunk back, Grant's cock slipping from her lips as Flynn pulled out between her legs.

He gripped her hips, spinning her around on the stage. Her head dangled off the edge, the rest of her lying flat against the warm wood. Grant knelt between her legs, lifting them into the air by her ankles while Flynn pinned her wrists above her head.

Flynn's cock prodded her lips, waiting for her to open. She did, tasting herself on him as his head slipped inside her mouth, her tongue working his cock.

The head of Grant's cock probed at her entrance, stretching her out further. He moved his shaft between her wet lips, rubbing the underside of his cock against her sensitive clit. Once he'd lubed his cock with her juices, he sunk inside her tight pussy with a heavy groan.

Lily moaned, the overwhelming feeling of fullness drowning her senses. Her tongue moved over Flynn's cock while Grant's fingers teased her clit in small circles. Small shocks of pleasure jolted her system like live wires, another orgasm threatening to take over as Grant's hips thrust in slow and powerful strokes.

Flynn kept his cock still, letting her taste and explore as Grant tried to coax another orgasm from her body with long, teasing thrusts. Lily wiggled between the two strong men, moaning as her pleasure spiked even higher, threatening to drop and pull her down with it.

"Come for me, Sugar," Grant's voice washed over her as his fingers moved faster over her clit.

Lily could feel her orgasm about to hit her, like watching a train coming for her. She screamed as her pussy latched onto Grant's thick cock. Flynn slid himself deeper inside her mouth until the tip of his cock slid into her throat.

Her orgasm rushed through her like lightning bolts, jerking her body in every which way, her limbs writhing in uncontrollable pleasure.

"Now, she's ready." Flynn's deep voice boomed over her like a thunder god. With surprising tenderness, he slipped himself from her mouth and lifted her into a sitting position on Grant's lap.

Grant laid back, letting her straddle his trim hips. He watched her with a sharp edge like a hawk eyeing its prey. His hands pressed into her hips and he guided her over his cock, slipping inside until he was buried to the hilt.

"It's in my pocket," Grant glanced over at Flynn, nodding toward his discarded jeans.

Flynn picked up Grant's pants and rummaged through them, pulling out a small packet of lube.

"What?" Lily asked, barely able to focus on Flynn's movements as he moved somewhere behind her.

"Lean forward, Sugar. It'll make it easier." Grant wrapped his strong arms around her shoulders and pulled her down until they were pressed chest to chest.

The dusting of hair on his chest tickled her nipples. She rested her head in the crux of his neck, exhausted and satisfied.

Flynn chuckled from behind her. "Oh, you're not finished

yet, Sweetheart. Now it's our turn." His finger rubbed luke-warm lube over the entrance to her ass.

Lily froze. "Will it hurt?"

She'd never…Not even once!

"You'll feel some pressure," Flynn said, his voice soothing her worry. "But I promise we'll be gentle."

"Are you sure you'll fit?" she asked.

Flynn threw his head back, the warm sound of laughter coating her inside like melted ice cream. "Oh, I'll fit. Just relax." He nodded to Grant.

Lily turned her head back around to Grant. His hand slipped between their bodies, searching for her clit and when he found it, he stroked it with soft, tender touches. Excitement built back up in Lily's lower belly.

Flynn's finger slipped inside her ass with ease. The sensation, though a bit weird, added to her excitement. Lily's skin flushed, her blood hot as he added a second finger.

A small ring of pain circled around his fingertip. "That hurts," she murmured against Grant's neck. "You're not going to fit."

"Shh, relax, Sugar. Your body will adjust." Grant's deep voice rang in her ears. His fingers picked up speed, heightening her pleasure. It mingled with the pain until the pain nearly subsided.

Flynn's fingers pumped slowly in and out of her hole, scissoring inside her and stretching her out. "I'm going to use some more lube and use a third finger. Relax, Sweetheart. You're doing fantastic."

Lily felt him plant a small kiss on her lower back before a third finger slipped inside her. Dull pain circled her entrance, her pussy squeezing onto Grant's cock as Flynn stretched her further. Lily shook her hips a little, trying to adjust to the full feeling in both of her holes.

As her body began to warm again, adjusting to his fingers,

Flynn slipped them out of her hole. Lily heard the crinkling of a condom wrapper a few moments before the head of Flynn's cock pressed against her ass.

Grant's fingers moved faster, pleasure spiking higher, threatening to spill over and make her come apart. "You can handle this, Sugar. I love you." He kissed her earlobe as Flynn began to slip his cock inside her.

Hot pain spread around her ass, and Lily cried out, biting into Grant's shoulder as tears sprang to her eyes.

"Focus on your clit, Sugar. Focus on me," Grant crooned in her ear. Grant eased his hips upward a bit, his cock jerking inside her wet pussy as Flynn slid in deeper.

Lily let her mind wander, focusing on the warm sensation of Grant's fingers on her clit, his thick cock filling her pussy. Lily's mind drifted away in a sea of pleasure as Flynn's cock slid home.

"Oh, fuck," he groaned. "God, Sweetheart, you're amazing. Fuck, I love you." He bent down, pressing a soft kiss to her shoulder blade. He reached under her, lifting her a few inches off Grant's chest.

Lily rested her weight on her forearms, staring down at the satisfied smirk on Grant's face. She bent down, kissing it right off him. Flynn's cock shifted behind her, penetrating deeper than before. She moaned into Grant's mouth, her tongue dancing with his as Flynn slipped from her, plunging back in. His hips slammed against her, jerking her body forward, higher on Grant's cock before sliding back down. As Flynn fucked her, her body ground against Grant in response.

"Please," Lily moaned, releasing Grant's lips and twisting sideways. Her gaze locked onto Flynn's blazing blue eyes.

A wicked twinkle sparked in them, his gaze fixed on where their bodies joined.

"God, yes, Lily," he groaned. He bent down, capturing her

lips against his for a fleeting moment before his hips hammered harder against her, rocking her against Grant's cock.

"Oh fuck," she shouted. Her body began to shake as another orgasm threatened to swallow her whole. She felt it building and braced herself for it. "Fuck!"

Her voice echoed around the auditorium, loud enough to wake the dead. Her body pulsed and squeezed the two cocks buried inside her. She twisted and writhed with nowhere to turn, trapped between two large men.

Flynn gripped her hair while Grant held onto her shoulder. Her hips were pinned between theirs and all she could do was feel the endless orgasm that threatened to drive her insane.

"Yes," Grant groaned.

"Come for us, Sweetheart," Flynn grunted as his hips thrust faster. "Yes, keep coming. I'm…I'm…Oh, God! Lily!" Flynn shouted as his cock twitched inside her, the condom ballooning around him, catching his cum. With a few more hard thrusts, Flynn kept her going.

"Lily," Grant groaned under her. He spread his legs wider, his cock slipping in and out of her in long, hard strokes. He panted beneath her as he spilled his cum deep inside her body. Her pussy milked him for every drop of cum.

Her body squeezed them, begging them for it. As her orgasm slowed, she felt Flynn's cock slip from her hole. She leaned forward, resting her weight on Grant's chest, heaving for breath. Her mind spun like a top, not sure when it would fall over or slow down.

"Oh my God," she murmured against Grant's neck.

The smell of men, sweat, and sex lingered in the air around her, turning her brain to mush in the aftermath of the most intense orgasm of her life.

"Agreed," Grant chuckled in her ear. The warm sound echoed deep in her heart.

"You were incredible, Sweetheart," Flynn said, lying beside Grant. He pulled her down onto the floor between them, their naked bodies wrapping around one another in a mess of limbs and smiles.

"You both were pretty great, too," she huffed, her lungs still trying to catch up with the rest of her body as she sunk into a relaxed stupor. "And you both...ouch!" she yelped. A small pain stabbed into her hip. "What was that?" She rolled back onto Grant, examining the spot on the stage where her hip had been. The head of a small screw stuck out a quarter of an inch from the floorboard.

"What the hell?" Flynn murmured, looking down at the floor.

"Good thing you didn't spin me around on that. That would have hurt." Lily grimaced as she stared at the offending nail like it had teeth.

"Why did we come in here again?" Grant asked.

The three of them fell silent as their thoughts raced back to why they had come into the auditorium in the first place.

The shouting. The fight. The infected in the boiler room.

"I'm not leaving," Lily said, a sudden chill lingering in the air. She shivered like she had stepped into a snowstorm buck naked.

"But, Lily," Flynn said, reaching for her.

"No, I'm not leaving. I'm not dragging Sammy around to find some magical camp where everything will be perfect again. It probably doesn't exist." Lily stood, shuffling around to find her discarded clothes thrown around the stage like props.

"You want to live in a school filled with zombies? That's safer than going out and finding a camp with people and supplies and other families for her to play with?" Grant rolled his eyes.

Lily turned to speak, her tongue drying up like sandpaper as she watched the two men move like panthers, reaching for their clothes and covering their lean, muscled flesh. Grant's cum trickled from between her legs.

"I…" She coughed. "I don't think it's smart to leave when we're safe here. There should be a way to get rid of the infected down there. We have lots of supplies and people and Sammy can have a more normal life here. It's a guessing game as to whether this camp exists. I'm not willing to risk my daughter's life on a guess."

The men tugged their shirts back on, staring at one another. With annoyed resolved they both sighed.

"I'm sure we can find a way to get rid of the infected. There can't be that many of them. Boiler rooms usually aren't that big," Flynn said.

"Fine. We'll stay," Grant glowered.

Relief spread through Lily, warming her to the tips of her toes.

"Thank you!" She rushed over to them, flinging her arms around Grant's neck, then Flynn. "I love you." She kissed Flynn on his soft pink lips, his stubble scratching her cheeks,

"Both of you." She turned back to Grant, rising on tiptoe to press a kiss to his tight lips.

Something darker than annoyance but not as hot as anger burned in his eyes. "We love you too, Sugar. I just hope we know what we're doing."

CHAPTER 17

*L*ily chewed on a gristly piece of jerky as she hunched over a copy of *The Hunger Games.* The deserted cafeteria was quiet except for the splattering of rain against the high windows. With the summer storm pouring over them, the packed dirt roads turned to mud which was too thick for the tires to pull through for a supply run today. Other than kitchen duty and collecting rainwater, today was a lazy Sunday for everyone.

As Katniss raised her bow to aim at a squirrel, a tap on Lily's shoulder jolted her out of the story. She swiveled, her heart hammering as she wondered how she had let her guard down.

"Jonathan, you scared me half to death." She flipped her book, pages turned down, onto the table and glared at him.

He chuckled, heaving himself into a chair beside her, the wisps of white hair on his head frozen in the still summer air. "Sorry, I didn't mean to startle you. I saw you sitting alone and thought we could have a bit of a chat."

Lily paused, her curiosity rising.

After over a month of being holed up in the school, their

small group got along with everyone else. Everyone adored Sammy, offering to babysit and play with her whenever they needed a pick-me-up. The little girl was as addictive as caffeine to these people. But, even with this small piece of attention, Jonathan kept his distance from them, like a scientist observing a group of lab rats in some experiment.

"Well, is there anything you wanted to chat about?" She shifted a little in her seat, crossing one knee over the other.

"I just wanted to see how you were adjusting here. Maybe see if you had any ideas to improve the place, or if there's anything we can do to make it run smoother here. We're a democracy after all." He smiled at her, one front tooth a bit more yellow than the rest.

Lily shrugged. "Um, I guess not. Everything seems to be just fine. Flynn and Grant seem happy here. Sammy loves it. This place is like her little playground. I can't remember the last time I felt that she would be safe if I wasn't in the same room."

Jonathan nodded. "That's good. I hope you don't mind, but I want to see if you could learn another one of our jobs around here. I want you to take a watch shift tonight. You and Raj. Think you'd be up for it, after dinner?"

"Watch shift?" Lily asked. Her interest piped up like a prairie dog from its hole.

"Yes, we have someone on watch twenty-four-seven. Just in case. You never know these days. A mass horde could be headed right for the school. We need to be prepared for anything outside those gates."

Lily nodded, but stayed quiet, waiting for him to continue.

"The bell tower at the top of the school, it's old, but it's good for a bird's nest. You can see about a mile around the school in every direction. If you're up for it, I want you to go up there tonight with Raj and learn how to take watch."

A weird feeling shifted in Lily's stomach like Tetris tiles. "Raj? Why not Grant or Flynn?"

Jonathan shook his head. "I haven't had them up there yet. I wanted to be sure…well, let me be completely honest with you. I wanted to make sure I could trust you three before I let you all up there. Normally there's only one person up there at a time. So, I needed to be sure you three were good company. I wasn't about to tell you everything about this place in your first few weeks after all."

Jonathan's mouth lifted in a faint smile, his eyes twinkling as he stared at her.

A punch of surprise jabbed at Lily. "You'd let us live here if you didn't trust us?"

Jonathan shrugged. "Your group appeared safe, but I knew only time would tell. I can see you are just about harmless, so long as Sammy's alright. I can't imagine how wild you'd be if she was hurt."

A flash of anger slashed through her vision. "Are you threatening my—"

"No." Jonathan held his hands up in front of him like stop signs. "No, not at all. I'd never hurt that sweet girl. No one here would. I'm just saying you're level-headed, most of the time, and that's good enough for me. I figured if Raj survives the night alone with you, then I'd see how Flynn fares up there."

"And Grant?" Lily asked.

Jonathan's gaze lowered. "Grant's a tough nut to crack."

"He's harmless," Lily said.

"He's seen things. Been through war. More than any of us, I'd reckon, and I don't say that lightly. PTSD can do funny things to people. Mess with their minds. I don't want to trust the entire camp's safety to someone I'm not one hundred percent comfortable with, especially while most of us are asleep."

Lily opened her mouth to argue, words and insults dripping from the tip of her tongue, ready to come out. But, she stopped herself. Her anger boiled in her veins but rolled to a low simmer as she thought about Jonathan's comments. He wanted everyone safe. He didn't hate Grant or have any vendetta against him. He wasn't throwing him out of the camp or having him watched.

He just didn't want him alone on guard duty while the rest of the school slept.

She didn't agree with Jonathan but, she was sure, with time, he would see just how good of a guard Grant would be to the school.

"Alright," she murmured. "I'll go. After dinner?"

Jonathan nodded, rising from his seat. "Yes, after dinner. Raj will get you when it's time for his shift. Anyway, I'll let you get back to your book. Good choice, by the way. I liked that series." Jonathan stared at the cover of her book before walking away.

Lily watched him walk through the cafeteria doors and back into the hallway, her fingertips drumming on the edges of the book.

With a nagging feeling gnawing at the back of her neck, she returned to her novel and tried to immerse herself again in another world.

She didn't look up again until she heard the squeaking of running shoes on the cafeteria floor. Glancing up, she saw Colleen, Rob, and Alexa stroll into the room.

"Hey!" Colleen waved at Lily from across the empty room.

Lily nodded, dog-earing the page of her book and laying it on the table. "Hey, what are you all doing here?"

"We've got kitchen duty today," Colleen smiled.

"You have kitchen duty. I have taste tester duty." Alexa winked at Colleen before sinking into a chair across from

Lily. "And now I'll have someone to keep me company while you two cook."

"You're going to cook?" Lily asked, turning her attention to Rob.

He nodded, taking a shy step behind Colleen. "Yes."

"I'm going to show Rob how to make the best canned chicken dinner he's ever tasted. Isn't that right, Rob?" Colleen's enthusiasm pulled the boy out from behind her.

He nodded, his eyes shining with excitement. "Yeah. And Will too. Right, mom?"

Colleen's smile faltered a little. "Yes, Will has kitchen duty with us too. Just make sure not to get in his way, alright?"

The boy nodded before trailing behind his mother into the kitchen.

As the door swung shut, Lily turned back to Alexa. "Does she not like Will?"

Alexa shook her head. "She says Will is a strange kid. I think he's just a boy going through some weird emo phase. I mean, he's seen a lot of bad things happen. We all have. I figured I'd cut the kid a bit of slack. His mom's an odd duck, though. Virginia. I don't know if she's always been like that, or if it happened after her husband died."

Lily shrugged. "I wouldn't know. I haven't talked to her much. I get the feeling she's very disapproving of my relationship."

Alexa rolled her eyes. "Some people are so judgy."

Lily leaned forward to keep her voice low. "Alexa, what do you know about Raj?"

Alexa shrugged. "Not much. Raj and Sanjay really only speak to one another, and always in Hindi. They won't speak English around everyone else. They'll talk to you in English just fine, but they like to keep to themselves.

But they look like they've been through hell and back. Raj is quiet, polite. Says please and thank you between grunts and nods. No idea how they ended up here. They were here before my family came. No one's said anything about them. Sometimes I forget they live here with us."

Lily sighed. "Oh."

Alexa smirked. "Sorry, I don't have much gossip about this place."

"I wasn't trying to gossip, so much as something to talk about during our shift tonight." Lily tapped the toe of her shoe on the table leg, glancing around the cafeteria.

"Your shift?" she asked.

Lily nodded. "Yeah, Jonathan came up to me earlier and asked if I'd take a night watch with Raj tonight so he could show me the ropes. But, I know nothing about the guy. I don't want it to be awkward."

"Well, let me say this. If you ask Raj a question and he just stares ahead and says yes or no, don't take it personally. He's not the talkative type. Sanjay is a bit different. You can have a pleasant conversation with him without feeling like you're taking up his time or saying something wrong."

A small ball seemed to drop in Lily's stomach. She had a feeling this would be a long night. "I'll keep that in mind. Thanks." She rose from her seat, the chair squeaking along the floor.

"Tired of my company already?" Alexa said, flashing a teasing smile.

"No, I just want to get a quick nap in before my shift. And I have to tell the guys where I'll be tonight."

Alexa stood and waved goodbye as she wandered off into the kitchen.

Lily pushed open the door to the hallway.

"Watch it!" a voice shouted at her.

Lily blinked, stunned and frozen in place.

An angry Will glared at her, standing inches from the edge of the open door.

"You trying to run me over or something?" he grumbled, pushing open the door beside her and hustling past.

"Sorry," she shouted behind her.

The teenager huffed and continued to storm through the cafeteria toward the kitchen.

Lily rolled her eyes, letting the door swing shut behind her as she strolled back to her room. Emo phase? More like young asshole phase. Though maybe Alexa was right. Maybe that kid had seen some gruesome stuff and just needed someone to cut him a little slack.

CHAPTER 18

"Colleen, I don't know how you do it," Alexa praised her wife over a warm bowl of canned chicken chili, the rest of the table nodding in agreement as they spooned more into their mouths.

"God, I'm so hungry," Flynn grunted, before shoveling in another bite.

Lily swallowed before speaking. "How's the bus coming along? Still having trouble with the transmission?"

Flynn rubbed the back of his neck with an exasperated sigh. "No, I finished rebuilding the transmission yesterday. I had to take pieces from the minivan, but that car was barely running. Today I couldn't get the emergency door on the bus to open. It's nearly rusted shut. If we need that bus, we'll need an emergency exit in the back. You never know."

"You've spent a lot of time working on that bus," Colleen noted.

Flynn nodded. "Yeah, I want to have it up and running as soon as possible."

"Excuse me, I don't mean to interrupt, but I couldn't help

overhearing." Virginia swiveled in a chair behind them, sitting with Will, Roman, and Carly. "Do you think you'll have the bus running soon? Do you think we'd be able to use it to go to that camp you mentioned and get out of here? Sitting around just isn't safe. One of these days, someone is going to find this place and—"

"Mom!" Will snapped. "Stop it. We're not going anywhere."

"But David wouldn't have wanted us to—"

"Dad's dead. Who cares about what he wanted." Will slammed his spoon down on the table and stood. He rushed out of the room before Virginia could say anything to him.

She turned back to Flynn, glaring at him like he started the fight. She opened her mouth to speak but seemed to decide against it, returning to her bowl of chili and ignoring their group.

Alexa twirled her finger near her ear and mouthed "Crazy."

Lily bit the tip of her tongue to stop her snicker from escaping.

"Lily?" a voice echoed behind her.

She swiveled in her chair, staring up into Sanjay's dark chocolate eyes. "Are you ready for your shift? If you're not done eating, we still have a few minutes."

"I'm finished," she said but stayed seated. "Where's Raj?"

Sanjay shrugged. "He needs some more sleep. Jonathan said we could switch shifts. So I'm going to sit with you tonight and he's going to cover for me tomorrow."

"Oh, alright." Relief rushed through her. At least Sanjay was the talkative of the two brothers.

She stood, leaning down to give Flynn a short kiss before pushing her chair back. "Give Sammy and Grant a kiss good night for me?"

"I'm not kissing Grant good night." Flynn smirked up at her.

"Well, that's a shame." She winked, leaving Flynn with a dumbstruck expression on his face. She could hear Alexa and Colleen giggling as she walked out of the cafeteria behind Sanjay.

They climbed the nearest stairwell to the third floor.

"So, where's the bell tower?" Lily asked, trying to make light conversation over the shuffling of their shoes on the tiled floor.

"Not far up ahead, between stairwells four and five. It looks like a broom closet." He kept pace in front of her, leading her down the hallway before stopping at a narrow door. "This is it."

He pulled on the knob, tugging a flashlight out from his back pocket. "There are no lights in the stairwell. The bulbs burned out, and they're not really worth replacing."

A thin beam of light lit the small stairway. His heavy boots thudded on each step, ringing in Lily's ears as she followed behind him. Little puffs of dust moved in the air around them, their footsteps waking the settled dirt beneath their feet.

Lily choked back a cough, trying not to touch the railing. "I don't think the school ever used it. I don't think this place has been cleaned since—"

"Since the school switched over to an automatic alarm bell system. I doubt this bell has been used in about thirty years."

"Oh," Lily said, closing the door behind her. She glanced around. The small bell tower was cramped with two flimsy folding chairs placed on opposite sides of the tower, each facing a different direction.

"There are slats over the windows. So, unless someone

knew where to look, they wouldn't see anyone taking watch. We usually sit up here one person at a time. It's safe enough to be alone, and we don't have enough manpower to rotate with two people up here at each shift."

Sanjay plopped himself in a seat as Lily walked around the small tower. A brass bell half her height hung in the middle of the ceiling, a long rope snaking down to around her feet.

Through the slats, the school grounds seemed to disappear into the trees. Miles of bright, green leaves stretched beyond that. The trees glittered with fresh rainwater, droplets catching the light like hundreds of gems in the distance. To the south was the entrance into the school, the winding gravel pathway that led up to the paved road. A couple of infected roamed nearby, wandering aimlessly. One had its ankle stuck in the mud and was stumbling around on the ground, trying to free itself.

"Someone's going to have to clear the fence again in a little while."

"I think Carly has fence duty tonight." Lily sat in her chair across from Sanjay.

He nodded, gazing out at the setting sun.

"So, how did you end up here with your brother?" she asked, trying to lighten the mood.

He shrugged. "Does it matter?"

"Maybe. Who knows what really matters anymore?" She tried to sound philosophical and profound enough to pique his interest, but his silence said otherwise. "I heard you were at the school when the infection started."

Sanjay shook his head. "No. We got here a few weeks after it hit the area."

Lily paused. "Oh. Well, where were you before that?"

He sighed, leaning back and keeping his gaze on the

sunset. "Getting ready for my sister's wedding. Preeti was supposed to get married about two months ago."

"Oh. What happened to her?"

"She flew off to New Dehli for the wedding." Sanjay's voice slid through the air like ice crystals. "Raj and I were supposed to meet the family in India after we finished some work. But then the infection started to spread and everyone canceled flights in a panic. We couldn't get a flight. Our whole family had flown over for the wedding. And that was the last time we saw any of them."

Sanjay's thoughts wandered off, his brown eyes gleaming as they glazed over and his mind took a stroll down memory lane.

"I'm sorry," she murmured.

"Thanks," he grunted. His gaze misted over like he remembered something he would rather have forgotten.

"So, what about Raj? He's pretty quiet with the rest of us." Lily shifted more in her seat, trying to continue some conversation.

"Raj is Raj. He keeps to himself. That's how he is, how he's always been. If he likes you, he'll talk to you. If he doesn't care about you, he acts like you don't exist. If he hates you...well..."

"Well?"

The word hung in the air.

Sanjay cleared his throat. "So, if you see anything suspicious, you report to Jonathan. If he's not there, then report to Marissa. She's kind of second in command."

"But—"

"Chances are it will just be a small swarm of infected. Nothing to panic about. But, we might have to go clear the area before they attract larger groups. If you see something major, something that can't wait for you to get to them, you ring the fire alarm downstairs. We'll all hear it and run out to the school bus and leave. Got it?"

"Yeah, I think so. But about—"

Sanjay rose from the chair, his stare still facing forward, away from her. "You won't need me up here all night. I'm going to check and see if Carly's out clearing the fences. Just don't fall asleep."

Sanjay's boots stomped on the wooden floor before he yanked open the door and rushed down the steps, leaving Lily alone in the bell tower.

A small summer breeze wafted around her, picking up smells of pine, fresh rain, and rotting flesh somewhere in the distance. Like driving past roadkill after a summer storm.

"Jerk," she murmured, kicking her feet up on the edge of a window and staring out at the treetops.

Just don't fall asleep…

Lily pulled her book out of her back pocket, which she had curled up in a way that would have given Marissa the librarian an ulcer. Lily thumbed back to the dog-eared page and began to read again, waiting for the sun to set and rise again, waiting until she could go back to sleep.

A grisly moan from down below sent a shiver trickling down her spine like melting ice. Infected? So close she could hear them?

Lily turned over her shoulder. Nothing. The moan echoed below, somewhere on the grounds in front of the school. The chair scratched against the wood as she stood and glanced down. Nothing. The grass bristled together in the dry summer wind like a brown wave below. Patches of earth and weeds dotted across the front lawn. But no movement. Nothing living or dead to be seen.

Had it been the wind? Something else? Maybe she heard the noise so often, she was imagining things?

She shivered at the thought. Hearing sounds when there was nothing there. Was she losing her mind?

She brushed the thought away as though it were a pesky fly. Pulling the seat closer toward the slats, she tugged her book opened again and forced herself to focus on the words.

Eight more hours to go.

CHAPTER 19

Alexa and Carly stayed in the library with the children while Lily, Marissa, and Colleen prepared for their presentation to Jonathan. They needed this school. The children needed it. Since their idea a few weeks ago, the kids seemed to be getting wilder and rowdier with each passing day. A mix of cabin fever, summer heat, and boredom was sinking into their little bones. This school was the perfect outlet for the kids.

But, breaking up Jonathan's routine—the washing, the cooking, the supply runs, the guards—was going to take some convincing.

"So, every day, but only in the mornings?" Colleen suggested.

"And we can rotate so only one of us will be missing from the group at a time. Colleen, you'll teach music for an hour in the morning at eight. Marissa will do language arts and spelling after music, and I'll try to add in some odds and ends, math and science and whatnot," Lily said as the three women studied the papers they had drafted as their makeshift schedule.

Marissa had written out the schedule, as well as a supply list. "We'll have to check around for empty classrooms and see what we can collect from the other rooms. I don't think we should use the library. That's become a playroom for them. I don't want to ruin it." She paused. "It's nice to see kids in the library again."

The mothers agreed. This small school would be a blessing for the children. Stability and education were what young children needed—not the monotony of cleaning dishes and mopping floors every day from now until God knows when. This would give them an outlet, for a few hours at least.

Sammy was still her bright, bubbly, four-year-old self. But, Rob had begun to look tired and too old for such a young boy. He remembered school, his old soccer games, playing video games with the neighborhood children, and times before the world changed. He never said anything, but the hollow expression in his eyes left a small streak of fear in the group. His youth and innocence were gone, cut down too early.

Lily shuddered. She hoped that light would never go out of Sammy's eyes.

"So, we have our game plan?" Marissa asked, derailing Lily's train of thought.

"Yeah, I think we're good." Colleen nodded. She stood and stretched her arms above her head.

"Yeah," Lily agreed. She folded up their papers and stuck them in the back pocket of her jeans.

"Let's do this then." Marissa turned on her heel and walked out of the library. Colleen followed. Lily glanced over her shoulder to the children playing in the corner. Some of the spark returned to Rob's eyes when he played. There was still hope for his future.

Lily nodded to Alexa and Carly before leaving.

The trio strolled down the hallway toward the dining hall. If Jonathan wasn't there, then he would be in his office nearby.

They found him in the hallway, holding a ladder steady while Sanjay replaced a light bulb. Jonathan watched the light bulb like he was ready to dodge it if it slipped from the young man's grip.

"Hey, Jonathan. Got a minute?" Marissa asked.

He kept his eye on the lightbulb. "Sure thing, just a minute."

The three women watched Sanjay finish twisting in the new bulb and climb down the ladder. The knot of hair at the back of Sanjay's head swayed a bit as he folded up the ladder and clapped Jonathan on the shoulder before walking away.

Jonathan hustled over to them. "So, what can I do for you ladies?"

"We were hoping to talk to you in private," Marissa said, taking the lead. She knew him the longest and had the most pull with him out of anyone else in the school. "We have a proposition for you."

"Well, then, let's find someplace to sit." He strolled past them and waved for them to follow. He led them into a small classroom furnished as an art studio. A bookshelf with nearly full bottles of paint and boxes of crayons and colored pencils were stacked up neatly in rows. More boxes with odds crafting items lined up along the windowsill. Glue sticks. Popsicle sticks. Pipe cleaners. Glitter glue. Stickers. A child's treasure trove. The supplies in here would last a long time with the two kids. And the room was perfect for an art class.

Jonathan heaved himself into a worn-down computer chair behind a small wooden desk, his watery eyes red and tired. "So, what did you girls want to talk to me about?" he asked.

"Well, first, we ask that you hear us out completely before you say anything," Colleen said.

"And if you have any questions, we'd be more than happy to answer them," Lily chimed in her part.

"But, we'd like to start a small homeschool program for the children," Marissa finished.

Jonathan's eyebrows crinkled together in one fuzzy line as he watched Marissa explain their idea of a morning school for the children. She described the hourly plans and gave him a rundown of the supplies needed, all of which would be found in the school. Her eyes lit up, her hands waving wildly as she talked, her voice getting higher as excitement mounted. At one point, her voice went so high, it squeaked and cracked, leaving Jonathan clutching his side and laughing at her antics.

"They need stability," Lily chimed in. "School gives them discipline. A feeling of purpose. Goals. It will give them an outlet and help us by keeping them on a tight schedule. They'll be more productive members of our group and let's face it, right now they're too young to be going on supply runs or clearing out infected near the fences. This will keep their noses out of trouble."

There was a long, slow pause as the women stopped talking and Jonathan stared them down like a bull ready to charge. He placed his fingertips together, resting his elbows on the desk. "Clearly you've all thought this through," he said. "And you're right. The children aren't much help around here. Sometimes they're a flat-out nuisance."

Lily jerked forward a small inch but kept her lips sealed. One of those *nuisances* he was bashing was her four-year-old daughter. Excuse Sammy for not being able to cook over an open stove just yet.

"But," he continued, "I think this might be a good idea, so long as it doesn't interfere with the flow around here. Any problems, I expect you to handle them." He pointed at Marissa.

She smiled. "Of course. No problem at all."

"So, it's settled then," he huffed, raising his large frame from the small chair. "You can start today. You still have a few hours before lunch. Go round up the kids and get started. And keep Rob out of the kitchen, would you? He loves being around food, but gets underfoot."

"Alright," Marissa jumped in before Colleen could speak. "We'll keep a close eye on him."

Jonathan nodded before walking out of the office. They heard his heavy steps shuffle down the hallway and disappear before they sunk into seats with goofy grins.

"So, our children are a nuisance?" Colleen's skin darkened to a pretty shade of watermelon. "He's going to regret saying that."

"I think we could get the children to come up with a few pranks. Might lighten the mood a little," Marissa suggested.

"So, want to go find a few rooms we can use?" Lily asked.

Marissa's eyes brightened. Of all the women in their group, the little librarian seemed the most excited by the project. "Yes, I know where we can get supplies. And I think I know just what room to use. There's a classroom right next to my bedroom. It used to be Mrs. Butler's old room. That hag was a crabby old bitch, but she decorated and stocked up like a crazy person getting ready for the apocalypse."

Colleen laughed. "Who would have thought the crazy people would end up being right about that?"

"They're probably safe in their steel laced cement made bunkers bingeing on cans of Spam," Lily said.

"Oh, don't say Spam. I'm starving," Marissa wrapped her arms around her flat stomach. "I'd kill for a good home-cooked meal again."

"You mean my Ramen tuna casserole doesn't cut it?" Colleen nudged Marissa's arm.

"Over a steak dinner? Sorry, but no. Now, let's go rally up the children. We've got work to do."

Colleen stretched her arms over her head with a loud yawn. "So, any idea where Roman and Will are? We should try to set up some reading time for the two of them."

"I think Roman would like that. He's a bookish kid. Will… well, we'll have to see. He doesn't strike me as the kind of kid who wants to read. He'd rather be on supply runs," Marissa chimed in.

Lily followed the two women out of the office. "What kind of boy is already so messed up that he'd rather go out shooting infected than stay inside, trying to learn?"

"Probably most of them nowadays," Marissa shrugged.

"Well, we can find them later. Right now, let's get Sammy and Rob. We can pick classrooms and let them help us find supplies," Colleen suggested.

Lily nodded while Marissa stared blankly down the hallway, her mind wandering somewhere, lost in thought. Lily didn't interrupt her.

Sometimes getting lost in your head was the best way to stay sane.

They strolled around a corner to the library, pushing open the door. Sammy crouched over a pile of building blocks, constructing some sort of house on wheels. Rob sat in the corner with his Transformers, crashing them onto a table with squeaky jet noises ringing from his lips.

"Who's ready for school?" Marissa bobbed on the heels of her feet with a small smile.

Sammy jumped to her feet. "Me! I want to play school." She ran to Lily who swept her up in her arms.

"I'll play," Rob said. He jumped from his seat and left the toys on the desk.

"Great, let's go!" Marissa cheered as she marched the group upstairs to the second floor.

"I think this is going to be my classroom." Marissa twisted the doorknob and pushed it open, hustling everyone inside.

Lily set Sammy down so she could explore the small room, but the girl held onto her mother's hand as she stared around like a child at Disney World.

Bright colors splashed over the walls, posters covering so much space they couldn't tell what color the walls were. A bookcase was loaded with bins of supplies. Stacks of books lined another wall.

"My bedroom's down the hall," Marissa said to the children. She glanced down at Sammy. "Want to see it?"

The little girl nodded in excitement. Releasing Lily's hand, she rushed down the hallway and began tugging closed doors, trying to open them.

"The next one, Sammy," Marissa called out.

Sammy rushed to the next door and pushed it open.

She froze. Terror painted over her face. Sammy screamed—a loud shriek that drove fear into the heart of every person in the hallway. Lily rushed toward her daughter, sweeping up the girl in her arms before staring into Marissa's room.

A small moan echoed around the tiny room. An infected's head screeched and moaned a few feet from the doorway. Congealed blackish-red blood glopped and oozed from the base of its neck. Its body laid spread eagle on Marissa's bed. The room seemed to have been ransacked. Books and papers scattered with bloodstains littered across the floor.

"Marissa," Lily warned as she stepped back from the infected's immobile but talkative head.

Sammy buried her head into Lily's neck, small sobs leaking out from her tiny lungs.

Lily cradled her daughter, rocking her gently like she had

was Sammy was a baby. "It's alright, Sammy. It can't move. It's not going to hurt you."

Rob clung to his mother's legs as he watched Marissa take a few ginger steps toward her bedroom.

"What the hell?" she breathed. Her body trembled as she leaned against the doorframe. She pulled a knife out from her boot and stabbed the head through its temple. It twitched once before going quiet. Only the sound of Sammy's sobs echoed around the hallway as Marissa shuffled around the room, checking for any more infected.

"Why?" she said. She paused, staring around the room, trying to soak in all the damage at once. "Why?" she screamed. Grabbing a paperback off a shelf, she tossed it against the infected's body lying on her bed. A loud, grating sob tugged on everyone's nerves as they watched Marissa slump to the ground in a heaving sob. "Who would do this?"

Lily and Colleen glanced at one another. Who would do this?

CHAPTER 20

Colleen walked the children down the stairway to the music room to keep them occupied. It took some coaxing to get Sammy to leave her mother's hip, but she finally agreed when Colleen promised to let her play on the piano.

Lily entered Marissa's destroyed bedroom with caution. If a bomb exploded, it might have left less of a mess. Books were ripped open, pages torn out and scattered all around.

Lily kept slipping from the sheets of paper stuck on top of one another, the congealed blood sticking between the bottoms of her boots and the papers. She shuffled her way over to the bed. The infected had been dead for weeks judging by its decayed skin.

"I can't tell how they got it in here," Lily said. She checked its wrists. No marks. No sort of cuffs. "Maybe with a pole, like the kind they use for dogs on the streets, but they sawed the neck up pretty bad. Butchered it. The skin's shredded. They cut the head off on the bed."

"Fuck!" Marissa shouted, kicked an overturned garbage bin across the room where it banged against a filing cabinet.

"Any idea who might have done this?" Lily asked. She couldn't imagine what it must be like to finally have a private space and have it be so violated. And worse still, this was an inside job. One of their own had done this to Marissa. But who? Why?

Marissa crouched down on the floor, glancing at the scattered papers. "No," she mumbled, standing back up. "I have no idea. I don't know why. I don't know…"

"Well, at least they weren't trying to kill you," Lily shrugged. "They wouldn't have cut off its head if they wanted you dead."

"That makes me feel loads better," Marissa huffed. "Some maniac doesn't want me dead. They just want to scare me so bad I give myself a heart attack. Or run me out of this place."

Lily sighed and scuffled over papers toward the doorway. "Let's get out of here. Maybe we can figure out who did this. But, you need to get out of here."

Marissa trudged over the papers, shaking her downcast head. Her shoulders sagged like someone had dropped the weight of the world plus a decapitated zombie onto her. Her puffy eyes looked raw and scratched as she shuffled down the hallway.

Lily wrapped an arm around her shoulders and steered her into a small teacher's lounge. Though layered with dust, this room was blood, guts, and gore-free. Lily sat Marissa down and opened the mini-fridge.

The stench of rotting lunches hit her nose like a garbage truck. Her eyes watered as she reached for a bottle of water and quickly closed the door, trying to ignore a couple of wriggling maggots near a crumpled paper bag in the bottom drawer.

She twisted off the cap and handed the lukewarm bottle to Marissa. "Drink," she said as she sat down in a puffy, dusty armchair.

Marissa took small sips as she stared at the musky carpet. "Who did this?" she mumbled, glancing up at Lily as if she might have the answer.

Lily shrugged. "I wish I knew. Maybe it'll be best if we figure out for sure who it wasn't and we can narrow it down from there."

"I can't believe anyone would do this." Marissa pressed her palms to her temples and squeezed her eyes shut.

"Neither can I. I don't know who would want to do that to you. But we should start trying to figure out who did it," Lily said. "Obviously, we're out of this. I would say so are the kids, Colleen, Alexa, Grant, Flynn, and Jonathan."

Marissa shook her head. "Right. And I don't think Will or his mother would ever do something like this. He listens to everything she says, and she's always watching out for me on runs. Carly can be a bit of a snob sometimes, but she doesn't have reason to target me specifically. If anything, she'd target you. No offense."

Lily sighed. "None taken. What about Roman?"

"He's just a kid." Marissa defended him, her back straightening up a little like Lily had just offended Marissa's own child.

"Yes, but he's a kid who's lived through hell. Think about it. He's all alone here. No one to keep him grounded. It's easy to lose your mind or think something is just a practical joke and freak everyone out," Lily said.

Marissa shook her head. "No, he's a quiet bookworm. He wouldn't hurt a fly."

"So, what about Sanjay and Raj?" Lily asked. "Those brothers… something about them gets under my skin. Like I wouldn't want to be alone in a room with them. They sort of scare me."

"I don't see why they would want to do something like this?"

"I don't think they wanted to hurt you. I think they just wanted to scare you." Lily shifted in the scratchy seat. A spring dug into her left buttock. "Maybe try to run you out of here?"

"But why me?" Marissa asked. "I know they hate newcomers, but I've been here even longer than they have."

"Maybe they're telling you to stay away from a newcomer here?" Lily pointed to herself, her eyebrow raised in question.

"No, I'd think they make it more obvious if that were the case. Besides, you've been here for a month now," Marissa said.

"But, I think we can agree? It was probably them who did this?" Lily asked. Marissa nodded. "We might not have motives, but we have a few suspects at least."

"But how did they get that thing in my room? How did they know about the boiler room?" Marissa asked.

Lily shrugged. "No one monitors where those two go. You can hear the moaning if you walk past the door. They're not stupid."

Marissa frowned. "No, they're not. Should we go to Jonathan? Tell him what's going on?"

"Not yet. I want to tell Grant and Flynn about this first. See what they think of the situation. Maybe they'll have some idea as to who it might be, for sure. Maybe they've seen something we're missing. Sanjay and Raj don't have a motive. I don't want to jump to conclusions too fast if it's not them."

Marissa nodded. "I'll give you a little time to talk to them. But I'm telling Jonathan after dinner. I'll need a new room. New mattress. New clothes. Fuck!" Marissa threw her bottle across the room, liquid spurting like a water bomb as it hit the wall, falling with a thud.

"Alright. You can stay in my room for now if you—"

"I'm going to the library." Marissa stood on shaky legs and darted out of the room before Lily could stand up from her chair. She'd gone.

*L*ily found her men near the garage, hovering around the broken-down school bus. Sanjay stood beside them with his arms crossed, watching Flynn work.

A sickening shiver racked Lily's spine as she walked a bit closer to their group.

The hood of the bus was propped open. Flynn stood on a small step stool, leaning over to check something under the hood. The upper half of his body disappeared as he bent over the large hood.

His ass in those jeans left Lily's mouth dripping. Damn, he looked good.

Her gaze flickered over to Grant and Sanjay. Sanjay glanced over at Flynn as he spoke with Grant. Lily could have sworn she saw a wicked glint in his eye. Thinking about slamming the hood down on Flynn's back maybe?

Lily shivered. She was probably just seeing things.

No one would want to hurt Flynn. He was one of the few people who could still make people in their camp smile. Sanjay would never...

"Hey, Sugar." Grant beamed at her.

"Hi." She beamed at him as she rushed into his open arms. "Can I talk to you guys?"

"Of course." His gaze shifted to Flynn, who stood up from the hood of the bus.

Flynn jumped down, wiping his grimy hands on his pants. "Is everything okay, Sweetheart? You seem spooked."

She nodded with another fake smile. "Yeah, I'm fine. But can I talk to you both in private?" She didn't look at Sanjay, but he took the hint with a heavy huff as he lifted his assault rifle from the ground and trekked off toward the school.

"What's wrong, Sweetheart?" Flynn asked. His hand reached out to tuck a stray strand of hair behind her ear.

"Something happened to Marissa," Lily said. "Someone left an infected in her room with its head cut off. They destroyed her room. Her clothes. Her books. Everything, it's just gone."

Grant and Flynn froze, staring at her with wide eyes, their jaws shifting as they digested the news.

"What?" Grant growled, releasing her like she'd burst into flames.

"Who did it?" Flynn crossed his arms, staring down at her with a worried spark in those topaz blue eyes.

Lily shrugged. "We don't know for sure. We thought about it and maybe Sanjay or Raj—"

"That son of a bitch." Grant stomped a few steps toward the school.

Flynn blocked his path, grabbing his arm. "Hold on, will you? Lily, are you sure it was them?"

"No," she said. "We're not sure exactly who would do this. Or why. But Marissa's shaken up by it. I don't know why anyone would target her of all people."

"Because, she's a weak target," Grant answered. "A woman alone in a group of people fighting to survive. Pick on the weaklings. I'm sure Sanjay and Raj would know that. We need to leave."

"But it'll be getting dark soon. We can't be caught out in the dark without a safe place nearby. It's too dangerous, and none of us know this area."

"Guys," Lily chimed in.

"Do you think it's any safer to stay here, under the same roof with crazy people who know how to bring in infected? People who have weapons? I'm telling you, we have to get out of here today."

"But, Grant," Lily said.

"I agree that we need to get out of here. Sooner rather than later. But we can gather up supplies today. Stock the bus. I've got it up and running. We can drive right through the front gate. We'll have guns if they try to chase us down. But if we go in the middle of the night, we won't be safe."

"But, I don't think—" Lily said.

"We already know where everything is. We can finish preparing in less than an hour and be on the road with plenty of time before sundown. I'm sure we can find a—"

"Would both you of shut up and listen to me?" Lily yelled, her face reddening the same shade as her wild hair. "I'm not going anywhere. I'm not uprooting Sammy again. No one was hurt."

Flynn sighed. "But, Lily, there's—"

"No, that's it. We don't know who did it. We can work something out, but I am not just going to pack up and leave. No one was hurt. This could have all just been a bad practical joke for all we know."

"No one would joke like this," Grant said. "It's sick."

"I know but—"

"We can leave in the morning. We'll each take shifts tonight and keep guard." Flynn said.

"What part of 'I'm not leaving' did you not understand?" Lily huffed, crossing her arms of the swell of her breasts. "We're staying, and that's final. Now both of you can either help us figure out who did it or keep quiet. But I'm not going anywhere."

Grant and Flynn paused. Grant opened his mouth. "The only tough part will be getting enough food to last us a few—"

"Ahhh!" Lily shouted into the humid air before stalking off.

As she walked past, an infected roamed up to the gate, its hands sticking through the bars, reaching for her.

Lily grabbed a crowbar that had been lying on the ground and swung between the gaps of the fence. With a sickening thud, the crowbar cracked open the infected's skull, its body crumpling to the dirt.

She chucked the crowbar aside and kept walking until she was inside the school. Her mind went hazy as anger pulsed through her veins in time with her heartbeat. Her feet kept moving, though she didn't know where she was going. She couldn't feel herself walking. She couldn't feel anything. Except anger.

After a few minutes, she found herself standing in front of the boiler room door, the soft, creaking sounds of death shuffling behind the metal door.

"Ahhh!" she shouted again, her fist punching into the metal, not even making a dent. She felt weak.

Small slivers of pain shot up her hand.

It felt good.

She punched again, the moaning growing louder. Something hit against the other side of the door, punching back. She hit it again. Half a dozen bangs on the other side followed. She teased the infected, hammering her fists on the door like Sammy used to when she had tantrums.

Bang! Bang! Bang! Bang! Bang!

The moaning grew louder, dull thuds sounding on the other side.

"Fuck you!" she shouted at the door before shuffling off.

CHAPTER 22

*L*ily rested her hands on the cold, wet tiles of the shower. Small checkered marks indented into her skin as she pressed her hands tighter, letting the muscles in her arms and shoulders fatigue. Cool water splashed onto the top of her head, rushing in small rivers down wet locks of hair, pooling around her feet.

Tired. She hadn't felt so tired in so long.

She was tired of arguing. Tired of running. Tired of scavenging. Tired of being strong every day for her daughter's sake. Tired of dealing with stubborn men who wouldn't listen.

She ran her hands over her wet hair, letting the last bits of greasy conditioner rinse out before picking up a bar of soap.

"Lily, are you in here?" Flynn's voice bounced around the walls of the women's locker room.

"I'm in here," Lily shouted through the gauzy plastic curtain.

"Um, is anyone else in there with you? I'm coming in."

The tentative pause in his voice almost made her laugh.

The apocalypse was here, and he was still worried about modesty.

"I'm alone," she said. She heard the soft padding of his boots on the tiled floor, stopping near her closed curtain.

His hand reached through the crease between the wall and curtain, pulling it back slowly.

Lily's hands roamed over her body, bar of soap in hand. Small, white suds trailed over her skin, goosebumps rising as a rush of cool air swept through the shower stall.

"I didn't know I was missing such a great show." Flynn smirked as he leaned against the wall. His gaze followed her hands as they moved over the delicate curves of her creamy skin. Water trickled down her, washing away the suds.

"You don't deserve a show after what you and Grant did earlier. You wouldn't even listen." Lily turned away, trying to ignore him. Her body couldn't ignore him, though. A sticky wetness was already pooling between her legs. Her heart thumped harder in her chest, her nipples tightening under his fiery gaze.

"Aw, now Lily, don't be like that, Sweetheart. We love you. We're just trying to protect you." He tucked his hands in his pockets, staring down at his shoes. His face gave away his guilt, like a kid who had his hand caught in the cookie jar.

"I was able to protect myself just fine until you came along," she snapped. She wanted to fight. Wanted to argue, but her blood had cooled enough from the shower. She didn't need another fight right now. She needed peace.

"You're right. But, I needed you. Even back then, I knew there was something about you. I needed you with me, Lily. You. Sammy. You were all I had. I was just getting by, and suddenly I found the two of you, and I had a purpose again. I needed to keep you both safe. You. Sammy. Grant. You guys are everything to me."

A mix of emotions flickered across his face. Happy. Melancholy. Guilt. But most of all, sincerity.

"I love you." The words spilled from her lips without her brain realizing what she was saying. She meant it. She didn't need to think about it. She really, truly loved him, and Grant. But, she'd wait to talk to him. He needed to cool off even more than she did tonight.

"I love you too, Sweetheart," Flynn echoed back.

A long pause followed, the two of them locked eyes on one another. A small hum of electricity filled the air between them, threatening to spark at any moment.

"Why are you still dressed?" she asked, nodding toward the shower. She crooked her finger at him and beckoned him to join her inside.

A mischievous grin broke over Flynn's face like a crack in a mirror. He gripped the hem of his shirt, lifting it over his head in one swift movement.

Lean muscle rolled under tanned skin as Flynn tossed his shirt to the floor beside him.

His large hands fumbled with his belt buckle and zipper before tugging his pants down his legs, kicking them off with his boots.

He'd gone commando.

His topaz eyes burned with a hungry spark that ignited a fire low in Lily's belly.

In three strides, he closed the gap between them and slid the shower curtain closed.

His hands slid under her jaw. His rough fingers cupped her neck with tenderness as he tilted her head upward to face him. His lips fell on hers. Their kiss grew wetter as the cool water sprayed over them. Droplets of water streamed down his hair, splashing onto her skin.

Lily shivered against him, his hot skin melding against her. Her hands wrapped around his waist, half of his body still dry, the other half dripping wet and warm. She pressed her body closer to him, sinking into his delicious kiss. Her sensitized nipples pressed into his hard chest. His tongue danced with hers, letting her mind slip away from her tiredness, away from the anger, and into something more comfortable.

A small ache between her legs grew into a hot and heavy need. Her body sagged against him as he leaned her back against the cold tile, a chill spreading through her back, his pulsing heat warming her front.

His hand traced a faint line from the column of her neck, over her collar to her chest. She moaned as his thick fingers spread over her breast, squeezing it with tenderness. Her nipple beaded against his palm, sending sharp tingles of awareness to her pussy.

Flynn sank slowly to his knees, his lips tracing a path down her chest, down her stomach, stopping just below her navel. His hand coasted down her body, leaving her breast. His fingernails traced faint lines that followed the path of his lips.

His hand gripped her thighs, tugging them wider.

"Flynn, I..." Lily gasped as he leaned forward, his hot tongue licking her clit. Her mind went blank, slipping out of reality as her body honed in on the pleasure that consumed her. Sparks tingled from her pussy, shooting up her body like fireworks. "Flynn," she moaned.

She reached down, tangling in his mess of dark hair between her thighs. Her hips arched closer to him, begging him for more.

He gave her more.

His hand coasted over the delicate flesh of her creamy inner thigh, climbing higher until his fingers pressed against her wet opening. He slid a finger inside her, eliciting small gasps and murmurs from her throat. He smiled against her pussy lips as his tongue continued to taste and explore her.

Lily groaned, her hips bucking against his hand as his finger slipped in and out of her pussy, fucking her slowly. Before her mind could get a grip on the sensations flooding through her, he slid a second finger inside her.

"Fuck!" Lily's head laid against the cool tile, cold water trickling over her breasts, down her stomach, dripping into his hair like some unholy baptism.

Need pulsed through her, hot and thick. An orgasm was already rising to meet her, cresting over her like a tsunami wave, ready to drown her in heat and pleasure.

"Please," she begged.

Flynn's tongue flicked harder. His fingers fucked her faster and her shout of pleasure bounced around the walls, ringing like a gong. Her body flung itself into the wave, letting herself drown in sensation and pleasure and ultimate satisfaction. She quivered, his hand and head keeping her body upright as she trembled against the shower tiles, her body wringing every ounce of pleasure it could from her. Her pussy gushed warm liquid down his hand, drenching her thighs.

"Flynn," she whimpered.

He leaned back, a satisfied smirk stuck on his face. "That's it, Sweetheart."

He slipped his fingers from her aching pussy. A cold emptiness filled her, making her shiver again.

He rose in front of her, his hard body towering over, dripping wet like a wicked water god. His triumphant smirk left her shaking again, another dull ache pulsing between her legs.

He reached out to her, but she stepped to the side, kneeling on wobbly legs until her face was level with his groin.

His hard, thick cock dripped with cool water. The tuft of hair above it glistened with dampness, like a sinful invitation.

She licked her lips once before leaning forward, engulfing the head of his cock into her warm mouth.

"Yes," Flynn groaned above her.

His hand reached down and tangled in her damp locks of hair as his hips bucked forward, driving his cock another inch deeper inside her mouth.

Lily slid her tongue around the head of him. Her tongue lingered on the underside of his cock for a moment before sucking him deeper into her mouth. His encouraging groans released a fire inside her belly. Her hands reached around him, her fingertips pressing into the tight muscles of his buttocks, keeping him still.

Her head bobbed up and down, sinking him deeper and deeper inside her hot mouth. Her tongue flicked over the head of his cock as she pulled back, a thick drop of pre-cum oozing from the tip. She swirled it around her tongue.

"God damn, Sweetheart." His dark voice shook her like an earthquake.

Need bubbled in her blood again, hot and consuming. His cock drove out all thought from her mind. She focused on his pleasure, on the taste of him, on the feel of his skin beneath her fingertips.

"Yes!" He pulled his cock from her mouth, his fingers twisting in her hair to keep her still. "Up. Now."

Lily rose on shaky legs, her gaze meeting his. His blue eyes danced with an icy fire. His lips set in a firm line, tense and ready to break.

He gripped her by the shoulders and twisted her around. "Hands on the wall."

His rough voice sent her excitement higher.

"Please," she moaned, bending forward and resting her palms against the cool ceramic tiles.

Flynn slid his thick shaft between the dripping folds of her pussy, the friction creating delicious tingles through Lily's body. Cold water trickled down the curve of her back. He pressed his swollen cockhead against her entrance, waiting.

She shimmied her hips against him, trying to coax him to sink deep inside her warmth.

With a heavy grunt, Flynn pushed his cock inside her warm body. He groaned as he slipped his cock out an inch and thrust forward again, jerking Lily forward as he stretched her.

Lily's mind swam as she focused on the fullness, the achy need tugging at every muscle in her body. Flynn slid from her, leaving her pussy empty and hungry for him. As he slammed his cock back inside her, she yelped, the fullness, the pleasure, consuming her.

His hand gripped her hip, holding her steady as he began to fuck her with slow, smooth movements, each one drawing more pleasure from her than the last.

"Flynn," she whimpered as his hand reached around her, slipping between her legs. His rough fingers found the sensitive nub of her clit, leaving her panting as he teased her. Her pussy throbbed with excitement, her orgasm building to a heady rush as his fingers moved faster, his hips thrusting harder.

"No," he growled into her ear, tearing his hand away before slipping his cock from her wet cunt.

Lily shivered from the emptiness, and the cold, and the confusion. She turned to stare at him.

His eyes were dark, like a summer storm cloud. His chest rose and fell like a trapped animal, ready to fight. His cock glistened with her excitement, almost dripping from the tip.

His hands reached under her, lifting her until she could wrap her legs around his waist. His fingertips dug into the soft flesh of her ass. "I want to watch you come." His lips fell on her in a demanding kiss as he lowered her body down, impaling her on his cock again. He stepped closer to the wall, resting her back against the cold tile.

A wicked shiver rushed through her as he heated her front, the tile cooling her back. Her damp hair stuck in thick, wet locks around her face and neck, sending rivulets of water down her breasts and stomach, disappearing where their bodies met.

Flynn slipped his cock farther out of her just as she rose. Her arms rested on his broad shoulders, wrapped around his neck.

Lily shook as she fell back onto him, his cock sinking deeper, filling her so deep it almost hurt. The dull aching pain mixed with her pleasure as her orgasm built back up again. Sparks of pleasure set off like sparklers along the base of her spine, lighting up the rest of her body.

She moaned his name over and over with each hard thrust, the sound bouncing off the shower walls. The slick sound of skin slapping skin, the pulsing beat of the water splashing over them, the hard grunting of the sexy man beneath her, hell-bent on forcing her body to cum.

It was overwhelming.

Lily shouted his name as she buried her head into the crux of his shoulder. She cried, her body convulsing over him. Her pussy squeezed him as his cock began to throb and pulse heavy inside her.

"Lily! Yes, Sweetheart. That's it. God, yes." His dirty words of encouragement stretched her orgasm out as he twitched one last time inside her.

Her body softened against him as his limbs trembled from exhaustion.

With tender ease, he set her down. Both of them sinking

to the shower floor as water sprinkled over their heads and chests.

Flynn stroked her upper arm, her head resting on his bare shoulder. Drops of cool water dripped from the tips of her hair, splashing against his chest and along the gym floor. "I love you, Sweetheart." His deep voice wrapped around her like a lullaby.

Lily sunk deeper against his chest. "I love you, too."

"Sweetheart, you need to talk to Grant," he said. "You can't just ignore what happened."

"No." She shook her head, droplets flinging from her hair as she straightened up. "He's stubborn. I did nothing wrong. He doesn't get to control me and tell me how to live my life just because he thinks he knows what's best. I know what's best for us and I—"

"Okay. Alright, calm down." Flynn raised his hands in front of him as though he was fending off her words. "I only meant you two need to discuss what happened. The words and tone you use are up to you. But you both need to talk to one another. Tell him what you're feeling, what's on your mind, and allow him the same courtesy. Listen to what he's saying. Sometimes you get a bit defensive, Sweetheart."

"I do not." She scowled.

He smirked. "My point exactly."

Lily opened her mouth to spit back a response, but sealed her lips shut instead. No point in arguing anymore. Flynn had apologized.

Anger still simmered under the surface, but Lily was too physically tired to bother. She yawned, exhaustion tugging at her senses, trying to pull her eyes closed. "I don't want to talk tonight. I'm tired."

"Alright." Flynn stood up. "But, promise me you'll talk tomorrow."

Lily nodded. She stepped out of the shower and toweled herself dry, slipping into a fresh set of clothes. She tossed the damp towel to Flynn, letting him dry off before slipping back into his jeans. He tucked his shirt into his back pocket, letting droplets of water fall from his hair, running down his bare chest.

They strolled hand-in-hand out of the gym and back up to their room.

In their bedroom, Grant sat on the mattress with a small smile on the corners of his lips while he watched Sammy play with her Barbie doll. Warmth floated in his chocolate brown eyes like golden honey.

Lily's heart and anger melted just a little bit more.

Flynn strolled in and nodded at Grant when he glanced up at him. Grant nodded back but said nothing. Some of the warmth vanished from his eyes as his gaze shifted to Lily as she stepped inside the room and locked the door behind her.

Flynn pulled a couple of desks over and piled them in front of the door as a makeshift barrier between them and whatever lunatic was still walking around in the school planting decapitated zombies in people's bedrooms.

"Sammy, it's time for bed," Lily said.

The four-year-old shook her head no, a big yawn stretching her lips. "But, I'm not tired."

"I know, but sometimes we still have to go to bed, even if we're not tired. How about I read you a story?" she suggested.

Sammy's eyes brightened. She flung herself from the floor and scurried into her closet-sized bedroom. "This one!" she shouted, waving an illustrated copy of *Beauty and the Beast*.

Lily's heart fluttered as excitement poured over Sammy's face. Her happiness was infectious. The men sat on the mattress, watching as Lily strolled over and tucked Sammy into her bed before cracking open the book.

"Once upon a time…" she began.

Her soft voice lilted a little bit higher, moving in a smooth, steady beat. She used to act out characters, exaggerating her voice. But tonight, she wanted Sammy to sleep. They could all use some rest after the day's chaos. Before Belle had changed into her golden gown, Sammy's eyes fluttered shut, her breathing slow and steady as she drifted off to sleep.

Lily rose, careful not to wake her daughter and she closed the door most of the way, leaving a small crack open. She stripped off her shoes and climbed into bed, sandwiched between Grant and Flynn. She turned her back to Grant, pressing against his chest.

She might still be angry with him, but that didn't mean she loved him any less. Before she could whisper goodnight, she fell asleep.

CHAPTER 23

"Changing of the guard." Lily sat beside Alexa on the front steps of the school. The sum-warmed stone steps heated her buttocks and thighs as she yanked up the cargo shorts she'd borrowed from Flynn. She wiggled as she watched the fence. "Anything weird going on out here?"

Alexa shrugged before handing over the sharpened pipe. "Nope. Just another calm day in paradise. Hey, have you seen Carly? Jonathan was asking for her before I came out here this morning. No one's seen her all day."

Lily shook her head, worry dropping into her stomach like a lead ball. "No, but I'll keep an eye out."

"I hate fence duty," Alexa murmured.

"I don't mind it," Lily said as she took the weapon. "It's kind of peaceful on a quiet night."

Alexa laughed. "Stabbing infected in the head is relaxing to you? Maybe you should talk to Jonathan the psychologist about anger issues."

Lily shook her head. "No anger issues. I'm a calm redhead."

Alexa's laugh stirred the summer air. "I bet Flynn and

Grant would say otherwise. All redheads think they're calm. They think they're the exception to the rule. Even Colleen. I've seen her go ballistic because I forgot to rinse off the plates before putting them in a dishwasher. Like, complete DEFCON one."

She paused before breaking into a smile. "You know, I can always tell right before she gets mad." Alexa threw her hands up in the air to imitate Colleen. "She does this and shouts 'Are you kidding me!' every time, just before she flies off the handle."

Lily giggled. "Well, your redhead has a bit of a temper," she teased. "Just a couple of weeks ago, I heard her screaming from the third floor. I could hear her all the way in the kitchen."

"That wasn't from anger. I'm just that good." Alexa winked and rose from her seat.

Lily shook her head with an easy smile. "Well, go enjoy your night. I've got the fence covered until sunrise."

Alexa nodded at her before disappearing through the front doors.

The front door shut, closing with a heavy click. No one else was around.

Lily carefully pulled a small pistol and silencer from her a side pocket of Flynn's shorts. She attached the suppressor to the end of the barrel and stared at the fence. Waiting.

Beyond the fence, the bushes stood still while the tree branches danced in the evening wind. Streaks of orange faded along the treetops as the sun set behind her, darkness threatening to cover her like a blanket. Overgrown grass rippled like a sea of green waves, splattered with weeds and fallen tree limbs.

After an hour of sitting and watching, boredom began to settle in her chest like a bad cold.

Lily stood and roamed across the field. She watched the

trees from around the corner of the school, the summer haze making the trees ripple like a desert mirage in her view. A small cluster of birds cawed and flew away.

Something was out there.

Lily began to whistle "Take Me Out to the Ball Game" as she waited, wondering what was just beyond the fence. Her fingers itched to unlock the gate and explore beyond the fence, but she knew it was better to wait.

She didn't have to wait long.

An infected stumbled out from a bush, fifty paces from the gate.

She stopped whistling and pointed her gun at its head, dropping the pipe to her side. The heavy metal thunked against the baked dirt and rolled behind her as she aimed through the sight. The infected's head wobbled between the two lines in her vision. She squeezed the trigger.

Pop!

The infected's shoulder jerked back as it continued to hobble toward her. She could hear its moans now as it drew nearer to the school.

She raised the gun, the weight pulling her arms down a bit as she fought to keep her hands steady. She peered through the sight, the infected's head swaying just over the line.

Pop!

"Damn," she murmured as the infected kept moving. She missed entirely.

Lily raised the gun again, her arms stiff as she braced herself for the kick. Ready. Aim. Fire.

Pop!
Pop!
Pop!

"Are you fucking kidding me?" Lily asked the infected as it continued to hobble toward her, so close to the fence its hands struck through the bars. Four bullets were lodged in its rotting flesh, thick blood oozing from the wounds.

Lily lifted the gun again, her shoulders sore and stiff as she took a step back from the infected, aiming at close range.

Click.

The magazine was empty.

"Fucker," Lily said. To the gun or the infected, she wasn't sure.

She bent down and grasped the pipe in her hand. She stuffed the gun back into her pocket. The metal pipe warmed her aching hands as she raised it and slid the sharpened edge into the infected's skull, right between the eyes. The skull resisted, then sucked in the pipe with a stomach-churning slurp.

She jerked the pipe back and watched the corpse crumple to the ground. Lily crouched down and carefully examined the dead body through the fence, poking at it with the bloody end of the pipe.

Two shoulder wounds. One leg wound. One stomach wound.

If it had been human, it would have been dead with that first shot. But killing an infected called for precision. Kill the brain, kill the beast.

Lily sat back and crossed her legs on the hard dirt as she stared at the corpse. How could she defend her daughter if she couldn't even aim?

A soft moan echoed farther down the fence, slowly making its way closer to her. The infected's mouth stretched down, a guttural groaning making Lily's stomach churn in disgust.

The body hobbled closer, its tattered police uniform stained red and brown. Even the officer's badge wouldn't shine with the layer of dirt caked over it. The infected stopped in front of her, its arms reaching for her through the bars.

Lily stared up at it, watching it in amusement as it tried in vain to push itself through the iron bars. Its jaws snapped at her like a rabid dog.

She rose to her feet and slid the pipe through the infected's right eye, the sickening pop churning her stomach again.

Death was a nasty thing.

She watched the officer fall to the ground on top of the first corpse, and for the first time, she wondered what happened to these creatures once they died.

Dampness smeared her cheeks as she wiped her eyes with her forearm.

"Fucker," she mumbled and turned to go sit back on the school steps and keep watch.

Fence duty. She hated it.

CHAPTER 24

*L*ily opened the door to their room, the hinges creaking as she stepped inside. Her gaze locked on Grant, who bolted upright from the bed, his hand reaching for the gun he kept beside him. His body relaxed as she closed the door, his gaze roaming over her.

"I thought you had school," he said.

"Oh, look, he speaks. It only took you two days to talk to me," Lily huffed. "At least it's a step up from bashing me over the head with a stick and dragging me back to your cave."

Grant flinched. "Okay, I get it. You're angry."

"You're damn right I'm still mad at you. You don't get to tell me what to do." Lily crossed her arms, staring down at him.

His gaze roamed up her body, his stare tracing the curves of her calves, up the swell of her hips, the dip in her waist, the delicate column of her neck, and finally reaching her eyes.

Suddenly the room felt too small for the two of them. His gaze left her feeling naked, exposed, and tingling in places she didn't want to think about right now. She was still mad at him, damn it.

"I need some fresh air." She opened the door again.

"Good idea. I'll come with you. Grab a gun and a few suppressors." He nodded toward the half a dozen handguns in the corner of the room near their bed.

"What?"

"I'm going to teach you to shoot. You need practice." He stood, towering over her as he squeezed past her, out the door.

The guns on the table all looked different. Different sizes. Different weights.

She grabbed a light one and another one that felt like it had some weight but she could grip the handle easily. She checked that the safety was on before pocketing them both in a spare holster. She grabbed a few of the silencers and tucked them in her holster too.

She left her bedroom and followed Grant outside without saying a word.

The sunshine warmed their shoulders as they strolled past their car, past the garage, past the bus.

Sanjay was loading the bus up with some supplies now that it was running. He glanced up at them but went back to slinging duffle bags into the back of the vehicle.

"I wonder what he's up to," Lily said.

"Jonathan told him and Raj to get the bus ready for any emergency now that it's running again."

"Where are we going? Won't we attract infected if we shoot outside?" Lily crunched a twig beneath her boot as she quickened her pace to keep up with him.

"We're going to the woodshop. If we close the door, it will be quiet enough."

Lily shrugged. "If you say so."

They strolled past brown grass and patches of weeds

before coming up to what looked like a small, red brick house. The word "Shop" hung on a sign in burnt letters, gently waving back and forth in the breeze.

The open door creaked as Grant pushed it wider, gun drawn in front of him. He stepped inside, glancing from side to side, checking the corners. He flicked the safety back on as he yelled, "clear."

Lily walked inside, shutting the door behind her. The dirty room was covered with sawdust and dried mud. Hand tools were neatly placed along the walls, each one in its proper place, all outlined by a thin line from a permanent marker. Workbenches were neatly lined up along two-thirds of the room, the front section designated for specialty tools.

Grant glanced around, pointing to a wall. "We'll set up over there. No windows." He moved a sawhorse over and set up a plank of wood to act as a table. He grabbed a couple of cans that rattled, probably full of nuts and bolts and screws. He placed five different sized coffee cans on top of the wood.

"So, ready to shoot?" he asked, stepping back across the room toward her. He picked up two sets of clear goggles from a bench and handed one to her as he slipped on a pair.

"You tell me," she said.

She pulled the foggy goggles over her eyes. She tugged the guns and suppressors out of the holster and set them up on the nearest workbench.

Grant pulled out two packs of earplugs and gave one to her. They stuffed the tiny pieces of foam into their ears, muffling the sounds around them.

Grant glanced at the guns and frowned. "The Smith & Wesson has a hard kickback." He picked up the lighter hand-gun and attached the silencer to it.

"So, is that the Smith & Wesson?" Lily nodded toward the heavier gun on the table.

Grant shook his head. "No, that's a CZ. You'll probably shoot better with that one at first."

"But it's so heavy."

"Yes, but it doesn't kick as hard. This one," he held the Smith & Wesson up higher. "This one might be a bit tough for you to shoot. It's small, so it's a bit more difficult to get a firm grip. And the kickback is harder, so you're more likely to slam yourself in the face when you fire this."

He placed the gun back down on the table. "Let's start with the CZ. You can try mine after that. It falls somewhere in the middle of those two. It's a Glock. We'll see how you feel after that one if you want to try the Smith & Wesson."

"Alright." Lily picked up the CZ in her hands and pointed it out in front of her.

"Hold on, put it down for a second. Is it loaded? Is the safety on?" he asked.

Lily checked and nodded before she placed the gun back on the table.

"First, if we don't put a silencer on it, we'll have a horde coming down on us from a mile away." He yanked and pulled on some parts of the gun before attaching a silencer.

"Here's the safety." He flicked a tiny switch on the side of the gun. "So, now the safety is on. Now, to see if the gun's loaded, you pull this back." He pulled the top of the gun back, revealing an empty chamber. "And let's see if the magazine is empty." He popped open the magazine from the handle of the gun. It was empty.

"Always treat a gun like it's loaded. Be careful and check to see if the safety's on. Otherwise, you could end up shooting yourself or someone else if you're not careful." He pulled out a box of bullets from his pocket.

"Now, here's how you load a magazine." He showed her how to press and slide in each bullet until the magazine was full. "Then you just slid it back into place. And you'll hear it and feel it click." He slammed the magazine back into the handle.

Something about the metal and the clicking and the weight of the weapon sent a thrill down Lily's spine. Her skin tingled, her nerves waking up and ready to try something new.

Something exciting.

"So, the gun's live now. First thing to remember, keep your finger off the trigger." He placed the gun on the workbench with the barrel facing toward the cans and stepped behind her.

Lily picked it back up, keeping her finger against the side of the gun and away from the trigger.

"Good. Relax your elbows a little. You don't want to lock your elbows, or the recoil is going to hurt your shoulders. You want a firm grip, but you don't have to hold it too tight that your knuckles turn white. Now, lean into it and look through the sight. Aim. Deep breath. When you're ready, fire."

Lily took a long, slow breath, looking through the sight. The "O" on the Folgers coffee can slid into focus. She tried her best to hold the gun steady. Another long, slow breath. She pulled the trigger.

Pop!

The gun lifted a few inches upwards, her arms jerking up with it. The clang of metal on metal bounced around the room. Lily's ears rang, her body shaking with aftershocks from the shot.

"Whoa," she breathed.

"Not bad. You hit it," he said, pointing over to a Maxwell House can that had a couple of small metal pieces sliding through the hole.

"But, I was aiming for the can next to it," she sighed.

"Well, try again," he said.

His voice grated on her nerves. Anger still simmered beneath the surface. They hadn't resolved their problems, and unless he learned to back off and trust her, she doubted that would be a problem she could get past.

He was over-protective, bordering on controlling.

And she would never let anyone control her. She wasn't a circus animal.

Pop!

The gun jerked again, but this time she was ready. Her feet were firmly planted in place. Her arms raised higher. Her body stayed tighter, relaxing her grip on the gun. As the bullet released, some of her anger shot out with it.

She lowered her arms back down and aimed again.

Pop!

"Nice going, Calamity Jane. You hit the Folgers can that time."

"Good." She smirked, leaning in for another shot. *Bang! Bang!* She shot until the gun clicked, the magazine empty.

"Want to try the Glock next?" He attached another silencer to the Glock and double-checked to be sure it wasn't loaded. He went through the same routine as before. Safety. Chamber. Magazine. Sight. Ready. Aim. Fire.

Pop!

The lighter gun jumped like a live wire in her hand. She tightened her grip as the muzzle of the gun tilted back down. The sound boomed in her ears, rattling around in her skull. Shooting without earplugs in must be horrible.

"So, how'd you do?" he asked, watching her reaction.

A small hole pierced the center of the O. "I got it!" she shouted in excitement, beaming up at him.

A moment later, she remembered she was supposed to be mad at him. She frowned and squared her shoulders, getting ready to aim again. She aimed for the X on another

Maxwell House can. Whoever the shop teacher had been, they sure liked their coffee.

After three more shots, she hit the X dead center. She shot until the magazine was empty and her arms ached from the effort of trying to control the kick of the gun each time. Her heart thrummed in her chest like a wild animal throwing itself against a cage.

"Want to try the Smith & Wesson?" he asked, pulling out another box of bullets. "This gun takes a different type of ammo." He lifted a small bullet from the cardboard box. "This is a nine-millimeter round. Powerful enough to shoot a zombie's eye out the back of its skull." He loaded up another magazine with bullets and clicked it into the light handgun.

"Safety off," he said, placing the gun down in front of her, facing downrange toward the cans.

She picked up the gun, nervous adrenaline pumping through her. The Glock had been hard to shoot. She tightened her grip, loosened her elbows, and leaned in for the kick.

Pop!

The gun lifted over her head with her arms still holding on for dear life. "Damn," she muttered, the bullet nicking the side of a can.

"Well, you blew its ear off," Grant shrugged.

"Great. Because if an infected is deaf, that'll stop it." Lily rolled her eyes and flicked the safety on. She put the gun back down on the workbench and turned to face him.

His large body towered over her. His eyes glinted like chocolate diamonds in the sunlight piercing through the windows. Suddenly there wasn't enough oxygen in the room.

"I need some air," she huffed.

"Alright," he said, stepping aside.

Lily yanked off the goggles and pulled the foam pieces

from her ears, resting them on a bench. She wandered out the door toward a small cluster of trees behind the building. The still, humid air clung to her like a second skin, sweat trickling down her neck, between her breasts, damping her hairline.

"You alright?" Grant asked, moving beside her.

"I'm fine," she snapped.

Grant gripped her upper arm swinging her around to face him. "Stop it. I know you're pissed off at me. Now, get it all out. None of this 'fine' bullshit you're pulling."

"Fuck you!" She yanked her arm from his grip. "You don't get to tell me what to do!"

"When? Right now? Or only when you're about to keep us here, where we're in danger and living with a lunatic. Your daughter is living with a crazy person. How safe is she?"

"You don't like it here," she spat. "You wanted to leave since the first day we got here. You can't stand the idea of finding a place to settle down again."

"Because this isn't going to work." His voice rose higher. "Maybe if you opened your eyes, you'd see that. We just strolled in here. What makes you think a larger group won't find this place and run us out? What makes you think they won't kill us for this shithole?"

"We can fight," she huffed.

"Or we could die," he said.

She rolled her eyes. "You're so dramatic. You just have to be right all the time. What makes you think we won't die out there trying to find your precious refugee camp?"

"We're not trapped out there. We're not stuck behind a small fence in a small building with an old man leading us, and a crazy person leaving corpses in our bedroom."

"We can figure out who did that and take care of it. We're not leaving because of one person's practical joke."

"How do you know that was a joke?" he asked. "How do

you know that wasn't a threat? A warning? Jonathan is supposed to be in charge and he hasn't done a damn thing to figure out who did it. We need to leave."

"We're staying!" She stomped her foot.

"Fucking stubborn woman." He leaned down and captured her lips against his, pressing hard, almost bruising them in punishment.

His lips seared against hers, possessive and hungry. Anger hummed in the air between them like music. His hand snaked up, wrapping her ponytail around his wrist, and held her head in place, tilting her face up higher.

Her heart thumped in her chest like a wild animal breaking out of its cage. Heat and need pulsed through her veins.

Her hands gripped his back, fingertips digging into the fabric of his tight t-shirt. She yanked, pulling it up higher until her fingers touched his flesh, her nails raking along his back in long, thin lines.

He growled, his lips lowering to her throat. The rough stubble along his jaw scratched her skin. His body overpowered hers, pushing her backward until her spine pressed against a tree trunk.

The dull ache along her back mixed with his wicked tongue, tracing small circles along the sensitive skin of her neck. A strong pulse throbbed between her thighs. She needed him inside her.

She gripped his shirt and tugged it up over his head, dropping it to the ground beside them. Her fingers fumbled for his buckle, tugged it open, and pulled down the zipper on his pants.

His hand skimmed the top of her shorts, dipping lower. He yanked, the fabric tightening to accommodate him as he reached down and explored. The tip of his middle finger teasing her clit.

She whimpered, the sound piercing the air around them. Her hand shook as she slipped his pants down around his muscled thighs, his stiff cock sticking out toward her, begging for her touch. Grant hissed as her hand wrapped around him, her fingers slipping up and down the hard shaft.

Grant released her. His fingers fumbled with the button on her pants before popping them open. He yanked the fabric down her legs before standing back up.

Lily kicked her shorts to the side, standing in front of him with just a shirt and her boots.

"I need you. Fuck me." She challenged him. Hot anger and desire and lust ignited every particle of air between them until a burning need consumed her.

Her hands gripped his shoulders, her nails digging into his skin. Her body hummed, ready for him. Dampness stuck to her thighs, small droplets mixing with sweat and trickling between her legs.

His eyes pierced her, hardening as he watched her squirm under his gaze.

Her legs trembled from the effort of standing upright. She knew just what would drive him over the edge. Her hands traced up her stomach before cupping her breasts through her shirt. She yanked down the top of her shirt, her breasts falling free from the wide-open collar.

"Fuck," Grant growled, his cock twitching between them.

"Please, Grant. Fuck me," Lily begged again.

Her fingers tugged at her stiff nipples. She cupped her breasts, feeling their weight in her hands. Her head lolled back as small sparks of sensation mixed with the need aching between her legs.

Grant stepped closer, gripping her thighs and lifting her into the air with ease. His fingertips dug into her ass as he shifted between them, his cock nudging against the wet entrance of her pussy.

He impaled her with his hard cock in one deep thrust.

"Fuck," she shouted in the air as he filled her, almost splitting her body in two.

He plunged into her, quick and deep, his body not stopping to let her adjust.

"Take it," he growled in her ear. His hips slammed into her over and over again, as he buried himself as deep as her body would allow.

Her mind lost to the pain and pleasure swirling like a hurricane inside her. Her breasts bounced in time with his thrusts. His gaze shifted lower, watching her breasts move with him. Her nails dug into his shoulders as she fought to keep her body upright.

Lily leaned back and gripped the tree trunk, holding her upper body to the tree behind her. Grant growled, his gaze glued to her large breasts, swaying with each hard thrust.

"Please," Lily whimpered. She was so close, but she needed more.

Grant's thrusts quickened. His hand coasted lower. He touched her, his gentle fingers moving in a slow rhythm over her clit.

"Yes, fuck yes," she moaned. Pleasure consumed her like fire, about to explode. His fingers quickened along with his thrusts.

"Fuck," Grant grunted, spilling himself deep inside her. His cock pulsed inside her, stretching her further.

"Grant!" she shouted as an orgasm ripped through her. The feel of his cum releasing inside her mixed with the intense pulses throughout her body, dragging her into heaven. Color exploded in shards of light behind her eyes as pleasure washed over her.

"Grant," she whimpered as he pulled himself from her body as her orgasm faded into aftershocks.

With careful ease, he set her down on her feet until she

was steady enough to stand. He grabbed her shorts and helped her slip them back into place as her mind still swirled in the afterglow of her intense orgasm. He adjusted her shirt, covering up her chest again before putting his pants back on. He tucked his shirt into one of the pockets and slumped down against the tree. He patted the ground beside him, asking her to sit.

They panted, both of them trying to catch their breaths, the still air around them choking them a little. "Fuck," Grant groaned, running his hand through his hair.

"Yeah," Lily murmured. She rested her head on his shoulder just above his tattoo, his chest still gleaming with droplets of sweat like diamond chips on his skin. Earth and sex perfumed the air. Why couldn't the rest of the world be this peaceful? This satisfying?

"I love you, Sugar." Grant slid a fingertip up and down her arm as he spoke, the soft words tickling her.

"I love you, too." She closed her eyes and just let the moment sink into her mind. Something happy to remember for the rough times ahead.

"If you want to stay, we'll stay. But I want to find out which freak is setting infected lose in this place. I won't sleep under the same roof as a madman."

Lily shifted, glancing up at him.

Madman. Infected.

Reality crept back into her skin like a parasite and shivers slithered down her spine. "Alright. Thank you."

"I'll do whatever I can to keep you and Sammy safe." He planted a gentle kiss on the top of her head. "I love you both. I'd never let anything hurt either of you."

"I love you. And I'm sure Sammy does, too." She smiled at him, thinking of how happy her daughter had been since Grant and Flynn came into their lives. She finally had a father figure to look up to and teach her things. Two of them. Two amazing men.

"Even though I'm not Flynn Rider?" he teased.

Lily laughed. "So, Flynn told you about how we met?"

He chuckled, the rich sound settling her belly like a warm bowl of soup on a snowy day. "Yeah. You have some nerve, going up against a guy with a sword while you were armed with just a candlestick."

"I thought he was going to hurt Sammy," she said. "I mean, now I know how wrong I was about him. But, still, I wasn't about to let a stranger near her."

"I understand, Sugar. I'm only teasing. So, does Sammy have any nicknames for me?" he asked.

"I heard her call you Thor a few times."

Grant's laugh boomed around them, a couple of birds flying out of a nearby tree. "God, I love that kid."

Lily's heart melted in her chest, dripping through her inside like melted candle wax. God, how could she have been so lucky to find him?

"We should get inside." Grant moved a little.

Lily untangled her body from his and adjusted her clothes, brushing the dirt off the back of her legs. She stood on shaky limbs, leaning against a tree as she finished wiping the mud from her skin.

"Let's go get the guns," Grant said. Standing up, he offered his hand for her to take it. She slipped her hand back into his and walked back to the shop, happier than she'd been in days.

CHAPTER 25

*L*ily strolled past the brightly decorated bulletin board, strung up with little paper stars that shone in the evening sunlight. Children's names were written in scrolling script by a teacher with perfect penmanship. Small, smiling faces peered up at her. These children would have only been a year or so older than Sammy.

Where were they now?

She shuddered as she walked past them toward the gym showers. Will and Virginia passed her, Virginia waving with a soft smile. Will gave her a grunt of acknowledgment. Typical teenagers.

She wound her way down the hall to the heavy metal doors. Sunlight streaked through the dirty windows into the gym, illuminating the floor in an orange glow. She smiled to herself, remembering Sammy's favorite game—the floor is lava. She'd bounce around from cushion to cushion, shrieking with laughter and excitement, pretending hot rivers of boiling liquid swam beneath her.

Lily strolled into the girl's locker room, hung her towel on a hook, and stepped into a shower stall in the middle of the room. She slipped her small bar of soap onto a holder next to a bottle of shampoo and closed the curtain out of habit.

As she twisted the knobs, cool water trickled out of the grimy showerhead. Water slid down her skin, streaks of dirt and sweat mixing and dripping off her body. She rubbed the bar of soap between her fingers, her hands tracing over her skin in small circles, washing away the dirt, grime, and tension.

She poured a dollop of shampoo onto her palm and massaged her scalp, lather working through the strands of hair. She dipped her head and hands into the stream of cool water, shampoo snaking through her hair until the lather disappeared down the drain.

She reached for a comb to start brushing out her wild hair, curly even under the hard water.

A low moan echoed around the bathroom.

Lily dropped the comb to the floor with a clatter. She wiped the water from her brow and turned the shower knob off.

Another moan, louder this time, sounded to her left by the entrance to the shower. Lily pulled back the curtain, stepping outside of the small shower.

An infected stumbled around the room, its dead eyes staring around, locking onto her. A loud, hungry groan screeched from its throat as the corpse hobbled its way toward her. Long, black hair swung from its head as it reached out closer toward her.

Lily stepped back, her foot skidding on a puddle. In an instant, she slammed into the ground, her arms reaching for something to help her keep her balance. Instead, she grabbed onto the curtain, which came down with her.

The infected hustled over to her, its body falling on top of her. Lily screamed, lifting the curtain over her head and neck like a large, damp blanket.

The infected clawed at the plastic, trying to break through, its jaws snapping just over her head. Lily kicked, her leg shooting up under the curtain, knocking the infected onto its back. She held the plastic out, flipping the infected onto its back, keeping the barrier between them. She straddled the monster through the plastic.

She glanced around, the corpse still struggling beneath her, trying to punch through the curtain. Nothing. There was nothing except a useless, flimsy comb five feet away on the shower floor. Lily jumped to her feet and ran out of the locker room and back into the gym.

Something. There had to be something to kill this thing. She moved over toward the equipment carts. Basketballs. A folded parachute. A bag of tennis balls. Rolled up yoga mats. Hand weights. Free weights.

Free weights?

Lily bent down, picking up a twenty-five-pound circular weight with a hole through the middle. The kind used in the gyms for lifting. Perfect.

Lily's gaze fixed on the girls' locker room entrance. A moment later, the infected stumbled out, its teeth gnashing together in its mouth. Its clothes stuck to its body, the short shorts tight around skin that hadn't start to decay.

As it stepped deeper into the light, Lily froze.

Carly.

The infected was Carly.

The infected stepped closer, its arms outstretched toward Lily as it hobbled nearer, ready for a meal.

Lily raised the weight to her shoulder, twisting her arms to the left.

The infected moved two feet closer to her.

Crunch.

The sound of the weight smacking against the infected's skull ripped through the air around them. The infected stumbled, falling back onto the floor. Lily lifted the weight in her hands, tilting the edge downward. She dropped the weight into its skull with a sickening crunch that turned her stomach.

Clots of blood and slivers of bone and brain scattered around its head, splattering Lily's feet and calves in red and purple gunk, like a Picasso painting. The infected's skull shattered into fragments, almost entirely in half. Its body twitched once then stopped. The weight fell to the right side, hiding half of its face. The other half was bloodied and smashed beyond recognition. There was a smear of pink lip gloss still on her gray lips. Her eyeball had popped, a pinkish mixture trickling out of her socket.

Lily vomited on the gym floor, her lunch mixing with the blood on her feet. She looked down at them and hurled again until her stomach was empty.

Was she alone?

She turned back toward the gym doors. No one was there.

She ran back to the locker room, her feet slapping along the floor. She twisted the knob to the nearest shower and scrubbed herself clean with the bar of soap that laid against the shower floor.

A minute later, she dashed back out, rushing into the gym with her towel and clothes in hand. No more surprise attacks. If someone sent another infected in after her, she wasn't going to be cornered with her pants down.

She dried herself with the towel and slipped into a change of clothes. She shoved her feet into her boots and laced them up quickly, her eyes darting between the door, to Carly's corpse, to her shoelaces. She tied them up and bolted back to her room, her towel discarded on the bleachers, her wet hair dripping down the back of her shirt

She had to find Grant and Flynn. She had to let them know what had happened.

Someone in their camp was a murderer.

CHAPTER 26

*L*ily rushed into her bedroom like a tornado. Her gaze darted around the room.

"Sugar, are you ok?" Grant asked as he rose from the mattress. Flynn stepped out of Sammy's bedroom with a stuffed tiger in hand.

Her skin clammed up like he was going to puke again. She couldn't seem to pump enough air into her lungs, no matter how hard she tried.

Grant gripped Lily's shoulders and held her to his chest. "Sugar, what happened? You look like you've seen a ghost."

Lily shook her head against his chest, some of the shock and adrenaline wearing off. She trembled like a leaf on a dead tree, slowly sinking onto the bed. She tucked herself deeper into Grant's arms, letting the heat from his skin sink into her bones. Suddenly she felt chilled like her skeleton had been replaced with ice cubes.

"Lily?" Grant stroked her hair, pressing his lips on the top of her head.

Heat seared her skin. "I was attacked. In the locker room,"

she mumbled. "Carly attacked me. Someone killed her. She was…"

A tear rolled down her cheek.

"What? What do you mean you were attacked? Did Carly attack you?" Flynn asked. His brows crinkling in confusion.

Grant leaned back to look at her more clearly.

"Yes. No. I mean….I don't know. Someone killed Carly. And she turned. She was infected. And she came after me in the shower. I killed her in the gym. Crushed her skull. Oh, God, why?" Lily sobbed into Grant's chest. "What the hell is wrong with these people? Someone killed Carly and set her on me. Someone wanted to kill me."

Grant's body tensed beneath her, his muscles turning to iron—rigid and cold.

Flynn moved beside Lily, his hands rubbing her back. "Sweetheart, it's alright. Relax. You're safe now. You're shaking. Sweetheart, relax, there's no need to panic."

"There was a fucking zombie in my shower, and you're telling me not to panic!" Her voice edged on hysterical laughter.

"Do you have any idea who might have done this?" Flynn asked.

Lily shook her head. "No. I think the infected in Marissa's room was one of the infected from inside the boiler room. I still don't know who did it. At first, I thought it might have been Sanjay or Raj, but I wasn't sure. I still don't know why they'd do it. None of this makes any sense. And where's Sammy?" Lily asked.

"I left her with Virginia in the library. She said she could watch her for a little bit until Marissa or Colleen or Alexa got back. I couldn't find anyone else."

Lily shivered, goosebumps rising on her skin. "Why am I so cold?"

Grant and Flynn shifted closer to her, their body heat barely penetrating her skin.

She shivered between them for a few minutes as they watched her slowly start to thaw out. "I don't know what to do now," she said. "I wanted to stay here. But, now…"

Grant glanced up at Flynn.

Flynn shook his head. "We should leave. Now." His large hand rubbed Lily's back, still trying to press warmth deeper into her skin.

"But… What if there's nothing else out there? What if there is no camp? What about Sammy? We can't survive on our own out there with no one to help us."

"Sugar, someone is trying to hurt you. Deliberately trying to hurt you. We need to keep you and Sammy safe, more than anything. If that means getting the hell out of here, then that's what we'll do. You can still teach Sammy. We'll find some way to give her stability. A good life. But we can't do that if we're always looking over our shoulders for a murderer."

"Do we know for sure it's someone inside here?" she asked. "I mean, we came in without a problem. Maybe someone snuck in here, and we don't know about it."

Grant shook his head. "Marissa and the others were on us no more than five minutes after we walked in here. We have people on guard duty around the clock. We'd find someone if they were trying to sneak in. Believe it or not, there aren't a lot of places to hide around here."

"Someone's been sneaking infected around the school. I think you're underestimating whoever it is that's doing this," Flynn pointed out.

"We need to let Jonathan know. Whether we leave or not, we need to let them know that someone is out there, trying to kill us. They need to be warned." Lily sighed, resting her head against Grant's shoulder, her fingers sliding up and down Flynn's strong arm.

"So, it's decided? We're leaving?" Grant tried to hide the hope in his voice, but he sounded perky.

Lily nodded. "Yes, we need to pack up and leave. Tomorrow. It'll be dark in a couple of hours, and we don't want to be caught on foot in the dead of night."

"Okay, but do you—" Flynn began to say.

Boom!

A thundering noise shook the building, a small gush of air wafting through the windows. Lily blinked, turning to face the windows. Sunlight still seeped through. Not thunder…

"What the—" Flynn glanced around.

Grant knocked over Lily and Flynn, his body shielding them.

"Get down!" He shouted, louder than the boom.

"Grant," Flynn huffed, pulling himself and Lily out from underneath Grant.

"Take cover!" Grant yelled, crawling on the ground toward the door.

"Sammy!" Lily shouted, wobbling to her feet. "I have to find Sammy. Please…" She turned to Flynn, tears starting to shimmer in the corners of her eyes like melted snowflakes. "Please, help him. Then help me find her."

"She was in the library with Virginia. Go. Now!" Flynn bent over Grant to try and soothe him enough to sit up.

Lily flew out the door, her heart pounding. She rushed down the steps toward the library door.

It was open. The lights were out. Lily rushed inside, but the small room was empty.

Where was Sammy?

CHAPTER 27

Running so fast her feet barely touched the ground, Lily bolted up the steps two at a time to the music room. To the classroom. To the kitchen. Back to their bedroom. No sign of Sammy. As Lily ran down the hallway, Roman rushed past her in a blur.

"Roman," she shouted out. "Have you seen Sammy?"

Roman froze, turning toward her. "The little girl's missing?"

"Yes," Lily nodded. Tears stung her eyes. Her heart pumped so hard against her ribs it might burst.

"I'll look for her too. I'll come find you if I find her. But, hurry, we're going to the bus. We'll be surrounded by a horde any minute now. That explosion was loud. Every zombie within two miles will have heard it."

Lily nodded, and they ran in opposite directions.

As she hustled down the hallway, another ear-shattering boom echoed from the opposite side of the school near the garage.

Was someone setting off bombs?

Lily rushed into the gym and the locker room. Nothing. She hustled back through the metal doors into the hallway.

An infected roamed down the other end of the hall, the soft moaning echoing off the walls. Lily tiptoed around the corner until she knew she was out of sight. She walked past the boiler room door.

It was open.

A wave of nausea punched Lily in the gut. Infected were on the loose, inside the school. No one could find Sammy. Grant was having a PTSD episode. The school would be surrounded by infected soon.

Lily rounded another corner, an infected moving in the same direction with its back toward her. She tugged the knife from her boot and slinked behind it.

She closed the gap between her and the corpse, a nasty squishing sound ringing in her ears as the blade sunk into the zombie. The tip pushed through its nose, nearly splitting its skull in two. The knife eased out as its body fell forward. Congealed blood oozed out around its head.

Lily walked past the corpse and hurried back down the hallway. Her shoes squeaked.

More moaning. More infected right down the hall.

Lily stopped in her tracks, ready to turn back when she heard Sammy's muffled screaming.

"Sammy!" Lily shouted, running in the direction of the moaning.

She whipped around a corner, almost sliding on the tile. Four infected pressed their hands against a wooden broom closet door. Sammy's soft shrieking came from behind the door.

"Sammy, stay inside. Don't get out until I tell you." Lily raised her knife again and sunk it into the nearest infected's eyeball before it had the chance to notice she was there.

The other three turned toward her, walking with loud,

hungry groans. Lily lunged for the nearest infected, her knife sinking into the middle of its forehead. Her leg pulled up and kicked against the zombie's chest, pushing it into one of the moving infected. A third roamed toward her with its arms outstretched.

The broom closet door began to open, Sammy's small head peeking out to see if the coast was clear.

Lily's gaze darted from the monster to her only child. "Sammy! Get back inside!"

Sammy snapped the door shut.

Too late.

Her moment of distraction left her defenseless as the zombie lunged toward her, knocking them onto the floor. The zombie rolled on top of the knife, the blade sinking into its side. It barely twitched, not noticing the blade. Its attention focused on the meal two feet away.

Lily rolled out of the way, jumping to her feet, and reached for her gun. She backed away.

If she fired, the rest would come down on them. She and Sammy would be trapped in the middle of the small horde.

"Come on. Come and get me," Lily shouted at the two infected struggled to get off the ground and move toward her. As they rose, Lily slinked down the hallway toward one of the open classroom doors. "That's it. Come on." One of the infected stumbled its way into the room a few feet in front of her. Lily glanced around.

A weapon. She needed a weapon.

She saw a drawer across the room marked "medical supplies." Kids still dissected frogs in biology class, right? There must be a scalpel in there somewhere.

Lily gripped a cord from a Bunsen burner on a nearby table and swung it like a lasso, the heater hitting the infected in the head, knocking it sideways.

The second infected roamed into the room, its eyes fixing on her, its yellowed teeth gnashing together.

Lily rushed toward the drawer, fumbling to pull it open on its old, rusty tracks.

Bingo. She pulled out of scalpel, long and thin. Hopefully, they kept them nice and sharp. She rushed toward the distracted infected, the blade sinking through its ear and into its skull. Its shocked eyes blinked once before falling over in a heap.

Lily slid the scalpel out with an ease that almost scared her. The last infected hobbled closer toward her. She rushed out the other door, back into the hallway. She hurried back up through the front door of the classroom, sneaking her way in behind the infected. It moaned as it roamed its way toward the back door where she had disappeared seconds before.

Lily closed the gap between them. She could see patches of pale skull sticking out from the infected's scalp. Dirty, purple, and crusty. She tried to stop herself from vomiting all over its back.

She took a long, slow breath as she raised her arm, the infected slowly turning around.

The scalpel sunk through its eyeball, squishing it deeper, into its brain. The zombie's arms flung out before falling forward. Lily stepped to the side as it tumbled down, the scalpel pushing through the rest of its skull, the blade sticking upward in a slick, red mess.

Lily turned back toward the other dead zombie, yanking her knife from its side, and wiped the blade on the corpse's tattered shirt.

She hustled back down the corridors through the front doors of the school. "Sammy!" Lily shouted, running back toward the broom closet. "Sammy, it's okay. They're gone!"

The door swung open, and Sammy flung her tiny arms around her mother's thigh, tears streaming down her face. The little girl sobbed as her mother bent down to hold her and carry her back outside.

"We need to go. We're leaving the school," she said as she jogged down the hallway. The little girl only nodded as she bounced in her arms.

Lily kicked open the front door, the evening sun blinding her for a moment. Her heart froze as she stared outside.

Roman was right.

A dozen infected were crawling their way out of the nearby forest on the side of the school. It wouldn't be long until the camp was surrounded.

Alexa and Raj were helping everyone onto the bus, hauling up boxes of food, and helping people walk on. Sanjay and Roman were in the car Flynn had driven to get here.

"Where are Flynn and Grant?" Lily placed Sammy down on the ground in front of her.

Raj shook his head. "We don't know. We haven't seen them. We need to go."

"Take Sammy. Make sure she gets out of here. I need to go find them," Lily said.

She'd never leave them behind.

She pushed the little girl in front of Alexa. Alexa threw her arms around Sammy as the little girl twisted in her arms.

"Mommy!" she shrieked like she'd been set on fire. "Mommy!" she screamed, kicking and twisting. All the while, Alexa kept a tight hold, nodding to Lily.

Lily's heart splintered in her chest, shredding her insides as she turned her back on Sammy. She rushed toward the other side of the school. Maybe they left the cafeteria.

She froze as she rounded the corner.

Will and Virginia hunched over, a gas chamber left on its side leaned against the brick wall. Virginia held a gun out in front of her, aiming at the chamber. Behind them, a dozen zombies were pushing against the gate, the chain link fence starting to give around them.

Two of them had made it onto the school grounds. Children, both of them. They couldn't have been more than twelve, their eyes gleaming a yellowish-white, their skin a sickly gray. Patches of flesh had fallen or ripped off. Their mouths hung open as they moaned, stalking toward the mother and son.

Lily groped around her waist, unlocking the Smith & Wesson. "Please don't fail me now," she murmured. She took her stance, relaxing her elbows. One long breath, flip off the switch. Ready. Aim.

Pop!

Will froze, his body hunched over the gas chamber before he crumpled to the ground. Dead weight.

"No…no!" Virginia shouted. She bent over the body of her son, looking up just in time to see the infected roaming toward her. She stood, backing away before both infected fell onto Will's corpse and began to feast.

The sound of ripping flesh and satisfied, deathly moans echoed in the air. The faint hum of the bus's engine revved to life.

"You," she pointed the gun toward Lily with a shaky hand. "You bitch!" she screamed, raising her revolver higher in the air.

Lily aimed for Virginia.

Pop!

Pop!

Both women fired. One slumped to the ground, the world black and lifeless. The other groaned, the bullet digging into her leg as she hobbled away from the corpses and the burning school building. She stumbled a few feet closer to the front of the school, the edges of her world fading to black.

Then the world went dark.

*L*ily jerked awake as her body bounced along Marissa's back. The tiny woman carried Lily toward the bus, the branches beneath her boots snapping and crunching along with the dried, brown grass. She recognized Marissa's boots. Sturdy, one always untied, with a large red stain on the toe of the right boot.

"She's wounded." Marissa huffed as she tried to rush toward the bus.

"Lily!" Flynn's voice shouted from a distance.

His strong arms wrapped around her, lifting her from Marissa's back with gentleness and stiffness from bone-deep fear.

"What's wrong?" Grant shouted toward them.

Lily slumped her head against Flynn's chest, the throbbing in her leg bringing her more into the real world. It hurt like a bitch.

But labor had been worse.

She glanced down, blood seeping into the top of her jean shorts. Her outer thigh was stained with the tacky red stuff, some dirt, and a dry leaf sticking to the crimson smudge like glue.

"She's wounded. I can still see the bullet sticking out though," Raj said, jogging alongside Flynn, Lily, and Marissa toward the bus. "We can stitch her up there. But we need to leave. Now."

"Wait!" Marissa shouted, turning toward the school. An infected stumbled from the front of the doors. A rotting corpse with long dark hair and gray skin. It hobbled, its ankle twisted sideways in a gnarled stump.

"Mitch!" Marissa's eyes gleamed with tears as she ran toward the infected.

"No," Lily shouted. "Marissa, no! Mitchell's dead. You can't."

"Shit," Grant murmured, chasing after Marissa. He pulled his gun out of its holster and stopped. He raised it, pointing it toward the corpse.

Pop!

"No!" Marissa shrieked, stopping in her tracks. "No. No. No, Mitch! No. Please. Baby, no." Marissa fell to her knees, her gaze fixed on the front of the steps. Heavy sobs ripped from her throat.

"We need to go," Grant barked. He stuffed his gun back in its holster and stepped closer to Marissa.

She leaped to her feet, running toward the school.

A dozen more infected began to step out of the trees, moving steadily toward them.

"Marissa!" Lily shrieked, wincing at the pain in her leg. Flynn stood holding her, frozen to the spot as he watched in horror. Raj stood beside him, his eyes round with horror as Marissa ran toward the corpse.

"Grant, get back here!" Flynn shouted.

Grant rushed up to Marissa, trying to catch her.

She darted away from him, leaping up the school steps

three at a time, falling to her knees beside Mitchell's lifeless body. She bent down, yanking something off the corpse before Grant caught up with her. He gripped her upper arm and began dragging her down the steps. He bent lower, hoisting her on his shoulder, and hurried back to the bus.

Marissa didn't bother putting up a fight. She bounced on his back like a sack of flour, her puffy, red eyes staring at the thing in her hand.

Flynn stepped onto the bus and carrying Lily with him. Raj followed.

Grant hustled inside, Marissa bouncing along his shoulder before shutting the door and gently easing her onto a seat. She slumped over, resting her head on her knees. Silent sobs shook her body, and her hand clasped around a broken necklace.

Jonathan heaved himself into the driver's seat and followed Sanjay and Roman's car out of the front gate. A couple of infected wandered up to the side of the bus. One moved in front, just in time to stagger under the bus's tire and have its skull crushed. The bus pulled out onto a dirt path and drove off the school grounds, the crunch of gravel filling the air before they hit the smooth road.

"Mommy!" Sammy cried as Flynn laid Lily down in the aisle.

"We need the medical kits. We need to get the bullet out and stop the bleeding." Raj moved into the aisle and squatted down beside Grant.

Grant stood and walked toward the back of the bus, tossing a medical supply kit to Raj. He shimmied past Lily to stand behind Flynn, crouching down on a seat next to her.

His face turned as white as cotton as he stared at her wounded leg.

Flynn reached over and pulled Grant closer to him, his

arm draping over Grant's shoulder. "You sure you're going to be okay watching this? Deep breaths, remember. You don't need to push your PTSD."

Grant shook his head. "No. No, I need to be here. I need to be here for her. I'm fine." He slumped deeper into Flynn's shoulder, resting his head there, and trying to gulp down slow, deep breaths.

"Grant, if you're going to wig out on me, go sit a few feet away. I used to be a med student. I know what I'm doing. Now, everyone, stand back." Raj rummaged through the medical kit in search of necessary equipment.

"Mommy!" Sammy shouted again.

Everyone but Raj turned to face the girl.

"Sammy, sweetie. Come here and give Mommy a hug," Lily smiled through the pain.

"Mommy," Sammy whimpered, and she jumped out of Alexa's lap and onto the floor. Her small arms wrapped around Lily's neck in a tight squeeze.

"Aw, I'm going to be fine, sweetie. I just have a bad boo-boo, okay? Raj is going to help make it all better. But, I want you to sit with Colleen and Alexa while he makes me feel better, okay? Can you be a big girl and sit with Colleen for me?"

Sammy nodded.

Lily looked up at Colleen, who nodded to her. "Help her," she mouthed. Lily gave Sammy a soft kiss on the cheek before releasing her, almost pushing her away from the blood and chaos happening in the front of the bus.

Sammy shuffled down the aisle, wobbling a little as the bus hit a patch of gravel.

"I'm going to need you to keep steady, Jonathan," Raj shouted from the middle of the bus.

"Grant," Lily gazed up at him, his eyes sparkling in the

fading sunlight. "Are you sure you're going to be okay here, watching this?"

Grant leaned closer to her as Flynn's arm fell from his shoulder. He reached out for Lily with one arm, while resting his free hand on Flynn's knee. "I'll be alright now, Sugar. I love you."

"I love you, too." She forced a smile through the pain. Her gaze shifted over to Flynn, his eyes glistening with worry. "I love both of you. Ouch! Mother fucker!" Lily panted as Raj rubbed alcohol on her leg, the liquid searing her flesh like he'd dropped gasoline and a match on her skin.

"Ah," she gasped. She couldn't scream. She would never let Sammy hear her scream.

Raj lifted her leg, resting it on top of a few stacked supply bags.

"We need to get that bullet out of you," Raj said, glancing up at her with a soft bedside manner smile before his head bent down, locks of dark hair falling into his face.

"Don't let her see me," Lily pleaded. "Don't let me scream." She stared up at Flynn, hovering above her.

He nodded and began to slip his leather belt out of his belt loops. "Bite down on this," he said, folding it over once and sliding it between her teeth.

"The wheels on the bus go round and round," Colleen began to sing loudly, her voice reverberating around the bus. She shifted Sammy on her lap so the little girl could watch the sun setting outside as they moved along the windy roads, back toward the highway.

"Round and round. Round and round." Alexa began to sing along.

"The wheels on the bus go round and round." Rob's voice joined the fray.

"All through the town," Jonathan chimed in at the end.

Everyone except Marissa and Lily continued to sing

as Raj pulled the bullet from Lily's wound. She shouted into the leather belt, biting down, trying not to twist away from the jagged pain shooting through her leg.

"This will only need a few stitches. It's shallow. Most of the bullet was sticking out," Raj said as he dropped the bullet onto the floor. He reached for a needle and thread, rubbing the needle and thread with an alcohol wipe.

"This won't take long, Lily. I promise I'll be quick."

Lily screamed into the gag again, her hand squeezing Flynn and Grant's hands so much she was sure she'd leave bruises. If it hurt, they didn't complain. Flynn wiped the sweat from her forehead and chest with a cloth from the medical kit.

"I'm going to have to clean it one more time, Lily. This is going to hurt." She cringed. Uncomfortable was a word doctors used if something was going to hurt. Hurt meant she needed to prepare for an extraordinary amount of pain.

Raj tipped the bottle of alcohol over the wound and pain exploded down Lily's leg, her mind slipping back out of reality, the world fading into blackness.

CHAPTER 29

*L*ily blinked, the world slipped in and out of focus. Her clammy skin grated against Flynn's dirty jeans as the world brightened back into color. Grant's muddy boots swam into her vision as she carefully eased her head to the side.

"Done," Raj said as he placed a gauze bandage over the wound and began dressing it with slight pressure.

Lily sobbed into Flynn's thigh as her body trembled a little.

"Shh, hey, it's all over, Sweetheart. You're alright now. Everyone's alright. We'll be fine. Do you want Sammy to come over now?" He ran his fingers through her mess of hair as she nodded against his leg. "Sammy, it's over. Your mom wants you to give her a big hug, baby girl." He shouted over his shoulder, shifting to the side to let the little girl rush past him.

"Mommy!" Sammy clung to her mother's neck again. Her mess of curls tickled Lily's chin.

Lily raised an arm, trying to hold onto her daughter in an awkward hug. With Raj's help, Lily lowered her leg and sat up, leaning against a seat. Sammy sat beside her, her little head drooping in exhaustion, her eyes fluttering closed.

"She's worn out. It's been a busy day." Colleen walked down the aisle toward them, a warm smile lighting her tired face. "Want me to take her?"

Lily nodded. "Thank you."

Colleen picked up Sammy and tucked her in close. She sat Sammy down on her lap as the little girl dozed off. Alexa gazed at her wife with liquid warmth in her eyes, her arms wrapping around Rob, who was dozing off on Alexa's shoulder.

"Let's get you off this dirty floor." Grant's arm slid underneath Lily, easing her up onto the edge of a seat. He shifted behind her, carefully arranging her on his lap.

Flynn sat beside him, their knees touching, as he rested Lily's legs over his thighs. His hands roamed over her skin, careful not to move too close to the gauze.

"Here, you need to eat." Raj held out a protein bar to Lily along with a bottle of water. "You look pale, and you lost some blood. But, not enough to worry about. You'll be light-headed for a little while." His stare shifted between the two men. "Make sure she gets some rest."

"Thank you, Raj." Lily smiled at him. "I don't know what I can do to repay you. If there's anything I can do, just ask."

A soft red tinted Raj's cheeks, his hand creeping up to rub the back of his neck. "Don't forget to sleep and stay hydrated." He shrugged before walking back down the aisle, sitting in a seat by himself.

"I really can't believe Will was behind this." Grant wrapped his arms tighter around Lily as the bus hit another bump in the road.

Flynn shook his head. "I don't think this was the kid's idea. His mother…"

"I think something happened on that supply run. The trip where David and Mitchell were both killed," Lily guessed.

"Right, why would the entire family go? We'd never all go on one run at once," Grant said.

Lily nodded against his chest. "Even Colleen and Alexa won't go on supply runs together."

"Maybe they were trying to escape?" Flynn suggested. "Maybe Mitchell tried to stop them from just leaving him in the woods, so they killed him? Maybe David's death was just an accident?"

Grant shrugged. "Maybe. But they're all dead. I don't think we'll ever know for sure."

"Poor Marissa." Lily glanced down the bus to the young woman with sorrow glistening in her eyes. "Let's not mention this to her, alright? She's been hurt enough. This can only make it worse."

The men nodded. A small silence seemed to creep inside the bus, everyone just listening to the bus rumble along.

"It's all my fault," Marissa sobbed over the silence. The adults turned to her as Marissa raised to stare at them. Her puffy eyes looked weary and red.

"I kept the infected in the boiler room. Those people. All those people in the school. Turned. My students. My friends. My co-workers. All of them. Bitten. Turned. Infected. I couldn't just kill them."

She sobbed, resting her head on her knees again. She let out a harsh cry before lifting her head again. "I thought they'd be safe. I thought we would all be safe. They were locked in. And Mitch…when they brought him back…dead, bitten. I couldn't kill him. I told them I would. I told them I wanted to be alone when I did it, but I just couldn't do it. I stuffed him in the room with the others. I couldn't let him go. I couldn't be the one to kill him. I just couldn't do it. I'm sorry. I'm so sorry."

"Shh, hey. Stop that." Raj strolled down the aisle toward her. "Marissa, stop. This isn't your fault. You didn't let them out. You didn't try to hurt us. None of this is your fault."

"But, Carly—" Marissa sobbed.

"We don't know what happened to Carly," Raj said, sitting beside her and clasping a hand over her shoulder. "We'll never know for sure. But it wasn't your fault. I'm sure Virginia and Will had something to do with it. Maybe they had an infected bite her or something. They were crazy, Marissa. They'd gone mad after David died. Always together. Always holed up alone, whispering. You did nothing wrong."

The rest of the bus blinked in surprise as Raj leaned forward, trapping Marissa in a bear hug.

When he broke away, he slipped into the seat beside her, keeping an arm wrapped tight around her shoulders. There was another long silence. The bus bounced along as it ran over some debris in the street.

"Show me the way to go home," Jonathan began singing from the driver's seat. Lily could see a small smile creeping onto his face from the mirror that hung from the ceiling.

"I'm tired, and I want to go to bed." Colleen and Alexa's voices sang along.

"I had a little drink about an hour ago, and it's gone right to my head." Flynn and Lily added to the music.

"Wherever I may roam, on land or sea or foam." All the adults except Marissa began singing along as the bus rolled further down the road, watching the dark horizon creeping up in front of them.

"You can always hear me singing this song…"

Lily glanced at the sunset behind them. Three infected wandered up onto the side of the road, trying in vain to hurry up and catch up to the bus, their arms reaching for them.

"Show me the way to go home!"

ACKNOWLEDGMENTS

First and foremost, I must thank my parents, to whom my first novel is dedicated. Thank you for being there, from watching me learn my ABCs, to teaching me how to hold a pen, to editing my terrible grade school assignments, and for not reading my smut. Thank you. I love you both and wouldn't be the writer I am today without your incredible support and encouragement.

To My Aussie, thank you for your support, patience, and love. Thank you for your edits and your time in reading my first novel and for encouraging me to keep going.

To my brother, you're an inspiration. I am so proud of you, and I become even more proud of you every day. You're the best big little brother a sister could ask for.

To my PRW group, thank you from the bottom of my heart. I don't know where I would be without you all, though I know one thing—I wouldn't be the writer I am today without you guys.

To my legal team co-workers…If you read this, thank you for not calling the HR department and telling them I write dirty books.

To my friends for reading, critiquing, helping, editing, and brainstorming with me along the way. Thank you for helping me tackle this mountain troll of a novel. "There are some things you can't share without ending up liking each other, and knocking out a twelve-foot mountain troll is one of them."

To the long list of men who have inspired this novel... Ben, Jerry, Jack, Johnny, José, Jim, and the Captain. I wouldn't have made it through this book without each and every one of you (some of you at the same time).

Finally, to anyone who has read any of my stories, thank you for being a reader. Thank you for following this story and I truly hope you enjoyed it. I promise, there is more to come and I hope you will follow me and these characters on their journey.

XOXO

-Caitlin Cherise

UNDEAD HEART COCKTAIL

2 oz. dark rum
½ oz. heavy cream
½ oz. cinnamon schnapps
½ oz. simple syrup
Sparkling apple cider

In a cocktail shaker, add dark rum, heavy cream, cinnamon
schnapps and simple syrup.
Add ice and shake for 30 seconds.
Strain into a champagne flute.
Top with sparkling apple cider.
Drink up and drink responsibly!

BOOK 2 IN THE UNDYING LOVE SERIES

Prologue

The bus rumbled along the road, darkened by night and littered with fallen tree branches and rotting corpses. The group huddled close together, their glances flickering over one another. Fear filled the bus once the sun had set, leaving a feeling of dread and worry mixing in their bellies. Only four-year-old Sammy and eight-year-old Rob slept. The adults kept their gazes out the window, waiting for something to happen.

In the dark, something bad always happened.

"I'm surprised there aren't more infected out there." Alexa nodded to the empty field that seemed to stretch for miles before disappearing into a cluster of tall trees.

"Oh, they're out there. You just can't see them in this darkness," Colleen, Alexa's wife, noted. Her hand slipped over Rob's head, his small body tucked into hers like he was an infant again. She smiled down at her boy.

Alexa leaned down and ran her fingers through Rob's thick head of hair, gazing at Colleen.

"We'll be okay," she whispered.

Raj rolled his eyes from the seat behind him. Any more mushy nonsense and he'd hurl all over the cuteness. He heaved himself from his seat and stomped up the aisle to the front of the bus. They'd been driving for three hours and this mystery camp that Flynn told them about was nowhere in sight.

"Any idea how close we are to this magical, wonderful camp?" Raj glowered, resting an arm on the driver's headrest.

Jonathan heaved his shoulders, rubbing a crick in his neck as he made a small turn to avoid a rogue tire lying on the side of the road. "Your guess is as good as mine. We've passed by it a dozen times where it should have been on the map. There's nothing here. I'm going to just keep driving east at this rate and see if it's a bit further. And if it's not there… Well, we have half a tank of gas already in this bus. We have a few gallons in the back with the rest of our supplies. Sanjay stocked up well before we left."

"You see my brother anywhere?" Raj glanced out the front window, the headlights shining like two dim beacons a mere ten feet in front of them. Beyond that, blackness consumed the road. How Jonathan could drive in this mess, Raj didn't know.

"Yeah, he should be just up ahead. Sanjay and Roman left on a full tank and they were just in front of us before it got too damn dark to see." Jonathan shifted in the squishy chair, his large rump spilling out over the edge.

"Good." A small wave of unease tossed in his stomach. His brother was out there in the dark with some punk kid to keep him company.

His only living family.

He would never know for sure if the rest of his family was still alive, over seven thousand miles away in India. If only his sister had waited until the end of the summer to get married. His family would all still be together. He and Sanjay could have protected them.

A bang up ahead derailed Raj's train of thought. A few hundred feet ahead, they saw lights flipping. The screech and groan of metal on tar filled his ears like a train whistle.

"Stop the bus," he shouted to Jonathan, yanking his gun from his pocket. He pulled the lever to open the door while Jonathan slowed the bus to a stop.

Raj jumped from the steps and rushed forward.

A Pontiac Sunbird was flipped on its side, the windshield cracked into a thousand pieces.

Sanjay's car.

The vehicle had flipped over, the roof crushed on the right side. Glass sparkled off the bus's headlights like dull stars on the black road top.

"Sanjay!" Raj shouted, his heart thumping so loud in his chest he heard it in his ears. His head hammered in time with his pulse. He moved to the driver's side and tugged on the door. Nothing.

"Sanjay!" Raj shouted again.

"Raj?" A weak voice mumbled from inside the car. Sanjay's voice.

"Close your eyes. I'm going to break the windshield." Raj punched through the windshield with the muzzle of his gun, knocking aside chunks of glass. He saw Sanjay twisted inside, blood gushing from his head.

"You're okay," he told Sanjay. "Head wounds bleed a lot and look worse than they really are." Something he learned as a med student. He tried to keep a lid on his rising panic ready to boil over. Knowing head wounds look worse than they really were and seeing his brother coated in blood were two different realities.

He bent over the windshield, gripping Sanjay's arms and tugging as hard as he could.

"Hold on," a voice beside him said, bending forward and gripping Sanjay around the middle. "Count of three," Grant said. "One. Two. Three." Both mean heaved, pulling Sanjay out of the car with heavy grunts.

His torso rose out of the windshield, followed by his legs and finally his feet. Raj maneuvered Sanjay over his shoulder.

"Let me out," Roman huffed, banging on the passenger's side door. Grant bent down and helped the teenager ease himself upright, gripping him around the waist and hoisting him out of the seat.

"You okay, kid?" Grant asked.

Raj turned and hurried off toward the bus. "Let's go," he shouted to Jonathan as he stomped up the steps.

"I'm waiting for Grant," Jonathan said, his brows crinkled together as he stared out into the darkness, waiting for Grant to return.

Raj eased Sanjay into one of the seats, Sanjay groaning as he swayed in the chair.

Pop!

Pop!

Two shots ripped through the air, startling everyone inside.

"Mommy," Sammy murmured, the little girl twisting around in her seat to find Lily.

"I'm right here, sweetie," Lily said. She turned around in the seat, careful not to move her injured leg as she glanced down at her daughter.

"Damn it," Flynn murmured, pulling his gun from its holster and rushing out into the darkness.

"Flynn!" Lily shouted as he bolted out of the bus. She heaved, but stopped, clutching her leg. The bullet wound she'd received earlier wouldn't allow her to bend her leg much, let alone chase after Flynn.

"They'll be alright," Colleen reassured her from across the aisle as Rob stirred against her lap.

"Infected," Grant huffed, rushing up the steps, Roman's body bouncing along his back. Flynn following behind him. "We need to go."

"Roman?" Jonathan asked as he closed the bus doors behind Flynn.

"He fainted." Flynn shook his head as Grant eased Roman into an empty seat. Grant bent over, his hands on his knees and he doubled over, gasping for breath.

Jonathan sighed as he drove along. Outside the window, they could see a few zombies begin to swarm the side of Sanjay's car.

Flynn gripped Grant on the shoulder, easing him into an empty seat in front of Lily. "You okay with those shots back there?"

Grant's pale face nodded. He tucked his head between his knees and began slow, steady breathing exercises. He shook a little as his mind fought with itself, tapering down on the PTSD episode that was lingering on the edge of his thoughts.

"Daddy?" Sammy's small voice piped up as she stood next to Flynn, watching Grant. She shimmied between the two men and wrapped her small arms around Grant's leg. "It's okay. The monsters won't get us."

Grant chuckled, his legs relaxing and slipping down to the floor. He picked up the little girl and tucked her on his lap. "You're right, baby girl. We're safe. You and your mom are safe. But it's dark out. You should go back to sleep."

"But the noise woke me up," Sammy murmured. She shifted on his lap, trying to get comfortable in his arms.

"I know, baby girl. I hate the noise too. It's alright." Grant tucked Sammy to his chest, his hands running through her mop of fiery red curls, just like Lily's hair.

"I'll leave you two alone. I'm going to see how Sanjay's

doing." Flynn smiled down at Grant and squeezed his shoulder one last time before walking off to see Lily.

"Look!" Jonathan said, pointing outside the window.

Up ahead, a cluster of infected moved, yet stayed put. Jonathan moved the bus a bit closer, the headlights catching on the poles. Several infected were impaled on long wooden stakes sticking up from the ground. A small bridge led to a fence crisscrossed with wire and long, wooden poles. A couple of towers stood behind the wire.

"They have to let us in," Raj said. "We don't have enough supplies here. I need to treat his head wound. He probably has a concussion and he's losing blood. He has cuts that need stitching. Now."

"Hold on, folks. This is going to be a bumpy ride," Jonathan said as he turned onto a pathway leading up to the camp. The bus shook like a wooden roller coaster climbing its way uphill. They held onto the edged of their seats as Jonathan drive a path to the front of the camp.

Raj tried to keep Sanjay's head steady. He yanked off his jacket, folding it up into a large square and pressed it to his brother's forehead to try and slow the bleeding. He murmured some soothing words to his brother in Hindi.

"*Aap theek ho jaenge,*" he murmured. *You will be okay...*

Sanjay began to fade in an out of consciousness.

The bus ground its way to a sudden halt as they reached the poles. One-by-one, they stepped out of the bus, staring up at the large wooden gate across the bridge like some medieval fortress in front of a castle. Below them was a trench. A couple of infected moaned at them from below, reaching up to try and grab at them, but they were too low to reach.

The group shuffled up over the bridge to the front gates where they saw a white banner splotched with black paint.

"Eden."

Caitlin Cherise writes the three "S"s: smart, sweet, and sexy. Her sensual stories leave readers with fluttering hearts and dirty thoughts. When she's not home enjoying a vodka soda with lime, Caitlin enjoys long walks through her gritty neighborhood in the heart of Philly or blasting heavy rock music in her house. Her readers love her, but her neighbors do not.

Website: CaitlinCherise.com
Facebook: @CaitlinCheriseWriter
Twitter: @Caitlin_Cherise

www.ingramcontent.com/pod-product-compliance
Lightning Source LLC
Chambersburg PA
CBHW061117100726
47911CB00013B/574